THE OYSTER

The Oyster, along with such notable publications as *The Pearl*, was one of the leading underground magazines of its day. It flourished in the 1880s and a large portion of it was made up of the reminiscences of Sir Andrew Scott. Although very little can be found out about Scott, it is clear that he had much fun in penning his conquests, and lived a riotous and exuberant life.

The Oyster continued to thrive until 1889. Along with *The Pearl* and other similar magazines, these underground journals provided a platform of resistance to the suffocating, guilt-ridden climate in which they appeared. Copies of these have fortunately survived to delight and amuse us as well as to provide an unusual and unconventional insight into the manners and mores of a vanished world, the reverse side to the coin of iron-clad respectability which appeared to characterise British society some hundred years ago.

Also published by New English Library:

THE PEARL volume 1
THE PEARL volume 2
THE PEARL volume 3

The Oyster

A Novel from the Victorian Classic Underground Magazine 'Printed and Published for the Uninhibited Members of Voluptuous Society'

NEW ENGLISH LIBRARY
Hodder and Stoughton

A New English Library Original Publication, 1985

Copyright © 1985 by New English Library Ltd.

First NEL Paperback Edition 1985
Third impression 1986

British Library C.I.P.

The Oyster: a novel from the Victorian classic
  underground magazine: printed and published
  for the uninhibited members of voluptuous
  society.
  823'.8[F]   PR5115.09

ISBN 0 450 05838 7

Printed and bound in Great Britain for
Hodder and Stoughton Paperbacks, a
division of Hodder and Stoughton Ltd.,
Mill Road, Dunton Green, Sevenoaks,
Kent (Editorial Office: 47 Bedford
Square, London, WC1B 3DP) by
Cox & Wyman Ltd., Reading.

PUBLISHER'S FOREWORD

THE PEARL was perhaps the most famous of all underground magazines which flourished in Britain throughout the mid-Victorian years. The first issue was published in London in July, 1879 and eighteen editions were printed until its sudden closure in December, 1880.

Although this monthly 'journal of facetiae and voluptuous reading' was given a brazen *imprimatur* of 'Oxford: at the University Press', in actual fact the magazine was brought out privately by a mysterious individual named Lazenby who—according to G. Legman, that indefatigable researcher and writer on erotica—published and indeed wrote much of the contents under the pseudonym of D. Cameron. Another contributor, says Legman, was the noted journalist and war correspondent George Augustus Sala but the identities of the other correspondents will probably never be revealed.

After the sudden disappearance of *The Pearl*, other similar magazines were quickly produced to take its place in the highly efficient subterranean marketing system that existed throughout the 1880s and 90s for the distribution of forbidden literature. Lazenby/Cameron offered *The Cremorne* whilst others of the same ilk that flourished during this period included *The Boudoir* and *The Oyster*.

And it is from *The Oyster*, one of the successors to the much imitated *Pearl*, that the novel in this volume is taken. Sir Andrew Scott began his reminiscences of his schooldays in an earlier issue (reprinted in *The Pearl, Volume Three*, New English Library) and this longer extract is very much in the same vein. Although prurient, it is well worth noting that like all the other material from *The Oyster* the novelette eschews sado-masochistic behaviour, flagellation and the even grosser sexual perversions such as pederasty and incest that cropped up regularly in many other such publications.

Whilst little attempt is made by our unknown author to write in any serious depth, and although the characters are at best two-dimensional, there is yet a pungent, lively spirit and a bawdy vitality in the writing which is rarely found in collections of popular erotica from this rather stuffy period of British history.

Certainly there can be little doubt that Sir Andrew Scott thoroughly enjoyed penning his memoir of youthful sexual frolics even if the apparent ease of finding ready and willing partners somewhat stretches our credulity. Perhaps we should heed the words of a more famous scribe of the time, Oscar Wilde, who once commented that: 'Memory is the diary we all carry about with us, even if it chronicles events that never happened and could not possibly have happened.' Yet it may be wrong to dismiss the narrative totally as mere boastful fantasising, despite the extraordinary ease of conquest displayed. Whilst a far stronger taboo on sex before marriage then existed, coupled of course with a very real fear of unwanted pregnancy, we know full well that many Victorian ladies were far less strait-laced than usually depicted either then or now. Amongst the upper crust, to take a well-documented example, there was often much flitting between bedrooms at country house weekend parties. Conversely, in all large British cities throughout the mid to late nineteenth century there were a shameful number of prostitutes (including a high number of under-age girls and boys driven to the brothels by abject hunger and often appalling poverty) to quench the sexual appetites of the lonely and the repressed.

So there may well be more than a kernel of truth in the narrative even if Sir Andrew has doubtless embellished his personal account of sexual discovery! He writes, it should be remembered, not as a social historian but primarily for his own enjoyment, and perhaps his account of how he came to write his memoir is quite true, and he did indeed compose the story sitting at a writing desk in the sumptuous library of his friend, Sir Lionel T——(whose name, incidentally, crops up in previous issues of *The Oyster*). One can only hazard a guess as to the identity of this gentleman, but he could well be Sir Lionel Trapes (1826-1908), a high-ranking Treasury official and patron of the arts who was a member of the circle that included '*Pisanus Fraxi*', alias H. Spencer Ashbee, the doyen of all collectors of erotic and gallant literature.

Scott, then, writes to titillate and amuse and not to instruct, and it must be admitted that he writes with some genuine style, keeping the simple story moving as briskly as he can between the frequent bouts of sexual grappling. He appears to have been a man of straightforward sexual taste although, somewhat unusually for this age, he regards oral sex quite equitably and takes no joy whatsoever from the idea of giving or receiving corporal 'punishment' in the bedroom.

The Oyster continued to thrive until 1889. The last recorded issue just preceded the first public news about the notorious Cleveland Street scandal, a *cause célèbre* that involved the exposure of a high-class homosexual brothel where Post Office messenger boys were encouraged to participate in sexual acts with some extremely well-known personages. Indeed, it has been suggested that the demise of the magazine was not unconnected with the hasty flight to France of Lord Arthur Somerset, a close friend and equerry to the Prince of Wales, who was heavily implicated in the Cleveland Street affair. Lord Arthur and Lord Euston were just two of a raffish group of men-about-town who were well known for their varied and robust sexual proclivities.

Other magazines appeared at regular intervals and these along with *The Pearl* and *The Oyster* provided a platform of resistance to the suffocating, guilt-ridden climate in which they appeared. They set themselves firmly against the notion that sexuality was an area over which the Establishment should exercise a stringent, rigid control and this led to a more sceptical, questioning attitude which in turn brought about the more relaxed and understanding liberal philosophy that by and large exists today.

The writers in these 'underground' magazines of our great-grandparents show that even during the stern days of Bowdlerism, when even piano legs were covered for the sake of a false and imaginary 'decency', there was still a fierce questioning of taboos, and there existed a simple desire to explore frankly the actual mechanics of sexuality.

There may be some who question the need to produce and to receive explicit works, but the modern acceptance of the view that adults must in general be allowed to read whatever they desire has its origins in such material as is produced in this jolly little book.

The identity of Sir Andrew Scott and others of his ilk will remain unknown. Although they should not, perhaps, be regarded as pioneers of freedom of expression, it is nonetheless most probable that they wrote purely for pleasure, and not merely for financial gain. Even so, it would be naive to suppose that the question of payment never crossed their minds. It should be pointed out, however, that whilst *The Pearl, The Oyster*, and other similar magazines were strictly illegal, there is little evidence of a rich black market for pornography, although there were doubtless several printers who would gladly have risked prosecution to print saucy material on an undercover basis. Lazenby and Cameron certainly made money out of publishing *The Pearl*, but what of the writers such as Scott? He writes with some erudition and is by no means averse to slipping in the occasional French, Italian or even Latin phrase, or regaling the reader with bouts of philosophising in between the more robust pieces of action. Some readers will recognise in his opening paragraphs the Platonic argument taken from the prologue of *The Republic* about the advantages and disadvantages of old age.

Without any genuine hard evidence to back up one's supposition, only mere conjecture can be made as to Scott's true identity. In the manner of the born gossip, he tantalisingly gives only the Christian names of his friends, most of whom appear to be titled. Indeed, he himself may well have been one of the idle, wealthy young men who took morning rides down Rotten Row, enjoyed huge lunches and lazy afternoons at their clubs and spent their evenings either at formal dinner parties or at the already popular music halls and theatres where hordes of ladies of pleasure awaited these sybaritic young drones.

My own view is that Scott was probably a writer. Not necessarily a professional hack on one of the fledgling popular newspapers that were surfacing throughout this era, but an occasional contributor to one of the many magazines and reviews that flourished during the 1880s. His apparent lack of interest in bondage and flagellation would appear to rule out George Augustus Sala, but he was most certainly a member of a similar semi-leisured circle willing and eager to spin out a tale for the amusement of his friends.

Copies of these and other works have fortunately survived to delight and amuse us as well as to provide an unusual and unconventional insight into the manners and mores of a vanished world, the reverse side to the coin of iron-clad respectability which appeared to characterise British society some hundred years ago.

Antoinette Hillman-Strauss
March, 1985

PREFACE TO THE FIRST EDITION

What it is that causes my lord to smack his chops in that wanton, lecherous manner, as he is sauntering up and down Bond Street, with his glass in hand, to watch the ladies getting in and out of their carriages? And what is it that draws together such vast crowds of the holiday gentry at Easter and Whitsuntide to see the merry rose-faced lassies running down the hill in Greenwich Park? What is it causes such a roar of laughter when a merry girl happens to overset in her career and kick her heels in the air? Lastly, as the parsons all say, what is it that makes the theatrical ballet so popular?

There is a magic in the sight of a female leg, which is hardly in the power of mere language to describe, for to be conceived it must be felt.

Most of my readers will be acquainted from experience with that magic which emanates from the sight of a pretty leg, a delicate ankle and a well-proportioned calf.

Your editor never sees a pretty leg but feels certain unutterable emotions within him, which as the poet puts it:

Should some fair youth, the charming sight explore,
In rapture he'll gaze, and wish for something more!

The Editor of The Oyster

11

Thus in the zenith of my lust I reign;
I eat to swive, and swive to eat again;
Let other monarchs, who their sceptres bear
To keep their subjects less in love than fear
Be salves to crowns, my nation shall be free;
My pintle only shall my sceptre be,
My laws shall act more pleasure than command,
And with my prick I'll govern all the land.

*Bolloxinion, King of Sodom or The Quintessence of
Debauchery*
The Earl of Rochester (1647-1680)

CHAPTER ONE

A FOND RECOLLECTION OF YOUTHFUL DAYS—
BY SIR ANDREW SCOTT

WHEN EVEN now I awaken in the still darkness of the night with a sudden start that appears to possess no apparent physical origin, when I am driven mad with passion and feel my hands stealing down to caress my ramrod-hard pego, then I know that the sweet dreams fast vanishing, alas, into the shelter of oblivion must have contained at least a fragment of fantasy about my darling Lucy, or one of the other young ladies who helped make my formative years so pleasurable during those dear days almost beyond recall.

I refer, my friendly reader, to the times spent as a schoolboy at the Nottsgrove Academy for Young Gentlemen situated near the pleasant hamlet of Arkley, deep in the wilds of rural Hertfordshire. Perhaps my first essay upon the delights of studying at that most progressive academy, penned for a previous issue of our esteemed journal, is not unknown to you. [See *The Pearl, Volume 3*.] Though the years have passed by, the pictures of Lucy will never vanish from my brain: her dear face next to mine, close enough for me to see her lips parting with desire; her ripe body touching mine, setting me on fire with carnal yearnings, clasping me with pleading urgency.

Ah, sweet recollections of lying naked on crushed and rumpled sheets, watching the early morning sunlight caress my sated, sleeping lover, listening to the muted sounds beyond the boudoir as the countryside wakes to another morn. Alas, often when old men meet together, many are full of woes. They hanker still for the joys of youth, remembering how in their spring years they would besport themselves with wine, women and song all hours of the day and night. Now, in the autumn of their time upon this planet, they think it is a great deprivation that those times are way behind them. Life was good then, they moan, whereas now they feel that they hardly live at all. I do not agree with this pessimistic outlook, for old age has the advantage of offering more time for contemplation and relaxation. I look back with much enjoyment upon my memories of a boisterous youth, and utterly refuse to allow my old age to be crabbed, for my recollections are to me as a fine summer's day of much sunshine and few clouds.

One further word before I open my store of the times that have passed. Hopefully we shall see the day when science and not theology will become the arbiter of personal morality; when pure reason, unfettered by the bumbling antics of well-meaning but ignorant clergymen, bound and limited by the dogmas of preconception, will seek and find sane and sensible standards of civilised conduct between the sexes.

For I hold that there is no distinction to be found between the sexual needs of the married and unmarried, as a young man's passion does not suddenly awaken at the moment of his betrothal. Nor are the desires of a widow permanently extinguished upon the death of her spouse. The number of predatory widows in London Society is proof enough, and the names of such ladies may be omitted here as they are well-known to all the many gentlemen who frequent the salons of Belgravia and Mayfair. So Lady Cecilia A—— and Mrs Hester S—— may with others of their ilk rest easy, as I do not propose revealing their secret lives in this manuscript.

Fortunately our century has produced an abundance of publications proclaiming the delights of the body in all its forms. And now I offer my own journey down the lane of memory as a humble addition to those other memoirs penned by that group of lusty scribes who have built up such a fine stock of gallant literature.

Finally, I would add only this—no apology will be forthcoming from me for putting into print this highly charged erotic narrative, as I feel assured that every devotee of voluptuous reading will derive as much, or hopefully even more, pleasure than that afforded your humble author in the writing of this epistle. I would like to thank my old friend and mentor Sir Lionel T——, himself an Old Nottsgrovian, for allowing me the use of his fine library to compose this work, and I end this prologue with the wise words of Boccaccio:

If in my tales there are a few words rather freer than suits the prudes, who weigh words more than deeds and take more pains to appear than to be good, I say I should no more be reproved for having written them than other folk are daily reproved for saying 'hole', 'peg', 'mortar', 'sausage' and like things.

No corrupt mind ever understands words healthily. And just as such people do not enjoy virtuous words, so the well-disposed cannot be harmed by words somewhat less virtuous, any more than mud can sully sunlight or earthly filth the beauty of the skies.

Those of us fortunate enough to have studied under the wise and caring guidance of Doctor Simon White will always salute the achievements of this remarkable scholar whose main educational aim was to break the shackles that bind us to a false morality. He showed his pupils that in his learned opinion, throughout man's past, throughout all known civilisations of both East and West, there have always been conflicts between the desires of some and the imposed wills of others. Sometimes, one class has been in a minority, sometimes it has been the other; but the rule holds good and indeed, it seems but only yesterday that I was back in my favourite chair in the prefects' room at Nottsgrove Academy, listening with the other senior boys to our dear old headmaster espousing his theories of philosophy with that characteristic passion and lucidity that were hallmarks of his delivery of a lecture to us. I should say that he encouraged argument and never attempted to indoctrinate us against our.

wills. But I digress, so I shall take up again the strands of memory to a day of excitement at Nottsgrove.

It was a lazy summer afternoon during my last term at Nottsgrove. The day's classes had ended and I was busily engaged in deciding what news to pen in my obligatory letter home (no excuses for the absence of such an epistle were ever allowed), when Doctor White entered the hallowed portals of the prefects' common room to pin up a notice of forth-coming sports fixtures upon the wall board.

After a moment or two my old friend Pelham Forbes-Mackenzie asked the good doctor some trifling question about a paper on modern philosophy that he was preparing for the summer examination—and of course this was more than enough to set our much loved and respected old pedagogue on course for yet another lecture about the faults of present-day civilisation.

'My dear old chap,' he boomed, 'never forget how we are unchained in body yet still shackled mentally to grossly outdated ideas that make our lives unnecessarily worrisome. But soon, Forbes-Mackenzie, very soon we shall face a climax in this continual struggle between, upon one hand, estab-lished authority with its clutch of beliefs and rituals and, upon the other, the soon-to-be-awakened intelligence of the until now uninformed, ignorant masses!'

All conversation in the room ceased, as we knew that the Doctor always enjoyed as large an audience as possible for his little speeches, and I sat back to hear him continue.

'To deflect the attack on these taboos which will be made when the general education of the common people is completed,' he announced, 'I believe that our so-called masters and betters will attempt to reinforce all those rules and regulations (which they themselves often ignore!) in an attempt to hold back the natural flow of self-understanding and enlightenment that mass education will surely bring.

'It is up to you all, the new leaders of the Empire, to resist these oppressive inroads before they are firmly established as the laws of the land, as unchangeable as those of the Medes and Persians!' he thundered.

'Above all, it is in your interests to fight the good fight! I know that you boys think of little else in your hours of free time except the desirability of fucking a pretty girl. Well, if the new barbarians achieve their ends, all you will ever be able to do is think about it until the time that you may marry!'

When our headmaster was firmly mounted upon his hobby-horse, it took a great deal of energy to persuade him to dismount! Of course, those readers who have perused my previous recollections of life at Nottsgrove will recall that we fortunate boys who studied under his care were given a most pleasing row across the sexual Rubicon by the doctor's young niece, Lucy, and by other young ladies of her acquaintance all, of course, to further Doctor White's belief in freedom in all social and personal relationships.

However, to return to that particular afternoon, Pelham turned to me after the Doctor had finally swept out of the room after finishing his oration and said: 'Andrew, my old chap, I believe that in your case, our headmaster has translated principle into practice as far as relations with the fair sex are concerned?'

'This is so,' I replied carefully. 'I received my first lesson from Lucy some ten days ago.'

'That's damned unfair,' complained my friend. 'I have yet to fuck my first girl and I am only three months younger than you.'

'Well, that is something you should perhaps speak about to a higher authority than I, for it is up to Doctor White to decide when a fellow is ready to lose his virginity,' I said, trying very hard to keep any note of gloating or superiority from my voice. Pelham was a hot-tempered chap and easily angered, but his temper was short and not malignant. His name, of course, may not be totally unfamiliar to readers of this chronicle as he later made a great name for himself in the 13th Hussars in India and later in Canada. A very striking and commanding figure, even as a youth, he possessed a strong, determined face—and as we will later find out, an equally determined pego! But while he had a fierce exterior, there lay behind it a warm and kindly heart, and I never knew a better friend, so I had no desire to upset his injured sensibilities any further as he furrowed his brow in anger.

'I do think it is time for my turn now!' he said crossly.

I urged him to speak to Doctor White whose administration, it must be admitted, could be a little slipshod if truth be told, as his memory was cluttered with so many matters to which he had to give his fullest attention. Thankfully, he accepted my advice and marched off directly to tackle the headmaster directly as to why he was still waiting for his first encounter in *l'art de faire l'amour.*

Later that evening, only half an hour or so before lights-out, one of the doctor's house-servants knocked upon the door of my study and announced that the headmaster wished to see me immediately. It was a warm July night and I was dressed only in a shirt and trousers and, as the matter seemed of such prime urgency, I slipped on a jacket and followed the man to the door of Dr White's private domain. I knew he would forgive my omission of a waistcoat and tie, as punctuality was a virtue he prized highly.

It occurred to me that in all probability my call was in connection with the truly heartfelt plea Pelham had made to Doctor White to be allowed to cross the Rubicon—and indeed, my premonition was soon to be proved absolutely correct. For when I knocked smartly on the door of the headmaster's private chambers, instead of a deep, somewhat gruff voice commanding me to enter, there was a soft sound of a muffled little giggle. Instantly I knew that the little minx Lucy was behind the door waiting for me—possibly alone but more probably with Pelham, as she had used my services before to demonstrate the art of fucking to newcomers to the sport.

Without further ado I opened the door and, as I had expected, there was the pretty little filly attired simply in a light blue cotton robe that she was very fond of wearing, especially as it had been a birthday gift from Doctor White. It was a wide, sweeping garment with ruffles, held together only by a blue sash of the same material. From underneath, the intoxicating aroma of her luscious young body poured out, mingling subtly with the French perfume I knew that she had dabbed between her bare breasts. And there, standing forlornly, without a stitch of clothing to his name, was poor Pelham looking a trifle shamefacedly down at the floor.

'My dear Andrew,' smiled Lucy. 'As you can see from the droop of his little pego, your friend is rather nervous. Perhaps he is a little frightened of me. Will you help me put him at his ease?'

'We can easily cure this malady, my sweet Lucy, by showing him how to fuck like a gentleman!' I said, already fired by the stunning beauty of this delicious girl.

'Those are my sentiments exactly,' she agreed, and as if by a prearranged mutual signal, we both stepped forward and engaged in a hearty embrace. As we kissed and our mouths opened to receive each other's tongues, Lucy tugged at the sash of her gown to untie the simple knot. The sash fell to the ground, the gown opened and she stepped out in all her naked glory. She stood before me like a statue crafted by a master sculptor come magically to life. Below the roots of her golden blonde hair, her creamy white skin was of an incredible softness. Her beautiful full breasts were as firm and round as two globes; her well-rounded shoulders tapered down into a small waist; her small feet, with delicate ankles, expanded upwards into fine calves, her thighs were full and proportionately made, whilst hanging down between them, forming a perfect veil over the pouting little slit, was a mass of silky blonde hair that contrasted so well with the snowy whiteness of her belly. As we writhed about in each other's arms, I managed to disengage myself of my clothes and my prick began to leap and prance about between her thighs, seeking an entrance into the hospitable retreat that awaited him. Her breasts rose and fell with the quickening pace of her breathing but I realised that I had to instruct Pelham in the full range of lovemaking. I therefore disengaged my mouth from her burning kiss and sank down to my knees, pushing her down onto the carpet. I squeezed those gorgeous orbs and ran my fingers over the stiff, engorged nipples that stood out like taps waiting to be drawn upon, then, as I heard her gasp with

21

pleasure, I buried my face in the thick brush of fluffy pubic hair. I grasped her lovely bottom cheeks as I flashed my tongue round the damp motte. She whimpered as her pussy opened wide and I slipped my probing tongue between the pinky sex lips. I felt myself flicking against her stiffening clitty as I licked and licked in long thrusting strokes. Her cunny was now gushing love-juice and as you may well imagine, my young pego was straining at the leash.

Lucy moaned with desire and I knew that such a sound heralded her wish to receive me fully. I raised my head and Lucy lay flat on her back on the lush green carpet with her legs spread wide to await the arrival of Mr Pego. She reached out and grasped my swollen rod, which was now in its prime state of erection. She caressed the throbbing shaft and I knew the time had come to conclude the overture and begin the performance in earnest.

I knelt between her sturdy white legs as she handled my prick so gently that I was concerned that I might come in her hands before I had tasted the full delights of her juicy quim.

'Come now, Andrew,' she murmured. 'Let's show Pelham how to do this exercise properly.'

As she guided my throbbing cock into her moist crack I noticed that Pelham's thick prick was now swollen upwards as he watched Lucy guide my cock into her warm, moist love channel. To hold her creamy buttocks was sheer delight and to suck her stiff little pink nipples was just too much for me. As soon as Lucy began to massage the underside of my balls I pumped wildly into her eager cunt and she groaned with delight as the gush of my juices sent wave upon wave of erotic energy passing through our bodies.

I knew that the delicious girl needed more fucking and that I had to be unselfish and let Pelham have his way with her. I heaved myself off Lucy and, after a questioning glance, Pelham gently lowered himself upon her, his body quivering with anticipation of the joys to come. There was a brief moment before his tight little arse was lowered and Lucy moaned when he finally managed to guide his excited cock into her. Although this was his first fuck, Pelham had a natural understanding of what was required and he did not rush in and out in a mad frenzy but thrust home slowly, then withdrawing and re-entering further. This had the desired effect upon Lucy, who was now in a state of high excitement. Her entire body quivered as she gasped: 'Oh, lovely, really lovely Pelham, ah, those long powerful strokes and—oh, yes —now Pelham, now. Make me come! Ram your darling cock into me! Shoot your sperm! *Ah*!'

Her bottom ground and rolled violently as she clawed Pelham's back and he grasped her shoulders and began to ride her as a bucking bronco. Her legs slid down, her heels digging into the carpet as she arched her back, working her cunt back and forth against the ramming of Pelham's thick, glistening tool. The moment was nigh and Pelham sheathed his cock so fully within her that his balls nestled against her chubby bum cheeks. 'Now, Lucy, my little pet,' he said huskily, 'Suck it out with your darling slit—every drop.' He shuddered as powerful squirts of creamy spunk exploded in her, on and on, until the last faint dribblings oozed out as he sank full down, his weight pinning her to the floor with the last weak pulsings.

My own rod was now standing as straight and erect as any Guardsman on duty, and Lucy could see that I was game for a third bout. She smiled at me and motioned me closer. 'I know what you want, Andrew,' she whispered. 'But Pelham's big prick has made me somewhat sore. Just stay where you are and I will relieve your agony.' She pulled my aching prick towards her gorgeous lips which opened to receive my red knob. Lucy squirmed away to leave Pelham lying on his own as her lips enveloped my shaft and sank down its length, making me shudder with pleasure. She quickened the movements of her mouth and her right hand snaked down and busily frigged away at her still juicy cunt. All too soon I was forced to whisper to Lucy that I was about to come. She craned her neck forward and forced the entire length of my tool into her throat, her lips almost touching my balls. As I shot off my cream into her hot mouth she cupped my balls in her hand, her buttocks bucking up and down as

23

she transported herself to the very pinnacle of delight. I spent copiously into her mouth and she greedily sucked every last creamy drop from my now shrinking affair.

Calm now being restored, I awarded the sweetly flushed girl a loving kiss, caressing her everywhere. Of course, it was now Pelham's turn to be ready for more fun and games but Lucy said she was exhausted and needed to rest. 'Doctor White is dining with Reverend Shackleton tomorrow night,' she giggled, 'and I have invited my good friend Amelia Fenland to spend the evening with me. I have a splendid idea. Let us all meet in Doctor White's bedroom after supper. Shall we say at half past eight?'

'That sounds wonderful, my darling. That's all right with you, isn't it, old man?' I said, glancing across to Pelham.

'Oh, yes, most certainly. I would love to—ah—but—ah— does Amelia—?' he stammered.

'Of course she does, you silly boy,' laughed Lucy. 'Amelia hardly has the chance to have a good fucking more than once a month as she lives with her Uncle Jonathan in Totteridge Village, and he is terribly strict and rarely lets her leave the house. So she will be more than ready for the fray. Go to bed now and don't be tempted to play with yourselves as I want you both in tip-top fettle tomorrow night!'

And with this stern injunction she kissed us both lightly and stole away back to her rooms. Although she was the good Doctor's niece, she spent few days in idleness, as she spoke both French and German with great fluency and marked all the foreign language essays of the fourth and fifth form boys.

We walked back slowly to our studies, but outside the door of the small sanitarium I heard a rhythmic creaking of bed-springs. I looked across to Pelham who had also heard the noise and we tiptoed to the door which I opened slowly and with care. I held up my hand and motioned Pelham to stay still. The room was dark except for the light of two small candles. Sitting on one of the beds, quite nude, was the gardener's boy, Jack, a fair-haired youth of about fourteen.

And also naked was his companion who was lying on the bed slowly frigging his standing prick as if keeping it in a state ready for use. I peered forward and saw that it was Gilbert Bell, a third-form boy who was supposedly ill with a severe cold. He too was fourteen or fifteen years of age, a tall slender boy whose girlish features had caused him to bear the brunt of much teasing by his classmates.

Jack lay down on the bed and began to rub his own prick up and down until it too was in a fine state of erection. He slipped the skin of the shaft down from the red mushroomed head and said to Gilbert, 'Well, shall we see who can come quicker, you or me? Mind you, it would not be a fair contest as you've been frigging your prick for at least five minutes already.'

'Alright, Jack, on the count of three. One, two, three, go!' And to my surprise they began fondling each other's cocks (fortunately Gilbert was left-handed) and, sure enough, within moments they both began to spend with the first spurtings of white juice shooting out of their pricks like miniature fountains.

Pelham was about to speak and no doubt halt the proceedings, but I put my finger to my mouth and motioned him towards the door. When we were back in the corridor and I had shut the sanitarium door, he exclaimed: 'Why didn't you let me stop those two dirty beasts?'

'Look, we've had a jolly time and those two will forget the pleasures of solitary vice once Doctor White introduces them to nice girls like Lucy!' I said, feeling generous to one and all in anticipation of frolics the next night.

'Well, I don't know about that,' said Pelham with a dubious note to his voice.

'Live and let live!' I said cheerily as we strolled back to our studies.

'Plato believed that punishment brought wisdom,' remarked Pelham somewhat pompously.

'Ah yes, and Aristotle viewed it as a kind of medicine,' I replied gaily.

'But then Oscar Wilde has written that punishment is often

more brutalising than the crime—which I find difficult to believe,' said Pelham.

'I'm not so sure,' I said thoughtfully. 'Would it have made any difference if you had swished young Bell! I have grave doubts about that and you remember what Doctor White is always telling us. Mankind's efforts to enforce conformity in social morality has had a truly disastrous record of failure.'

'I suppose so, for it is true that no-one has yet devised a system of punishment that immunises society from evil or revolt.'

'So there you are. Good night, Pelham. I've just remembered that there's only a morning's lessons to be slept through tomorrow, as in the afternoon we are playing cricket against the Savages from High Barnet.'

'Good night, Andrew. Yes, we can sit and snooze whilst our team thrashes those yokels and then there is the evening to look forward to. My, I have only one regret.'

'What's that?' I asked.

'That Doctor White did not let Lucy initiate me into the arts of love last term!' he laughed. I joined in his merriment and we both undressed quickly and prepared for bed. Tomorrow would be a day worth waiting for!

I will pass over much of the happenings of that day, though I recall well how we eyed the clock frequently, waiting for the tedious hours to pass till the time appointed to meet our partners for the evening's frolics. Suffice it to say that somehow we managed to pay sufficient attention to our lessons in the morning to escape detention or extra evening preparation. We spent most of the afternoon lolling in the grass watching, as I had forecast, Nottsgrove's senior cricketers easily vanquish the team of gentlemen farmers from neighbouring High Barnet.

After a light meal, Pelham and I decided to take a short stroll through nearby Arkley Woods.

'We should have some fun tonight, old boy,' I said to Pelham, who looked somewhat thoughtful as we walked towards the quiet of Oaklands Lane.

'Yes, Andrew, I am looking forward to it tremendously,' he replied. 'I am just a little worried that Mr Priapus will fail me as he did with Lucy.'

I laughed and reassured him that he had little about which to worry. 'My dear old chap,' I said, 'The first time or two you will naturally be nervous, but once you become accomplished all will be well.' I could see by the bulge in his breeches that he was already thinking about the joys to come that evening, and I laid my hand on the pulsating swelling. 'My goodness, Pelham,' I said. 'I am sure that your prick is even bigger than mine. Let us compare and see who has the larger.'

Without ado I opened his trousers and let out his naked red-headed cock which stood in all its manly glory, stiff and hard as marble with the hot blood looking ready to burst from his distended veins. He then pulled out my own not inconsiderable affair which was, as it happened, fractionally shorter in length, which must have given Pelham further confidence for the evening's entertainment. We handled each other's tools in an orgy of delight during which I spunked creamy jets of froth onto his hand. I then dropped to my knees and played and sucked his delicious prick till he spent in my mouth with an exclamation of rapture, as I eagerly swallowed every last drop of his copious emission.

When we had recovered our serenity we walked back to the school, still pulsating with unsatisfied desire, to await with scarcely concealed impatience the appointed time of half past eight o'clock. And who could find it in his heart to blame us for wanting to speed the passage of time as the hands of the clock seemed to move so slowly! Ah, the fire of passion that coursed through our youthful bodies is now but an ember, though my torch is still capable of lighting a fire or two! Many a good tune is played upon an old fiddle!

CHAPTER TWO

IN MY experience, most pretty girls are not friendly towards one another, thinking perhaps that an equally attractive companion may turn some of the attention of the gentlemen present in the company. In fact, Lucy was not one of this flighty breed, and she chose her friends of the fair sex for their true qualities rather than any other. And indeed, this was well shown that marvellous summer evening.

The sultry day had ended with one of those wonderful sunset skies—with such gold as Cuyp himself never painted—though if truth be told both Pelham and myself were far too agitated to enjoy fully the beauties of nature. I cautioned my friend not to eat too hearty a meal. Somehow, we contained our impatience until the time came for us to wander through the cool of the old schoolrooms to our arranged meeting place. As we reached the bedroom door I could see Pelham trembling with excitement.

'Look, old man,' I said to him, 'Don't worry if you have, ah, starting problems again. Just relax and let yourself be swept along with the tide, so to speak.'

'Yes, Andrew, thank you for the advice,' he said. 'I suppose you can see that I am nervous.'

'Well, just don't fret yourself,' I said firmly. 'Fucking is as natural as swimming. All you have to learn is to do what comes naturally and all will be well.'

'I hope she's a pretty girl, this friend of Lucy's,' he muttered. 'Would you like to be a good chap and pair off with her and leave Lucy for me?'

I smiled as I guessed that Lucy would not be satisfied until we had tried every known sexual permutation but I judged it

28

best to leave Pelham in ignorance of the full joys awaiting him behind the door which stood before us.

'Don't worry, Pelham,' I promised. 'I'll stay with Amelia whilst you and Lucy do whatever takes your fancy.'

I knocked lightly upon the door and I heard a little giggle and then Lucy called out for us to enter. I opened the door and ushered Pelham in. The room was dark as the girls had closed the curtains and only two lamps lit the large room. I closed the door and locked it behind me. Although the girls were obviously there, we could not see them. Then we heard another muffled giggle from the far side of the large bed and I grinned—so that was where the two hussies were hiding!

'I can hear you though I cannot see you!' I called out, 'you are discovered, my pretties!' At this Lucy rose from her hiding place and to my amazement the delicious girl was quite naked! Although I had seen her in a state of nudity before, I gasped with admiration at her uptilted breasts, her flat stomach and the thick blonde mass of hair at the base of her belly. In a trice I rid myself of my shirt, trousers, socks and boots, and I moved purposefully towards her. We embraced and now it was my turn to tremble with delight as I felt the touch of her lips and the soft probing of her tongue in my mouth. My cock was now as stiff as a poker and ready for action. Though I could hardly wait to plunge Priapus into her waiting love bush, I knew what Lucy preferred me to do beforehand. So with a gentle effort I reclined her backwards upon the bed and moved my head down between her splendid white legs where the luscious, pouting lips of her cunny, quite vermilion in colour and slightly gaping open, invited my attention as she drew her legs further apart.

I was down on my knees in a moment and I glued my lips to that lovely little crack, sucking and kissing furiously to the infinite delight of the delicious girl who sighed and groaned with pleasure. It was now impossible to hold back, and getting up on my knees I brought my straining shaft to the charge and, to Lucy's high squeal of delight, fairly ran it right through into the depths of her throbbing pussy until my balls banged hard against her bottom. We lay still for a few moments whilst Lucy's pulsating pussy squeezed my cock so beautifully that I almost swooned away with pleasure. She then heaved up her bottom and I responded to this move with a shove of my own and we commenced a most exciting struggle. My manly staff fairly glistened with love-juice as it worked in and out of her sheath, whilst the lips of her cunny seemed to cling to it at each time of withdrawal as if afraid of losing such a delightful sugar stick; but this did not last long as our movements got more and more furious; and then suddenly she was transformed into a wild animal, screeching as she bucked and jerked uncontrollably beneath me. Then, with a little wail she slumped backwards, her buttocks and thighs clenched as she shook all over in a rapid drawn-out series of tiny spasms. Her cunt squeezed my prick even tighter, and the continuous pressure was now too much for me to bear. I could feel the boiling sperm rising and then it surged out of me, spurting from my prick deep inside her secret parts in an orgasm that seemed to last and last as I pumped my creamy white froth into her juicy, dark warmth.

We lay there panting with exhaustion from our labours and to my surprise I could see young Pelham and Amelia standing stock still watching us in some kind of awe at our performance. Like Lucy, Amelia was quite naked. She was a tall girl blessed with long tresses of light auburn hair, slightly golden in tint, deep brown eyes set off by dark eyebrows and long dark eyelashes, a full mouth, richly-pouting cherry lips and a brilliant set of pearly white teeth. And what magnificent swelling young breasts she possessed, round and firm with a lovely whiteness of belly which was set off below by a bushy Mons Veneris, itself covered lightly with silken, reddish hair through which I could just perceive the outline of her slit. Her breathing had quickened with excitement brought about by the passion that she had just seen displayed in front of her, her eyes were unduly bright and her nostrils flared out like those of a stallion coming upon a mare in heat.

'Come on, you two slowcoaches,' called out Lucy. 'Why, Pelham, you still have your clothes on. That is almost an insult to Amelia. Don't you want to fuck her?'

'Oh, of course I do!' Pelham stammered out.

'I think he is just a little bit shy,' said Amelia gaily, as she stroked the huge bulge between Pelham's legs which showed well that his equipment was now in the finest working order. She gave the bulge an encouraging rub up and down with her hand and this had the desired effect of setting a match to the tinder.

This was indeed all the encouragement he needed and in a veritable flash he was undressed and I noticed his thick cock with its enormous red head was bolt upright. Amelia and Pelham rolled beside us in the huge bed and now it was our turn to take the part of spectators at the match.

Amelia was experienced enough to see that her partner was fast approaching the climax of delight so she climbed onto his lap facing him and squeezed her knees alongside his muscular thighs. She put one arm round his neck and felt for his cock with her other hand, adjusting her position as she slipped his rock-hard tool between them, fitting it snugly into her quim. When she was sure that the few inches were safely inside, she hugged him tightly, kissing the corners of his mouth, and whispered: 'Push your prick into me darling—harder, that's right, you won't hurt me, keep pushing!' She worked her hips up and down, riding slowly but firmly on the throbbing shaft, letting it sink all the way into her juicy snatch, holding it there completely engulfed.

Pelham was in his own private heaven now—too excited to remember that he was performing in front of an audience and, within a minute, I saw him shudder as the spunk began to gather for the finale. Amelia began to grind her bottom round and bounced up and down on his mighty cock. Pelham thrust upwards as his prick began to spurt, giving complete and utter satisfaction for them both. But Amelia was now a-fire and, to my astonishment, she shot out her right hand and grabbed my cock which immediately responded by standing smartly to attention as she rubbed it up to its peak condition.

'I hope you don't mind, Lucy, if I get Andrew to fuck me,' said the little minx with a great show of politeness.

'Not at all, my dear friend,' replied Lucy. 'Please feel free to do so whilst I suck that lovely young prick of Pelham's which looks as if it still has some life in it.' And so saying, Lucy moved across me to kiss the end of Pelham's rod which was still oozing tiny drops of semen. Her tongue encircled his knob, savouring the juices and she drew him in between her rich, generous lips, sucking lustily as Pelham instinctively pushed upwards as her warm hands played with his heavy, hanging balls.

I was now more than ready for a further fray and I lifted myself onto my knees between Amelia's legs and quickly hooked them over my shoulders so that her bottom lifted entirely from the eiderdown and was immediately cupped in my hands. A low gurgle of anticipation escaped her and my tongue protruded, licking gently up between the lips of her slit whilst she bucked and writhed with pleasure. Heady as the salty musk taste of her was in those shell-like folds, I savoured too the lingering cream of her libation which had oiled her cunny as much as Pelham's pego had done just minutes before. 'Ahhh! Aaaah!' she cried as I found the pink bud of her clitoris which had erected itself like a miniature penis. My searching tongue made smaller and smaller circles till it probed that very centre of sensual enjoyment. Her rounded bottom began to move in rhythm with my explorations as I lashed juicily around the pearly flesh and gently nibbled at the swollen clitty, causing ripples of cum to spill over my tongue which I greedily slurped up.

Her heels drummed against my shoulders, her torso twisting, the silky cheeks of her plump bottom squirming in my palms whilst the tip of my tongue flicked remorselessly back and forth over her bud, diverting now and again to the sopping aperture of her cunny itself. Her quim literally mashed itself to my mouth bringing a fine salty sprinkling of her pleasure whilst I held the peach of her bottom cheeks drawn apart. 'Are you ready?' I whispered. 'Oh, yes, yes, put it in, dear Andrew without delay,' she gasped as raising my head, I slithered across her lovely body as her legs came crashing down on the bed. She opened them wide then curled them round my hips as she raised herself to meet my hungry

32

pego. So willing and so ready was she that she clung to me as if she would draw the very last breath out as I thrust harder and harder, plunging again and again as she pulled me even deeper inside her. She reached climax after climax as my throbbing cock slid in and out of her now dripping pussy. Oh! the joy as she rotated those lovely buttocks, getting my prick to penetrate her to the very extremity! My body grew moist with perspiration yet still she held on with her legs as her cunt wildly received my boiling spurts of sperm as it jetted spasm after spasm of spunk into her writhing love-box. She squeezed my balls gently as I withdrew and the last creamy drops trickled down my thighs. I rolled back exhausted but Amelia pointed my head to the left where, holding the thick shaft at its base in both hands, Lucy was still sucking Pelham's cock! It was obvious that they too had reached the crossing of the Rubicon as his prick jerked up and down and Lucy sucked as much as she could of the gushing cum as she gobbled the ruby head and her hands jerked up and down the shaft of his thick prick. Once he had shot his load we all lay back quite exhausted.

'Let's all snuggle up under the eiderdown,' said Lucy sensibly, as we would be foolish to catch cold after our fun. Pelham lay on the outside next to Lucy whilst I was sandwiched between the two beautiful girls.

'Oh, I love sucking cocks,' said Lucy smacking her lips. 'I would like to suck and suck but even Pelham here, who is one of the best, squirts off too quickly.'

'Yes, that can happen,' agreed Amelia. 'But I also enjoy it very much stroking a cock gently, playing around until it is really stiff. Then I like to suck it, but I don't really enjoy the spunk coming in my mouth.'

'But that's almost the best part,' said Lucy. 'I just adore a man who can shoot cream again and again. I find it so satisfying swallowing spunk as it squirts into my mouth. Nothing tastes as clean and fine as fresh sperm. You really should persevere, my dear, if for no other reason than that way you will never become pregnant!'

Amelia sighed and nodded agreement. 'I suppose I must

try harder,' she said. 'Mind, I can say that I have never had any complaints. You enjoyed fucking me just as much as being sucked off by Lucy, didn't you, Pelham?'

'Oh, indeed,' said Pelham gallantly. 'Both of you are absolutely top-hole, aren't they, Andrew?'

'Absolutely so!' I said heartily, reaching out to rub Lucy's mound with my right hand whilst my left hand strayed towards Amelia's hairy cunny and I gently inserted a finger and began slipping it in and out of her juicy snatch. She wriggled slightly and laid her hands on my semi-tumescent organ, but continued her conversation.

'I like to hold a stiff prick,' Amelia said. 'I like to put it in my cunt and to hold his balls while we are fucking. I think many girls lose much pleasure by not letting themselves relax.'

'That's just what I told Pelham to do—to relax completely,' I chimed in.

'I think I need to do that right now. I feel quite shattered,' groaned Pelham.

'I think Andrew still has something left over,' laughed Amelia as she rubbed my foreskin up and down leaving the ruby-domed head uncovered.

I thought it best not to show Pelham I could still fuck again so quickly so I moved Amelia's hand away.

'Let's rest for a little while,' I suggested.

'Oh, very well,' said Amelia. 'I think that shows that we are not really the weaker sex, are we, Lucy?'

'Certainly not, my dear Amelia, far from it,' smiled Lucy.

Now I remembered how arousing it could be for Lucy to recount one of her erotic encounters and I suggested that she told us a story from her past.

'Oh, very well,' she said. 'You two might feel jealous but one of the most satisfying sexual affairs I ever took part in concerned another girl.'

'This should be worth hearing,' I replied. 'We'll all listen quietly to you.'

Lucy sat up and began her tale. She was a born storyteller and we listened in silence as she began:

'Only recently a clever girl said to me that if you want to

understand something you must face it naked. She was expressing herself in philosophical terms as the role of philosophy might well be said to extend and deepen our own self-awareness. This is true also in the field of sexual relations. We must experience everything in the conceptual framework to truly aid our understanding, and it is proper for intellectual groups to make this particular sort of effort at self-comprehension. Until recently, if I may now recall my own personal experience, I had never enjoyed the experience of an amatory affair with one of my own sex, for at my school I always had a bedroom to myself. However, at a reception given by my uncle, Doctor White, some months ago, I found myself deep in conversation with a jolly girl named Kate Wilson. I don't think any of you have had the pleasure of meeting her, though her papa is an old acquaintance of Doctor White from their days at Cambridge University. He is now a diplomat and Kate travels with him often in Europe. Last year they were away nearly three months in Central America. However, I digress, and must return to the point of this tale.

'Kate was an extremely pretty girl with lovely firm and rounded breasts, a narrow waist but with a generous posterior and long shapely legs. Her complexion was somewhat darker than mine due perhaps to the considerable amount of travel she had undertaken, but it was set off well by silken hair almost as blonde as mine. She had large sensuous eyes and her flesh was as firm and smooth as ivory. We were the only females present and I soon gained the permission of Doctor White to escort my new friend to my rooms as the conversation was not of interest to us. I showed her around and as she inspected my bedroom she pounced on a copy of *The Pearl* which I had inadvertently left on my bedside table.

' "Heavens, how did you come by this book?" she asked. I began to stammer a reply but she chuckled and said: "Please do not be alarmed. I am neither shocked nor am I against people reading what they will. But the trouble with these smutty books is that they are all about men and women poking. Am I not correct?"

35

' "Yes, I suppose this is true," I answered. "Ah, but have you read about the joys of loving between women?" she continued. "I am sure that you have never read anything about that, let alone experienced such pleasure." I had to confess the truth of her observation though I had heard Doctor White mention this phenomenon in a lecture.

' "I am somewhat ignorant," I said. "Although my uncle tells me that there is a famous German professor who calls love between girls moral insanity because of its essential contrariness. And Professor Mantagazza classes it 'an error of nature'," I continued glibly. 'Such conduct is called a sickness by doctors though I am more tolerant, even if I still believe that there is nothing to beat the gorgeous feeling of pleasure occasioned by a thick tool entering one's damp cunt."

' "How do you know?" said Kate hotly. "In the women's club I belong to (the Holly and the Ivy Circle just off Regent Street), most of us feel that there *is* something better." And before I knew it she kissed and hugged me so lovingly that at first I felt slightly confused and, although we were all alone and no-one was in the least likely to disturb us, I felt my face burn with pink blushes as her hot kisses on my lips made me all atremble. Her touches fired my blood and the way she sucked my tongue seemed truly delicious.

'Suddenly we were locked together on my bed and her hot moist lips pressed down on my mouth as I responded as our tongues licked deeply inside each other's mouths. We rocked to and fro until she suddenly pulled away, stood up and undressed. I must tell you that the sight of her beautiful naked body sent shivers of desire up and down my spine. Her full breasts stood firm and her brown teats and rock-hard nipples contrasted excitingly with her smooth golden skin and large amount of crinkly hair covering her love mound that bulged between her long slim legs. I threw off my own clothes and in a flash she was on top of me, rubbing my titties to full erection between her fingers. She then gently eased her hands down between my legs to allow access to my own yearning cunny that was already moist, even before she began to stroke

36

my clitoris until my little button protruded stiffly. I lifted myself up and buried my face between her breasts making her titties shake with desire. I then lay back and massaged her deep breasts, stroking her titties to new peaks of hardness.

'Our pussies ground together as she sucked one of my own hard nipples making me squeal with excitement. I rubbed my pussy even harder against her until we were both practically on the brink of the ultimate pleasure. Kate gurgled with pleasure and she lowered her head towards my sopping quim and slipped her warm, wicked tongue through my cleft, prodding my little clitty, tonguing me to a little series of pleasure peaks. Our hands were everywhere, grabbing and squeezing and writhing together as our bodies locked, demanding release. "Lucy, my darling, where's your hand? Here, put it there, rub your finger on my crack, just there," she whispered. I frigged her passionately until I ducked my head between her splayed thighs and buried my mouth in the moist and succulent padding of curls in which nestled her cunny. I had a glorious view of the paraphernalia of love. A splendid mount covered with curly black hair; the serrated vermilion lips of her cunt slightly parted from which projected quite three inches a stiff fleshy clitty as big as a man's thumb. I opened the lips with my fingers, passed my tongue lasciviously over the most sensitive parts, took that glorious clitoris in my mouth, rolling my tongue around it, and playfully biting it with my teeth. It was too much for Kate and with a cry of, "Oh! Oh! You make me come, darling Lucy!" she spent profusely all over my mouth and chin.

'I continued to move my tongue along the velvety grooves of her cunt, licking and sucking the delicious juices that ran down like a stream, mixing with my own saliva. With each stroke of my tongue, Kate arched her body in ecstacy, pressing her fully erect clitty up against my flickering tongue. "Oh, Lucy!" she gasped, wrenching my mouth from her trembling slit. "Heavens! Pull my clit! Hard! You won't hurt me!" Gripping it in my fingers I tugged vigorously as she

37

writhed her hips wildly beneath me. After a brief rest she rolled me over onto my back.

' "Now it's my turn to repay the delicious pleasure I owe you," she sighed, kissing me rapturously, and sucking my tongue into her mouth so that I could scarcely catch my breath. With her fingers she opened my crack as wide as possible, then directing her fingers to the passage she probed into my most sensitive regions as only a woman would have known. Her fingers tickled round the hood of my clitty and when the little red love-bean broke from its pod, I at last had the courage to caress her own sweet body. Gladly she let her heavy breasts rest in my keen hands. I squeezed her tawny nips and then I came before I really wanted to, soaking her fingers with my pent-up juices. I sighed with utter bliss as my hands ran over her delicious body with frantic ecstasy. I cupped her breasts and stroked her buttocks and my fingers ran up the groove in between them and round and round . . . and then she pushed her head deep down between my legs and she was tonguing me to new peaks. She drove her wicked tongue right into the ring of my cunt and tossed it round the quivering walls, withdrew it, then plunged it in again deeply, rapidly in and out, in and out.

'Frantically she attacked my engorged clitty—a short, thick point of pulsating lust—as I groaned with sensual desire. She pulled away momentarily and then in a trice our bodies were locked together as she directed her own stiff clitty to the juicy passage she had opened up and she seemed to stuff it all in, lips and all, closing my cunt lips upon it and holding them together tightly with her hand. I can hardly express to you how novel and delightful this new conjunction was to me. We were both so heated as our spendings mingled together that we reached new heights of erotic fury. Without separating for a moment she rubbed and pushed about inside me, the lips and hair of her darling cunny titillating the sensitive parts in the most thrilling fashion. We swam in a veritable sea of lubricity until at last, sated with pleasure we lay panting together, almost swooning from the frenzy of our emissions.

'It was a warm evening and we recovered our strength

while we lay naked on the bed. "Was not that perfect bliss, my dear Lucy?" asked Kate.

' "It was certainly a most pleasing experience," I rejoined. "However, I still maintain that a really good fuck with a boy is even nicer."

' "I have enjoyed ordinary fucking," said Kate, "and it is true that it is certainly more pleasurable than most other activities."

'Then, to my horror, there was a knock on the door, and I remembered that I had asked one of the fifth form boys whom I tutor in French to give me the exercise I had prepared for him earlier that day. "Who can that be?" asked Kate with a note of worry in her voice. "It is Charlie Watkins, a fifth form boy who has an exercise to give me," I whispered. "Well, let's use him to see if you prefer boys to girls after all," she said.

'My blood was still up so I padded across to the door, still quite nude, and opened it wide. There stood sturdy young Master Watkins, a regular Adonis of a boy, rather slim, tall and dark, with a beautifully plump rosy face, dark hair and dark fiery eyes.

' "Come in, Charlie, don't be afraid," I said gaily. "I would like you to meet Kate, a dear friend of mine who would like you to fuck her. I'm sure that you will be a good sport and join in the fun."

'His eyes sparkled as I had never seen before. I should have guessed that he had yet to prove his manhood, and before I could close and lock the door, the bold boy had slipped out of his clothes and was on the bed with Kate.

'She reached down and encircled his fast-swelling young cock. I watched as she massaged it until it grew stiff and erect. She was now completely engrossed and unaware of my presence as she leaned over and took the ruby-headed knob between her lips, jamming down his foreskin and lashing her tongue round the rigid shaft. Then she sucked hard, taking at least half his tool into her mouth while her hands played with his rather small balls. She opened her mouth further and took the dome and stem further into the depths of her mouth, extending her tongue down to lick the soft underfolds of skin along the base of the shaft. She sucked with a firm motion as she slid her lips up and down the rock-hard cockshaft, gulping noisily as the head of his grand tool slid along the roof of her mouth to the back of her throat.

' "That is exquisite," groaned my fine young man, and from the manner of his fast breathing and twitching cock, I knew that he could not last too long and was fast approaching his climax. Kate had surmised this as well and she pulled her head up and whispered urgently: "I want your cock inside me. Lie down on your back, I want to ride you."

'He did not wait to be asked twice. He lay on the bed with his cock poking straight up. Kate quickly straddled him with her now ravenous pussy engulfing his prick, sliding down the not inconsiderable length of it until it was buried to the hilt. As soon it was lodged deep inside, she became frantic, sliding up and down, swaying back and forth with her hips as he arched up to meet her wild thrusts. This was too much for poor Charlie who began pumping faster and faster and his face reddened as his breathing quickened even further. My own juices had just begun dribbling down my legs for as you can imagine, this was most exciting to view, when Charlie came with great spurts of spunk that shot out of his prick all over Kate's lovely flat belly.

'This was too much for me to bear and I jumped on the bed and took hold of the sperm-coated cock, grasping hold of the now semi-erect monster. But after only a few quick rubs up and down, Charlie's cock was up to its full majestic height again and I lay back and opened my legs to receive him. He lowered himself gently on top of me and his lovely rod slipped into my hungry cunt. He began pumping up and down in a steady rhythm and my body surged upwards to meet his as every pounding jab struck home. I managed to slow him down, making sure that on each stroke the whole of his marvellous cock slid in and out of me like a piston. His eyes were closed and he had a dreamy look on his pretty face as his hands fondled my breasts. I whimpered with joy at every thrust and the climax came, shooting through the whole of

40

my body, taking away every other sense as I tossed and turned in delight. My hands thrust into his back, my cunt thrusting upwards in a mad effort to cram even more of that magic hardness further inside me as his balls banged against my bottom. I tensed to drain every last drop until, as my clitty throbbed from its explosion of fulfilment, his tool jerked wildly inside me and he shot a superb load of creamy jism into me as our juices mingled happily and our hairy mottes crashed together as we reached that fabulous plateau of pleasure.

'He rolled back exhausted but I thought that the young fellow-me-lad could perform at least one service. My hands ran around the cluster of thick black hair around his tool and I let my mouth travel along that lovely blue vein that ran along the shaft to the uncovered dome at the end of his glorious knob. Even though Charlie's prick was limp, it still looked capable and as you know, I love to fondle a prick and feel it throb and swell as my hand grasps the shaft and begins rubbing it up and down. Very soon, Charlie's cock had swelled up and I gently kissed the purple dome as I eased his foreskin up and down until his strong young weapon stood smartly to attention.

'His prick was throbbing furiously now in my mouth and I greedily gobbled the pulsating tool as I looked up to Charlie with twinkling eyes. He lifted himself to cup my breasts with his hands, deftly flicking my nipples with his nails. I began to give him sharp little licks on his swollen rod followed by a series of quick kisses up and down the stem, encompassing his hairy balls and running to that amazingly sensitive zone between his prick and arsehole. I thrust his cock in and out of my mouth in a quickening rhythm—deep into my throat and out again with my little pink tongue licking at the tip at the end of each stroke, lapping up the drops of creamy white fluid that were beginning to ooze out of the tiny eye at the top of his lovely knob.

'As soon as I felt that he was on the verge of coming I made ready to swallow his love juice. Charlie thrust upwards and his cock shuddered violently between my lips—and then in one long spasm he released his spunk, first a few early shoots and then crash! My mouth was filled with juicy, gushing foam as his cock bucked uncontrollably as I held it lightly between my teeth. I let it flow sweetly down my throat, gently worrying his now spongy knob with my tongue to stimulate it as much as possible and then, very gradually, I allowed the wet shaft to slide free.

'The three of us continued to suck and fuck until sheer exhaustion compelled us to separate. I discovered that Kate had already arranged to sleep in one of our guest-rooms whilst it was not difficult to smuggle Charlie back to his dormitory. In this short narrative it would be impossible to describe everything we did at great length, but I can assure you that our worship of Venus and Priapus led the three of us to hours in Paradise!'

This voluptuous narrative had stirred my blood and Amelia, whose appetite for *l'amour* was the equal of my own, quickly perceived that I was aroused. She stroked my now rampant prick, admiring its smoothness, its large uncapped head red and glowing with the heat that was raging inside it. So, gently laying her down and placing a pillow under the half-moons of her firm bum cheeks, with my hands I gently pushed her legs as wide apart as they would go, exhibiting to my gaze the gaping lips of her cunt, ready and open to receive my throbbing cock, which by now had raised its foaming head erect against my belly. Laying myself down upon Amelia, I made her take hold of my prick and put it in, but so firm and erect was it that she could barely bend its head down to the entrance of her dripping cunny. So magnificent was the erection that I had difficulty in entering the dear girl despite the stretching her pussy had previously received from our exertions. Drawing myself back to wet the head of my charger with some spittle, I slowly shoved away until my balls banged against her bottom hole. I moved slowly in and out at first, building up to such a speed that we soon both melted away, giving us both the maximum enjoyment of a joint spend.

Watching our couplings stirred both Pelham and Lucy and I sensed that both were now ready for one last joust of a splendid evening's entertainment. Lucy lay face down and buried her pretty face well into the pillows. Immediately Pelham raised himself to kneel behind the delicious girl, clasping his arms around her waist and manoeuvring his glowing, iron-hard prick between the cheeks of her lovely bottom.

'What an adorable bottom,' he exclaimed. 'May I have the pleasure of inserting my rod *au derrière*?'

'Of course you may,' smiled Lucy. 'But do be careful as you poke me as we have no cold cream readily available.'

He made no answer but thrust his cock towards the wrinkled little bum-hole that beckoned his throbbing tool. Lucy whispered to me to aid my friend who was totally inexperienced at bottom fucking.

'Ease into her slowly but firmly, old boy,' I murmured. 'Here, let me assist you.' I took hold of his pulsating shaft and eased the glowing dome of his noble weapon between Lucy's superb cheeks which were waiting to be split. He pushed forward but found difficulty in penetrating, so with my fingers I moistened the gleaming, rubicund dome with spittle and again placed it aright. This ministration achieved the desired effect and his prick quickly enveloped itself between the in-rolling cheeks of that mouth-watering bum. A little fearful at first in case he injured the darling girl, Pelham pushed slowly at first but then realised that he was now absorbed well enough in her tight little orifice and began to work himself with vigour, pushing his whole body forwards and backwards, making her bottom cheeks slap loudly against his belly as she moaned deeply with delight. His prick was now fully ensconced in her warm, tight arsehole and he screwed up his eyes in sheer bliss.

'My love, my desire!' he cried out as he bent over Lucy to fondle and weigh her lush breasts and erect titties. As she waggled her arse provocatively she lifted her head from the pillow and we could all see that there was no doubt of her total enjoyment of Pelham's thick rod pounding in and out of her gorgeous bum.

'Now, Pelham, now!' she gasped, and he needed little effort to obey as he flooded her bum-hole with such vibrant shoots that one could almost view the ripples of orgasmic joy that ran down Lucy's spine as she shuddered to her climax. As she artfully wriggled her bottom, spout after spout of creamy spunk filled her juicy hole as with a succulent *plop*, Pelham withdrew his glistening shaft and sank back upon his haunches as the exquisite spendings melted away to a tiny blob of white spunk on the tip of his cock.

We continued to fuck, suck and gamahuche until almost half past eleven and the lustful orgy drew to a close. Our passions were sated and we were all more than ready to fall into the arms of Morpheus. Pelham and I wished the girls a loving goodnight and made our way back to our rooms. We both slept extremely well until the rising-bell awoke us from our slumbers. A new day had dawned and this day too had its charms which I will now recount.

CHAPTER THREE

IT WAS a glorious summer day and, as good fortune would have it, my day was free of scholastic work as Doctor White had decreed that on such a beautiful morn, his senior charges would be best occupied in activities of a physical nature. Although his progressive ideas were shared by few of the parents, they all agreed that the good Doctor was always mindful of his boys' physical as well as mental well-being.

Ah, yes, *mens sana in corpore sano* (a healthy mind in a healthy body) was a maxim dear to his heart—and this is why that fine July morning saw me stride out through the fields, my rucksack on my back filled with my luncheon sandwiches and a jacket to slip on in case the weather changed, which at first seemed unlikely.

It was just after ten o'clock when I left Nottsgrove to walk to a favourite spot of mine, Lapping's Meadow, some two miles north of High Barnet. As I walked briskly along Oaklands Lane I became aware of what I believed to be a figure behind me that seemed to be keeping pace for pace with me. The sensation of being followed is a disagreeable one and I began to wonder if I were to be attacked by a footpad, though such crimes were virtually unknown in that sparsely populated area.

I quickened my steps and at once was conscious that the figure behind me was doing the same. Soon the path was clear of trees and I became ashamed of my first apprehensions. After all, the Queen's Highway was free for one and all to use. The steps dogged me as I walked on enjoying my exercise. But though it had been bright and clear when I left the school, as I crossed the main Barnet road the air began to smell of rain. It was still warm when I sat down on a mossy bank between the road and the fields of a jolly local farmer, Mr Morrison, whose sixteen-year-old daughter, Louella, was a young lady much admired by all at Nottsgrove. She was one of Tennyson's rosebud garden of girls, a miniature of conventional English beauty with gold-dusted light-brown hair and soulfully expressive dark brown eyes, a most exquisite and charming girl who had attended the occasional cricket match between Nottsgrove and the local club of which her brother Harry was a noted member.

I allowed my rucksack to rest against the slope of the hillock and the skin of my back exhaled warm moisture. I stretched my arms above my head and yawned, at peace with the world. But then the first drops of a summer shower blew against my face and I stood up reluctantly and readjusted my pack. I was about to walk across the field to take shelter in a barn only some two hundred yards away when I stopped abruptly as I saw the figure that had been following me for the previous mile or so. It was none other than Louella Morrison and I blushed to think that this lovely girl had frightened me into thinking that I was in some kind of danger.

'Good morning, Miss Morrison,' I called out. 'Have you been following me? I thought I heard someone behind as I was walking.'

'Indeed I have, Andrew,' she replied shyly. 'I would have called out to you but you looked deep in thought and I had no wish to disturb your meditations.'

'That was most thoughtful of you but, indeed, my mind was engaged upon nothing more than admiring the scenery. Now, alas, the rain has interrupted any such thoughts I might have had. Let us walk briskly to your father's barn and shelter ourselves from this unfortunate shower,' I said.

'Yes, let us do so,' she replied with a little smile. We stepped out smartly, when Louella stumbled and, with a grimace of pain, hobbled along as quickly as she could.

'Miss Morrison, I am so sorry, let me help you,' I said and took hold of her arm and placed her hand on my shoulder. 'Is that better? Come, let us see if you can walk.'

'Thank you, Andrew,' she said, but I could see that she was in pain.

'Permit me,' I said and taking hold of her with my left arm behind her back, lifted her off her feet and carried her to the barn door which was slightly ajar. Once inside, I gently let her down by a pile of newly-mown hay. 'Are you alright?' I enquired.

'Well, yes, I think I am. Let me take a few paces. Ah, that is better, I think it was nothing more than a slight strain and I am fully recovered. Thank you so much for helping me.' And to my astonishment and delight she gave me a full kiss on my cheek.

'Why, Miss Morrison—' I stammered.

'Oh, please, call me Louella,' she said. 'After all, I call you Andrew and you do not take offence at the familiarity, I trust?'

'Not at all, no, of course not, Miss, er, Louella.'

I shrugged off my rucksack and sat down next to the girl on the huge pile of hay that performed sterling service as a couch. We were both somewhat weary from our walk and we refreshed ourselves with a drink of bottled water that I had placed in my rucksack. The shower had now ceased and the barn was warm so I removed my jacket and sat in shirtsleeves and trousers. We sat together then in silence and I could not but admire the heavenly creature next to me. Her dark hair was drawn back in a bun and, as she loosened it, I noticed that her skin appeared faintly olive-tinted but otherwise of such clarity that it seemed illumined from within. She was wearing a blue jacket which, being fashioned tightly to her torso and waist, allowed me to see the perfect development of her breasts, while her lower limbs were clad in a long, pleated skirt. Her features were finely shaped and her full rich mouth beckoned mine. Our mouths joined and in a trice we were kissing and cuddling with the greatest passion.

She pulled away from me suddenly and said: 'Andrew, I

know it is your birthday next week. I have a present. Would you like it now?'

Puzzled, I replied: 'Yes, Louella, I would, but where is it?'

She undid her jacket and threw it to the ground, then putting her hands underneath her dress, she pulled down her drawers. 'Help me off with my skirt and petticoats!' she breathed, and I needed no second bidding as my cock now reared up hard against my trousers as the skirt dropped to the ground, swiftly followed by the rest of her clothes, until she stood completely naked in front of me. I could at first only stare with wonder and then with unabashed lust at her small but exquisitely formed uptilted breasts and smooth white-skinned belly, below which twinkled a dark, rounded mass of curly black hair.

Without further words, we sank back into the hay, entwined in each other's arms, exchanging the most ardent of kisses as the clever girl began to unbutton my trousers, releasing my straining cock which sprang up like a flagpole between my thighs. She lay me down on my back and then bent forward, rubbing my rigid member against her breasts, squeezing along its length, moving to straddle across me so that her pert young bum cheeks were but inches from my face as she lowered her head, parting her full lips to take my cock into her deliciously wet mouth, sucking slowly, deeply, softly. She manoeuvred until her lips completely covered my engorged member, sucking lustily as she slurped down to the very base. The cheeks of her bare bum so close to my face fired me to even new heights of passion. The moist lips of her quim parted to my groping fingers and her bottom cheeks began a merry dance. Without delay I forced my head upwards and slipped my tongue between those pouting cunt lips which caused the lovely girl to moan with delight as she sucked steadily on my pulsating prick. She wriggled her hips anew and the curled point of my tongue found the wrinkled little bum hole into which I inserted it a trifle, as a fond murmur of pleasure escaped from the owner of the altar of love to which I was attending. My hands moved over her body in tantalising strokes and her clitty throbbed against my fingers as they slipped in and out of her pussy with ease, coated in the love juice which trickled from her in a stream.

I knew that I could not keep this position without exploding and I gently eased her off me until she lay on her back. I eased her legs apart and knelt down between them. She pulled down my head to her sweet cunny and my tongue searched out her fine stiff little clitty which projected quite an inch and a half from the pouting lips of her vagina. I sucked it in ecstasy and titillated her sensitive parts so well that she spent profusely in a moment or two, holding my head with her hands to make me go on. It was perhaps the most exciting gamahuche ever as my tongue revelled in her creamy emission till she begged me to stop and instead insert my now bursting prick.

I grasped her thrilling young body and guided my rampant cock into the soft, clinging pussy and she grasped my bottom cheeks to pull me inside her. Soon we were locked in hard, sweeping strokes as my long stiff prick slid in and out of her sopping cunt. I sank myself into her warmth, glorying in the smooth unfaltering motion of her hips, in the strong confident lifting of her body as she joined me in a wild bout of passion. I felt myself swell further within her as she kept driving up against the power of my punching hips, bouncing back from each drive, over and over again as she met every onslaught with complete delight. She bucked beneath me as I felt the juices boil up inside my throbbing tool and with one mighty *wham!* I plunged yet again into her juicy pit and the darling Louella arched her back to receive the thick squirts of frothy white cum that spurted out of my pulsating prick.

My climax rocketed through me with such force that I was totally unable to fight against the current as the hot gobs of jism continued to pour from my cock. I could only whimper as the spunk dribbled down from the tip of my glistening knob which I slowly withdrew from its enclosing sheath. 'I regret that I came too quickly for you!' I panted.

'Oh no, you dear boy, I have spent copiously too, but I am sure that we can repeat the game, can we not?' She smiled back at me, sweetly, with a slight nod of her head. 'This is really marvellous. I want you to fuck me again and never stop!'

'I'm sure they never taught you such words at school;' I said. 'I am most surprised.'

'Oh, every girl knows the word. Now come on, Andrew, fuck me hard! Fuck me in the mouth and fuck my cunt!'

And in a moment our lips were glued, our tongues caressing. The hairs on my chest had brushed her nipples to erection and my fingers found their way to tickle her bum-cheeks. She pushed me down onto my back and tongue-teased my prick erect. The sight of her pretty face, her mouth bulging with my rock-hard cock, prepared me soon enough. But before I could move, it was Louella who swung a leg over her mount and lowered herself upon the phallic saddle.

'Now, Andrew, now!' she cried. 'Oh, my dear love, fill me!'

Smoothing out every little wrinkle inside her cunt, it seemed to me, my prick drove upwards to her soft depths as she rode gracefully and easily, leaving me little employment. My hands roved around her slender shoulder blades and found the light contours of her spine. Following these down, I came to the cleavage of her bottom and fiddled between her cheeks to excite her doubly. She drew my hands from there, in protest, as I thought. But it was only in order that she might lead my right hand in a light smacking rhythm upon her rump. My frisky filly wanted the double pleasure of riding whilst at the same time feeling that there was a jockey upon her to spur her on! Gently and rhythmically I spanked her backside as she rode. The effect was such that I could feel warm, pearly droplets of love juice bedewing my prick as it drove into the very depths of her pussy.

Suddenly she released a muffled scream of ecstasy into my mouth and the crisis was precipitated for us both. From the swollen knob of my cock great gusts of jism jetted into her dripping cunt. Indeed, it must have felt as powerful to her as to me—a rare event if we are to believe Doctor Featherstone-haugh—for Louella had her second orgasm within seconds of the sensation of my sperm squirting into her.

We lay there quite exhausted at last though my cock still threaded her and gently we turned on our sides, remaining entwined. Presently we drew apart and hastily dressed as we had no wish to be compromised by discovery. Louella whispered to me that the house just half a mile along the road was empty but that she possessed the keys and that we could continue our pleasures there. I eagerly assented, remembering that the cottage belonged to a Mr Greenhalgh, a writer, who spent a considerable amount of time in France.

Indeed, the little cottage was quite empty when we arrived at the front door. Flowering myrtle crept up the sides and wild roses perfumed the air about it. The flowers smelled of love and excitement, an incredibly sweet and moving odour.

Louella bent down and extracted the key from under the doormat. 'That is a most unsuitable place to leave a key,' I exclaimed. 'Any robber would look for it there after ascertaining that the cottage lay empty.'

'Ah, yes,' replied Louella. 'But in fact Mr Greenhalgh gave the key to me and I left it under the mat only earlier this morning.'

Oh, sweet girl, *la bella donna della mia mente*! We kissed with burning passion as we entered the hall. I looked around as Louella led me into the drawing room. As Mr Greenhalgh used the cottage infrequently, he furnished the rooms quite sparsely. The furniture, all very old, consisted only of a large sofa with a huge bent wooden back, an oval table in front of the sofa, chairs along the walls and two or three cheap prints in yellow frames, representing girls with birds in their hands —that was all.

But the room sufficed for our needs. The sun was now shining fiercely and its rays burned through the wide windows heating the room so that we stayed warm, even as we tore off our clothes to stand before each other absolutely naked. My truncheon was already standing to attention as stiff as any guardsman, its bulbous dome bursting through the foreskin to pulsate, exposed, as the lovely girl gently clasped the shaft of my hot prick as I took her in my arms. I swept her off her feet and, with her lips still glued to mine and now fiercely rubbing my cock up and down, she put her other arm round my neck as I carried her over to the waiting sofa. I laid her down on her back and, still refusing to relinquish her hold on my throbbing rod, she continued to tongue my mouth so vehemently that I felt the boiling juices already collecting in my balls.

Somehow she sensed that my climax was nearing and she quickly withdrew from my mouth and pulled me on top of her. She motioned me to put my prick near her lush red lips and she eagerly sucked upon the red knob, noisily and uninhibitedly lashing her naughty tongue all around my rampant pole, slowly but surely encompassing inch after inch until I could hold back no longer and I began to fuck her mouth in long, slow strokes until at the downstroke, every piece of that delicious morsel was in her mouth and throat and my balls banged against her juicy lips. Such delight could not continue indefinitely and soon, all too soon, I felt the gush of sperm that was not to be denied and I spunked gob after gob of thick white foam into her throat. Louella greedily slurped every drop of love-juice from me, licking every blob from the tip of my knob until my fine prick lay limp on my thigh.

The sofa was wide enough for us to lie closely beside each other, so I rolled off her and we lay motionless in each other's arms.

'Did you enjoy that sucking-off?' enquired the delightful Louella.

'Oh, my darling, the joy was almost more than I could bear,' I replied truthfully.

'I am so glad. My dear friend Sophia taught me how to suck a stiff prick but I feared that she was more expert than I.'

'Sophia? Do you mean Sophia Lyttelton, your cousin, who came with you to Nottsgrove last April when we invited local ladies and gentlemen to see our school amateur dramatics?'

'Yes, that is the girl, Andrew. Do you remember her? She is prettier than me, is she not?'

I looked at my new love with indignation. 'Certainly not,' I said heatedly. 'She is by no means as lovely a creature as you.' This was certainly the truth although I did recall Sophia as being a most uncommon beauty. She was a tall, slim girl, not yet sixteen with wavy golden brown hair, a high complexion and intensely blue eyes, a pretty little nose and a fine bow mouth. So that little minx had instructed my Louella in the art of sucking a penis! I was quite flabbergasted, and told Louella of my surprise.

'It may shock you, dear Andrew, but Sophia has been sucking for almost a year now. In fact her first *amour* was with my brother Harry.'

'With Harry? He is only a year older than you is he not, my precious? This is indeed a surprising conversation for me.'

'Well, that may be so but Harry is quite a handsome boy and, despite your denial that Sophia is prettier than me, I know how attractive she is to men. Since Harry's cock has been able to stand, I have noticed that his breeches bulge whenever he is near my cousin!'

'Good heavens! Are you sure that they have actually—'

'Most certainly. Why, I saw them together only last month. You remember one Sunday the temperature rose to what must have been record heights. My parents were out for a walk and the three of us were left alone. Shall I continue, Andrew, as I have no desire to bore you with an uninteresting story?'

'No, no, go on, go on.'

'As I said, then, we were alone and the sun was beating down with all its might. Sophia suggested we take a short walk down to the river where it would be cooler. Our way to the river bank was by a path through a plantation of tapering firs which had been planted some years earlier and which sheltered the path in winter from the elements. By reason of the density of the interwoven foliage, it was a mite gloomy there, even during a hot, cloudless afternoon. To describe the place fully it would be best to call it a vast, low, naturally-formed hall, the plumy ceiling of which was supported by slender pillars of living wood, the floor being covered by a soft, dun carpet of needles, mildewed cones and tufts of grass.

'We all stripped off our clothes as Sophia and Harry wanted to bathe in the river and she had brought some towels with her. Nothing loath, I laid my clothes neatly in a pile but when I looked up I could see Harry and Sophia were already walking hand in hand towards the river bank and his cock was already in a state of some excitement.

'I pretended not to notice and stepped off the river bank into the cool water, which was more invigorating. But to my amazement, Sophia and Harry had set down a towel on the bank and were sitting on it, embracing passionately. Harry was squeezing her titties in between running his hands licentiously all over her naked body, whilst she had hold of his rampant cock which stood staunchly up with its bulbous dome unhooded as she rubbed his shaft to iron-hard stiffness. Then, shaking a fringe of hair clear from her eyes, she bent down and took the stiffened tool in her mouth. I could see that she sucked slowly, with every refinement of tongue, tickling and working round the little "eye" on the dome. Then, afraid that Harry would spend too soon, she left off her lubrication with a butterfly kiss and turned over on her belly, pushing out her firm young rump towards Harry's glowing face.

'By now I, too, was excited and my hand went down between my legs and I began to rub my own pussy which was already deliciously damp as I was standing in water up to my belly button. My excitement increased when Harry wet the head of his prick with spittle and, as he drove it down between Sophia's bottom cheeks, I heard her gasp with fright. She knew, however, that she should not tense herself against the knob and she relaxed her cheeks as Harry drove forward again, this time reaching her puckered little bum-hole, and he grunted with delight as he pushed in at least two or three inches of his prick, which fortunately was not too thick.

'Sophia obviously possessed an exquisitely tight rear-dimple and his cock rode in and out of the tight sheath of her bottom as at the same time he twiddled her nipples and kissed the back of her neck. Delightedly I watched his lusty young tool plunge in and out of the now widened rim of her bum-hole, pumping and sucking like the thrust of an engine. She reached back and spread her cheeks even further as the pace quickened and the movements of her rump became more hurried until Harry shot his jets of spunk deep inside her bottom.

'All the while my fingers were working in and out of my pussy as my thighs squeezed together, but though some love juice dribbled out, it was not nearly as satisfying as a good honest fuck and Sophia had obviously reached the peaks of delight. They now lay silent except for their long-drawn breaths as the call of birds and the smell of mown grass came from the sunlit world around us.

'Then Harry sat up and, with a frown, told us that he had just remembered that he was already late for an appointment with Mr Atkins, the farm manager. The matter of business would detain him only a half-hour at most but he had to make his excuses. We said we would wait for him to return and he dressed quickly and ran as fast as he could after his exertions towards the farmhouse. Meanwhile, I decided to return to the bank and I picked up a fresh towel and dried myself as Sophia lay back, exposing her firm young body to the sun.'

Listening to this sensual tale had made my cock rock-hard and the telling had stimulated Louella who responded eagerly to my advances. She wriggled herself on her belly and twitched her rounded bottom cheeks provocatively at me. I immediately positioned myself for the charge and Louella took hold of my swollen prick and lasciviously placed it at the entrance to her puckered rosette. I pushed hard and she cried out in surprise more than discomfort. 'Go on, go on, Andrew. I want a nice thick pressing of juice up my bum.'

So I went to work with a will and her bottom responded gaily to every shove as I drove home, my balls bouncing against her smooth rounded bottom. I worked my sturdy prick in as far as it would go and it tingled deliciously in her velvety depths as her nether cheeks were drawn irresistably tight against my flat belly. I had corked her to the very limit. She squeezed to eject me from the constrictions of her bottom-hole but only served to heighten my pleasure. I moved in and out in a slow shunting movement as I snaked my right hand round her waist and, diving into her curly motte, I massaged her little erect clitty, with much luscious kissing as she turned her dear head towards me. I could feel her love juices flowing as she worked her bum to bring me off in a flood of gushing come which both warmed and lubricated her superb backside. As I spurted into her I continued to work my prick back and forth so that it remained stiffly hard and, with a 'pop', I uncorked it from her well lubricated arsehole. We lay exhausted, recovering our senses as the warm sunshine bathed the room in a rosy glow. My, my, the tenderness of those hours will ever remain with me—*me tamen urit amor; quis enim adsit amori.**

By now we were hungry and we eagerly devoured the sandwiches and consumed the lemonade I had luckily packed in my rucksack. I asked Louella if she could come to the school that evening as I had no preparation before me and I wanted to fuck Louella again as soon as possible. We agreed to meet that evening at the entrance to the school and, after a fond farewell kiss, I dressed and began my walk back to Nottsgrove. At first I walked brightly with a gay demeanour, but the nearer I got to the school, the more my conscience pricked me—for how would Lucy take to the idea of my introducing a fresh girl into our sport? I knew that Lucy preferred me to fuck her above all others and she would be hurt if I showed that my heart was bound up with another. This was a delicate problem which would have to be solved and I

* Love consumes me yet—for what bound may be set to love? *Virgil.*

wondered how I could do so without hurting anyone's feelings. Never do tomorrow that which can be done well this day—this was a maxim that Doctor White was fond of repeating to us. There was much to be said for grasping this nettle at the first opportunity and I resolved to do so. Perhaps a mutual friend could come to my assistance, I mused, and by the time I reached the gates of my dear old *alma mater*, a plan of action had formed in my brain.

CHAPTER FOUR

I MAY have mentioned in a previous epistle to this esteemed journal that Doctor Simon White was a keen horticulturalist and was often to be found during his few hours of leisure preparing learned papers upon the delights of flora and fauna. And it was just such a paper that he was working on when I called upon him in his private study. It was typical of the man that, although deeply engrossed in the preparation of his thesis (those readers interested in his works may read them in the quarterly magazine produced by the Royal Horticultural Society), he looked up and greeted me in his usual affable fashion. Every boy at Nottsgrove knew that the headmaster's sanctum was somewhere they could go to at any time to discuss a personal matter of any description.

'Andrew, my dear old chap, come in,' boomed the good doctor. 'I haven't had a chance to speak to you for some days, and I wanted to know how Forbes-Mackenzie behaved himself during his recent initiation?'

'Oh, very well, sir, very well indeed. He played his part to the full, showing every kindness and consideration to his partner.'

'That is good to hear, Andrew, I am well pleased. Far too many young men partake of the joys of fucking but forget to ensure that the lady who is providing such exquisite delight is also entitled to some happiness, especially as she may be running the risk of an unwanted swollen belly! I hope that we won't have any problems on that score.'

'I don't think so, sir, as Lucy and Amelia were both experienced enough to—'

'Amelia?' interrupted my old mentor. 'Surely you don't mean that the lovely young wench Amelia Fenland partook of the delicacies of the feasts of love?'

'Well, yes, sir. I must apologise for mentioning a lady's name in such a context,' I stammered.

'Yes, to be sure, you must hold your tongue about such affairs,' said Doctor White. 'However, no damage is done as I shall not repeat your indiscretion. I am a little shocked to think that she would enjoy sharing with Lucy. Indeed, I did not know that she had even crossed the Rubicon, so to speak. I hope this was not the first time she was threaded?'

'Oh, no, sir,' I replied, somewhat relieved that I had not compromised an extremely pleasant girl. 'She was well versed in the arts of fucking, sucking and every facet of the noble sport.'

He nodded, pleased with the information as he had no wish to proselytise any young person to his own liberated philosophy—nor did he wish a breath of scandal to mar the glorious reputation of the old school.

I sighed with relief as the conversation had taken a turn in exactly the path I needed to bring up the ticklish problem that was bothering me.

'Sir, there is a problem bearing some relation to such matters which brings me here,' I said.

'Nothing too serious, I hope?' said my old mentor. 'Sit down, my boy, sit down. You know as do all my scholars that you may talk to me in complete confidence about any problem, great or small.' He motioned me to take a pew and he settled himself in the deep French armchair that the Old Nottsgrovian Society had presented to him some six years back upon the occasion of his fortieth birthday.

'Well, Andrew,' he said encouragingly. 'Spit it out and let me hear what is troubling you. As you know, I take a special interest in you and other boys whose parents are often abroad, acting *in loco parentis* especially in personal and private matters.'

Reassured, I blurted out my thoughts—how I thought so highly of Lucy yet only that morning I had banished her from my mind when the beautiful Louella offered me her delicious body and I had totally succumbed to her blandishments.

'When I am with Lucy,' I said earnestly, 'we enjoy each other's company tremendously. We talk, we laugh and when we are locked together in times of passion, we cling together in a stillness, lost in each other's presence, speaking few words, scarcely moving.'

'And yet you felt similar feelings when you were with Louella?' prompted the headmaster.

'Yes, sir, I must admit that I did,' I said somewhat shame-facedly. 'I feel that Lucy will be most hurt if she knows that I am showing favour to other girls.'

'Your worry does you credit,' said Doctor White gravely, although I could not help but perceive that he had a slight twinkle in his eye. 'But have no fear, Andrew. Lucy thinks highly of you and indeed of all her lovers. She will not fuck lightly, Andrew, and there are many students and I suppose members of staff who would give their all to have their pricks inside my niece—and I don't really blame them either! But Lucy takes her pick of the pricks that are offered to her and she has yet to find the right man to marry. When she does, I am afraid that you and all the others will have to find another mistress as she will then transfer all her favours to the lucky man who will stand beside her at the altar. But rest assured, Lucy has no thought of marriage for some time and you may enjoy your romps with a clear conscience. However, in all fairness, I think you should ask her permission before you bring another girl into your, ah, activities. She may not know the girl which could cause embarrassment or, even worse, she might not like her which could cause problems all round, not least for yourself.'

'I believe the two girls are not unacquainted, sir,' I said.

'Make sure, make sure—that is my advice, Andrew,' said Doctor White with a grin. 'And here is some final advice. Let the two of them get together first with you in a relaxed and comfortable environment. Louella is coming to Nottsgrove tonight? You know that guests must leave by ten o'clock, you randy young puppy? I expect you to obey the rules, you know! However, if I were you I would entertain them first with refreshments in your room. Then, perhaps you could read to them. Oh, yes, that would be an excellent plan, and I have a splendid volume of classical literature you may borrow. I suggest you read a portion of the work of Mr Cleland which you will find on page three hundred and five.'

'I should read to them, sir?' I said, rather puzzled by this somewhat strange advice.

'Certainly, Andrew,' said the Doctor, rising from his chair. 'Most certainly you should do just what I tell you. After all, think on the words of the great Virgil:

Tale tuum carmen nobis, diuine poeta,
quale sopor fessis in gramine, quale per aestum
dulcis aquae saliente sitim restinguere riuo.'*

And with these words ringing in my ears, he sent me packing, clutching his book under my arm. I pondered yet again as to whether Doctor White had taken my problem seriously for there was, I was sure, the hint of a smile playing around his lips as he wished me good afternoon. But was there really any alternative, I asked myself with resignation? In truth, there was none and I knew that I should have to screw up my courage to the sticking point and face my beloved Lucy. I would tell her quite straightforwardly and with as much candour as I could muster that I had chanced upon meeting a very pleasant young lady that morning and that I had invited her to spend the evening with us. There was no way to avoid adding that I had enjoyed a marvellous fuck with the lady, Louella Morrison, who perhaps Lucy had met before. If Lucy chose to be annoyed by the idea, I would have to inform her that I could not now break my word to Louella and that if she, Lucy, thought I was a cad, so be it. I would accept her strictures in silence and beg her forgiveness. Of course, what

---

* For us your song, inspired poet, is like sleep on meadow grass for the fatigued, or in the heat quenching one's thirst from a leaping stream of sweet water.
Virgil, Eclogue V.

really concerned me was the selfish fear that Lucy might be so angry with me that she would never again enter my study at night for a mutual spending of love juices and that our liaison would terminate for ever—but this was a risk I was forced to take and there was now nothing for it but to face the music!

I was so engrossed in turning over these thoughts in my mind that I can scarce recall how I spent the next hours until I was free to meet Lucy in a favourite place of ours, behind the cricket pavilion after tea-time. This was a most handsome structure paid for by Alderman Sir Michael F——, Lord Graham G—— and a wealthy group of sporting Old Nottsgrovians.

I kissed Lucy and without delay told her that something was bothering me and that we had to talk.

'Is this a matter of importance?' she enquired.

'It most certainly is,' I said heavily. How was I going to tell her?

'Does this weighty matter concern me?' she twinkled lightly. 'Oh, Andrew, what can it be?'

'Well, my dear,' I struggled out. 'The matter of concern, ah, it is, er, a very, how shall I say this, a most personal, ah, affair—'

'Concerning the fact that Louella Morrison had hold of your darling prick this morning!' she finished triumphantly with a little giggle.

Good heavens! I thought with horror. Surely Doctor White of all people would never break a confidence!

'Oh, Andrew, you are a chump!' she continued. 'Why, you silly goose, did it never cross your mind just how fortunate a coincidence it was that Louella was able to follow you? That she knew that you would be taking a walk this morning? Did you never think how ready she was for that glorious fuck in the hay? Was it by mere chance that Mr Greenhalgh's cottage was so invitingly near and empty, too? My, how convenient all the pieces in the puzzle fall so neatly into place, don't they, my dear boy!'

I stared in shocked amazement at my darling girl. Why, she

had known all the time and from her words it appeared that she had even connived in the whole affair! What a thoughtful, sweet girl she was, I thought, as she looked at me merrily with a roguish smile upon her pretty little countenance. Of course, she realised that I would enjoy nothing better than a nice fresh fuck from out of the sky, so to speak, and I swept the lovely girl into my arms and we embraced heartily, lost in that strange stillness that only lovers enjoy. Readers, I shall always remember the smell of the green grass, slightly damp still after the morning's showers, the smell of the fresh summer air and the softness of Lucy's firm young breasts crushed against my chest. My lips found that little hollow in her neck, my arms went right round her to hold her tightly against me. Ah, what joy, what bliss! My hands roved across her and her flesh quivered beneath the journeying hands and it was as if the earth itself came alive as at the touch of a gale or a storm of rain.

The scent of sweet Lucy was like that of the earth, the sighing of her breath like that of the wind in the trees. As I fastened my mouth upon hers and laid my hand on her breasts, I was under an enchantment, her spell and the earth's spell. For a moment I clung to her still more closely, and then we sank to the ground and my hands went under her skirt where, to my amazement, I found that she was quite naked underneath. As we continued to kiss passionately, I threw up the skirt to expose the naked charms of her pussy to the world. My hands pressed against the inside of her thighs and she allowed me to spread them wider and she covered my face with her own hands as she felt my breath between her thighs. My mouth touched the love-lips and my hands slid under her adorable bum cheeks, lifting her to my waiting mouth. I carefully examined the soft lips of her cunny, covered with downy golden hair and then I began to lick her and I trembled with excitement as my naughty tongue sought out and found the secrets of her quim. Her juices dribbled like honey from her parted labia and her clitty turned from pale pink to deep red as I flicked it gently with my wet, darting tongue. I delighted in the taste of her flesh as I licked and sucked at the stiffening little clitty and the juices began to flow over my face as I sniffed that erotic female odour, my nose buried in her damp motte. As I sucked and sucked bringing Lucy to new peaks of delight, I moved my own body to the side so that her eager hands could unbutton my now bursting fly. My cock shot up, rampant, as she plucked it out of its covering and pulled me across her as she reached across and sucked the tip of my red-capped cock which waved in front of her. She grasped it with both hands and took it firmly in her mouth, slurping lustily on the shaft as my body went into paroxysms of delight. I could not contain my orgasm and I shot my seed right into her mouth. Lucy's mouth was like a suction pump and she swallowed every drop of my copious emission but still my prick was ramrod stiff and then I heard her whisper: 'Andrew, my dear, I am ready for you now.'

She held me as I lowered myself on top of her and our bodies were joined from mouths to groins as her nipples brushed against my chest and I could feel their rough hardness, even through the material of her frock. I pumped again in time with her jerking hips as she clutched my own heaving bottom, inserting her finger into my bottom hole to spur me on to push my pulsating prick even further inside her sopping wet cunny. As I drove again and again she bucked her hips urgently to meet every thrust of my jabbing pelvis and she lifted her bottom to work it round and round, her hips rotating to achieve the maximum contact.

Desperately she clutched at me as I felt the boiling sperm gather in my shaft as my balls banged against her rounded bottom. She threw back her head in abandon and then a primordial sound came from deep within her as her climax spilled and coursed through her body. Her clitty rubbed against my own thatch and I groaned as I could hold back no longer and, with a crash, I pumped spurt after spurt of hot jism into her womb as wave upon wave of ecstasy thrilled through every fibre of my being. I pulled out my soaking tool, which was glistening with its coat of love-juice and was still dribbling out spunk, as Lucy swooped down and sucked the very last morsels of come from me as my cock slipped down into its natural state and the red-capped dome slithered back inside its covering of foreskin.

'Oh, I would love another fuck, Andrew, but make haste, button your fly as some people might be walking by,' she giggled.

'I would love to fuck you again, my love,' I replied gallantly, 'but you are right. However, you could suck me off if we go inside the pavilion.'

'No, my darling boy, I want you in peak condition for tonight's little frolic. Tell me, will Pelham be joining us?'

'I think not, unless you want him to be there.'

'Oh, no, although a good thick cock like his is always welcome. But let tonight be just for us alone.'

'And Louella,' I added. 'We must not forget her.'

'No, I won't forget her,' sighed Lucy. 'I suppose I must share your gorgeous prick with her but as they say, half a loaf is better than no bread.' And after a final little kiss of farewell we parted, as she had to correct some French papers for Doctor White and I had to bone up on some German verse that I was to be tested on in a lesson the next day.

I tried very hard to force the lewd images of the two girls from my mind as I studied, holding the book with both hands, and ignored as best I could the continual pressure of the erection that pushed up from between my legs. But after an hour I could bear it no longer and sat down on my bed, opened my trousers and let my stiff cock spring out from my trousers. I grasped the throbbing shaft, rubbing it furiously as the red-capped dome slipped its bulbous head out of the top as I played with myself until my seed shot forth in a fountain of frothy sperm. It was not an unpleasant sensation but what a difference there was between tossing myself off and enjoying a glorious fuck!

After a light meal of cold roast meats and salad (thanks to Doctor White's interest in horticulture we grew much of our fruit and vegetables in the school grounds and everyone will know how delicious home-grown produce can be), I decided to take a short walk around the quadrangle before retiring to my study for a short rest. After all, I would shortly have the honour of pleasuring two lovely, lusty girls and I would need all my vital health and strength if I were to give full satisfaction, especially as I had been hard at work during the day!

But as I was about to open the door to my study I heard my name being called. I turned round and saw a good friend and fellow sixth former, Paul Hill-Wallace, striding towards me. Paul was spending his last days at Nottsgrove as he had already gained a place at B—— College, Oxford, to study philosophy. He was a brilliant chap and was still working hard at his studies when most ordinary mortals like myself would have used the spare time purely for leisure pursuits.

'I say, Andrew,' he said. 'Could you spare me a minute or two?'

'What is it, Paul?' I enquired somewhat crossly. 'I am rather busy just now.'

'This won't take long and I would appreciate five minutes, old boy. Doctor White has set me a fascinating paper to prepare for next Thursday and I would like to hear your views upon the subject.'

'I am honoured,' I said rather sarcastically. 'What can I say about any matter of substance to such a distinguished scholar as yourself?'

This was a most unkind and unwarranted remark and Paul looked a trifle hurt.

'Don't be a rotter, Andrew,' he said. 'This will take only a few minutes. Come, let me in and we'll jaw about it and then I will promise to leave you alone.'

He was such a charming fellow and I felt so ashamed at my lapse of manners that I nodded and welcomed him into my room. Paul was my age, just seventeen and a half, and he was blessed with a lean yet powerful frame. His lustrous brown hair was set upon a fresh and handsome face—I am no expert in such matters but Lucy's cool judgement may be safely relied upon here—and he was of a generous spirit. Paul was always top of the class in all subjects yet he would willingly share his store of knowledge with his friends when it came to homework and he helped make our studies far less of a chore through his good nature. I must confess that I was flattered to be asked my opinion upon a matter of scholarship by so able and clever a chap!

'Please excuse my rudeness,' I said as we settled into our chairs. 'May I offer you some refreshment? No? Well, then now, I am delighted that you should ask me to assist you. How may I help?'

'Well, the essay I must prepare deals with the role of the novelist in society. I must discuss the importance of the novelist and of fiction in the continual changing pattern of the politics of the modern nation state.'

I gulped and quickly decided upon a course of action. 'What is your opinion?' I asked, throwing back the question to him.

'I am somewhat undecided which is why I would welcome another opinion. I am sure that you will agree that it is hardly surprising for a philosopher to use the novel as one of his modes of expression. However, we must of course distinguish the novel proper, such as the works of Jane Austen or of Proust, from the novel of ideas such as *Candide* or the plain tale such as *Moll Flanders* and the modern metaphysical tale of which there are innumerable examples. The novelist proper is in his way a kind of phenomenologist for he has always implicitly understood, what the philosopher has grasped perhaps less clearly, that human reason is not a single, unitary tool, the nature of which could be discovered once and for all. The novelist has had his eye fixed upon what we do and not upon what we ought to do or must be presumed to do. He has the natural gift of a precious freedom from rationalism which the academic thinker achieves, if at all, only by a precarious discipline. The writer of fiction has always been a describer rather than an explainer. Would you not agree, Andrew, with such a hypothesis?'

I struggled for words for, truthfully, the only word I fully understood was 'tool' and in his context I knew that Paul was not using the word in its vulgar form. 'I'm sure you are right, old fellow. Do continue,' I said, settling myself down in my chair for a nap. Even during the early years of my life I had learned a simple yet important rule which was that when people asked you for advice they desired not your true opinion but, in reality, a confirmation of their own views and dear old Paul (who is now, incidentally, a distinguished don with several learned tomes to his credit which to my shame I have never perused) carried on and on until I felt my eyes drooping and within a short time I was deep in the arms of Morpheus.

I awoke when I felt my shoulder being gently shaken and a voice coming through the mists of semi-consciousness saying: 'Andrew, Andrew, wake up. Oh my, oh my!' Then I heard giggling and I woke up with a start. There in front of me were Lucy and Louella, both heartily laughing, and Paul was also standing there with a smile upon his face.

'Ladies, you must forgive me,' I blurted out. 'Paul was giving me a dissertation upon the role of the novelist when I, er, I—'

'Went to sleep on me!' Paul grinned and it was typical of the fellow that he had not taken offence at my rudeness. 'Now, don't worry, Andrew, Lucy has introduced me to this charming young lady and indeed has invited me to take tea with her guest. You too of course are invited and I can continue my argument if you so wish.'

I smiled weakly and stood up. I saw the volumes that Doctor White had loaned me on the table and I took hold of it. 'Lead the way,' I said. 'And it will be my turn to entertain the company with a reading from a great novelist.'

'That sounds extremely interesting,' said Lucy and I thought I detected a note of irony in her voice but I refrained from comment as we walked towards her rooms which were on the other side of the building.

After we had made ourselves comfortable, Lucy said: 'Did you really mean what you said about giving us a reading?'

'I always mean what I say,' I replied loftily and picked up the book I had taken with me.

'Who is the author?' asked Louella.

'His name is John Cleland,' I said, looking at the cover. 'He was the composer of an erotic novel called *Fanny Hill* but this extract is from a piece extremely appropriate for Paul as he will soon be an undergraduate at Oxford University and this is entitled *Memoirs of an Oxford Scholar*!'

Lucy, Louella and Paul settled down whilst I began to read:

'I released her, kissing her again, allowing my hungry lips to travel down to the warm spot in her throat where the twin pulses race in uneven tempo.

'My impatience to possess the one who had occupied my dreams impelled me to lift the dear girl, my lips still pressed upon hers, to the waiting bed. Gently, so as not to distress the tender sentiments I saw reflected in her eyes, I unloosed my Chloe's gown and, her passions keeping pace with my own, she unfastened the stays and lay back, her lovely body but barely concealed by the near-transparent shift. I made haste to remove my own shirt and breeches, and seeing Chloe's hand move towards the fastening at the bodice of her shift, I helped her to undo them—and to remove the last hindrance to my first sight of that body for which I had so long suffered in denial.

'Her bosom, now bare, was rising in the warmest throbs and presented to my eyes the firm swell of young breasts, such as must be imagined on the most beautiful of goddesses. Their whiteness, their delicate fashioning, were all that man had ever dreamed of in his most fantastical imaginings. Their rosy nipples, surmounting the pale mounds of taut flesh, added to the final ravishment to my eye and the most exquisite of pleasures to my roaming hands. She lay there, silent, unresisting of the examination of her body by my love-filled eyes and my pleasure-ravished hands. Her tender acquiescence to my probings encouraged me to pursue to completion my long-held goal. Taking her small hand in mine, I guided it down to my rod which had by now stretched himself to a fair tallness. The head was extended and blushed a fiery crimson showing the hot rush of blood to its tip. Chloe gasped, pulled away for an instant, then sighed as I placed her sweet hand firmly around the erect shaft, then springing up straight from the wreath of curls that lay at its base. She held her hand still, then by my tender encouragement began to

69

stroke the member softly. Anon, with great fearfulness, she reached her hand down to its base, lingered there in the curly thicket and thence strayed between my thighs. I knew the softness of her fingers as she felt with wonder that globe of wrinkled flesh that held the honey of passion's flowering. Her hand clung to the root of my first instrument, that part in which Nature contained the stores of pleasure and I made her feel distinctly, through the soft outer cover, the pair of round balls that seemed to float within.

'The visit of her warm hands to those impassionable parts had raised my desires to a boiling heat and I, near to over-flowing with ungovernable passions, set upon the attainment of my goal.

'Her thighs were already open to my love assaults in obedience to the irreversible laws of Nature. I lowered myself between them, and for the first time did the hard bone of my instrument feel the wiry curls that hid Chloe's full-pouted lips. Pressing on, that instrument drove at her breech, conformed to the dictates of Nature, yet shielded over with Nature's own device. I pushed vigorously, yet came against a wall which would not open to admit me.

'I begged my Chloe to bear with patience as I reached for a pillow to put beneath her buttocks, thus to make a point-blank aim at the most favourable elevation. Again, I lowered myself between Chloe's spread thighs, and rested the tip of my machine against that tiny cleft. So small was the slit that I could scarcely count upon the accuracy of my aim. But assuring myself, I stroked forward with violent energy. My rod's immense stiffness surged forth with implacable fury, wedged against, then rent, the seal that had denied me access. This furious stroke gained me entrance to the tip alone but following well the initial insertion I at once stroked again vigorously and aggressively, increasing the advantage just gained. Inch by inch, achieved with violent thrusts, I was at last in possession of that treasured prize.

'At last freed from the demands of my own throbbing loins, I looked into my Chloe's face and saw that she had pushed the sheet into her mouth to prevent her disturbing the house

70

with her cries of pain. I gently removed the cloth from her hands and kissed her lips. Now deep inside her, the fury of my passion drove me to complete the journey on which I had started forth with such difficulty. I thrust and stroked heedless of the pain it caused the darling virgin. With an immense shudder, my liquids burst forth from me. As I withdrew my slackening member, I saw that the love-froth was tinged with blood and that Chloe had fainted with the anguish of the tremendous onslaught.

'When she returned to her senses, she caressed and kissed me tenderly, explaining that I need not regret the pain that I had caused her.

'Immediately my member, responding to impulses deep within me, begins to transform himself into the stiff gristle of amour. I kiss Chloe again, she responding the more ardently. She wraps her arms around my neck, thus allowing me the freedom to undo the laces that close my shirt and, at length, to remove my breeches.

'I slip into the bed, already warmed by her pulsing body. Slowly I begin to make advances toward my adored wife, when she takes me by surprise—moving abruptly and lowering herself upon my member, by now extended to his fullest proportion. Following her impulse, she runs the slit of her Venus-mound directly upon the flaming point of my sword, thus piercing herself through the centre and infixing herself upon it to the very extremest degree. Thus, she sets upon me, straddling me with her open thighs.

'I, in delight, pulled her down to receive the token of my kisses, at the same time increasing the rising sting of pleasure. I toyed with her pert breasts thus arousing her to a sweet storm of wriggles which apace aroused my own sensations.

'Up and down she moved, in the inverted position of mortar and pestle. And then she swayed herself from side to side thus extending even further the arena of our mutual enjoyments. The volleys of heaves and counterthrusts increased to a violent rhythm over which neither of us had any more control. In anticipation of the ultimate moment, I pulled my Chloe down over me with a fevered emotion and, in an

71

instant, we both discharged, flowing mightily from within, the one on the other.

'I lay back, so overcome was I with the ecstasy of the moment, and Chloe, inflamed to an intolerable point, lifted herself off my still semi-erect weapon and sank down on to the bed, stretching her love-moist body against my own, also wet with the exudations of passion.

'We remained thus, silent, for some time.

'Chloe's thighs, by now obedient to the inclinations of both Nature and passion, happily opened again and with now a glad submission, offered up that tender, ruby gateway to the portal of pleasure. The velvet tip of my aroused organ met the deliciousness of her secret haven. I entered her, inch by inch, to the utmost of my length and, for some sweet moments, remained there, my sword impaling her.

'She embraced love's arrow in eager, dear suction around it, compressing it inwardly. Every fibre of her love-bowl strained too to be conjoined with my weapon of love. We gave pause, the better to delight in the sweetness afforded in that most intimate point of union. But the impatience inevitable to such a position soon made itself felt—and drove us to the mightiest action.

'I drove into her with a fierce tumult and she responded with the most violent rejoinders. The more insistent, the more furious became my action, the more heartfelt and frenzied her reactions.

'Oh happiest of mortals! We were joined in that most intimate of all positions. The rhythm increased to a super-human intensity; and my body, suffused with the boiling blood of passion, convulsed with the agitation of my ultimate rapture. My discharge, which I thought would be diminished by the previous exertions, seemed only to be redoubled. And Chloe's discharge similarly seemed to be amplified by such previous encounter and we were near drowned in the waves of liquid sweets which emanated with the immensest force from our bliss-parts.

'We lay back, she in a pallor of faint and I, almost beyond the reaches of my mind in delight.'

It is not a false modesty but a true regard to the fact of the matter when I say that it was not my rendition but the beauty of Mr Cleland's imagery that thrilled my listeners. I noticed that Lucy and Paul were sitting closely together and that Paul's right arm was around Lucy's bosoms and his hand was squeezing her left breast passionately while she had her right hand placed strategically upon the bulge between his thighs which she was almost abstractedly rubbing gently as she said: 'That was quite wonderful, Andrew. Why, this has made me feel quite randy.'

'I would rather like a fuck too, Andy,' chimed Louella, climbing to her feet to nuzzle against me.

'I am sure we would all enjoy some relief,' said Paul. 'Did you notice that he stirred our sexual emotions so greatly without once using an improper word?'

'He is, or rather was, quite a special novelist,' I said, smiling, as Louella began to unbutton my shirt. I turned to kiss her passionately and she slipped her hand inside my open shirt to run her hand deliciously up and down my chest and stomach. Our mouths were glued to each other as we staggered across to the bed, still engaged in the most passionate of embraces and then, almost before I knew what was happening, Louella was unbuttoning my trousers and taking my rigid prick in her hands. 'Take off your clothes!' she whispered urgently and she undressed even more quickly than me. We lay naked on the bed and my cock was now ramrod-stiff as the darling girl knelt in front of me. When her tongue touched its end and her fingers toyed with my heavy balls I knew that already she was accepting the taste of semen. She could hardly get her mouth over the uncapped redheaded dome but she licked ecstatically until I could bear it no longer. Gently I pushed Louella's head away from my cock and lustfully grasped her to me, smothering her throbbing lips with burning kisses. As her tongue darted in and out of my mouth, a thrill of lust came over me and I pulled my face away to bury it in the silky brown motte that covered her juicy Mons Veneris. It was delicious, divine. My heartbeat quickened with erotic excitement as my tongue raked her

73

clitty then slipped down to probe deep into her cunt. Almost of their own volition, her legs splayed wider, bent at the knees, as she sought to open herself still more to me. I slurped lustily as I drew the lips of her cunny into my mouth, delighting in the taste of her flesh, licking eagerly to suck more and more of the thin fluid that was flowing from the depths of her cunt. I was in the seventh heaven of delight as I sniffed the unique female odour, my nose buried in her cunt hair. She gasped, jerking her hips upward as her stiff little clitoris was drawn further and further forward between my lips and her hands went down to clasp my head, holding my mouth tightly against her. Her legs, folded across my shoulders, twitched convulsively with joy.

'Andrew,' she gasped. 'I . . . I . . . I'm ready for you now.'

My head jerked up from between her thighs, my eyes alight with eagerness and love for this tender young creature, and gently I stretched myself on top of her. She reached down between our bodies to guide my raging prick to the slippery entrance that was to welcome it. My whole being tingled with excitement as the swollen head of my tool teased the love-lips of her juicy, wet love furrow. Slowly I edged my prick deeper and deeper into the pubic mound as wave upon wave of exquisite pleasure enveloped us both. I let my hands rove across her heavy breasts, arousing the nipples until they too stood proudly erect as I began to fuck Louella, first slowly but then increasing the speed until my prick was hammering like a piston, my balls beating a tattoo against her bottom. All too soon I felt myself approaching the ultimate pleasure stroke and, though I tried to postpone the ultimate moment, my body was being wound up tighter and tighter until finally it exploded into one climactic release as I shot my hot, sticky juice deep into the sweet girl who was writhing beneath me as she rotated her hips wildly, lifting her generous bottom to obtain the maximum contact. I groaned as I felt her finger-nails digging into my back and the tiny throbs in her cunny as my seed spurted jet after jet of love juice inside her. Desperately she clutched at me, her mouth seeking mine, arching her body towards me and somehow her clitoris rubbed against my own luxuriant growth of pubic hair. 'Ooooooh, ooooooh, Andrew, my love that was the best fuck ever!' she cried, her eyes closed in her own private ecstasy.

My lusty cock had fired the sweet girl's sensuality to such an extent that she wanted me in her again. She took hold of my now shrunken prick but it would only spring to a semi-erection in her hand. 'Give me a minute to recover, my dear!' I panted.

'You may have half that time,' she teased, tweaking her nipples until they stood up like little soldiers ready to do battle. She then slid her hand down to her pussy and began rubbing herself gently as I watched with fascination. She parted the lips of her cunt with two fingers and massaged her clitty with the middle finger, her head thrown back and the other hand massaging her magnificent breasts. Shortly, her bottom started to wriggle in rhythm, her eyes closed and she was in her own private world. Her head started to roll from side to side and she moaned with bliss as she began to come to climax. Her rubbing went in jerks, her bottom cheeks tightened and slackened and by now my prick had perked up and Louella fondled my now rampant cock as we kissed passionately. She pulled my shaft beautifully as my forefinger tickled the crisp pubic hair of the lovely girl, tenderly moulding the soft, yielding lips, and then my finger slid into the dainty quim that was already moistened to a delicious wetness. Her hands roamed all over my torso as I frigged her with now one, two then with three fingers as she clutched my bum cheeks to bring me across her. Our bodies touched from head to toe as she guided the huge purple head of my tool to her dripping love hole and the silky stiff prick eased inside its natural home. Her teeth sank into my shoulder as my first strokes jerked her body to new peaks of ecstasy. I pounded home the strokes faster and faster as we rocked together, climbing to unbearable heights as our spendings mingled, and again and again my raging cock slid uncontrollably in and out of that juicy cunt. Our orgasms crashed through almost simultaneously as she milked my cock of spurt after spurt of hot, sticky spunk.

Yet my rod was still hard and the shaft throbbed with energy as Louella squeezed it gently. She lowered her pouting mouth and slid her lips across the dome, with one hand massaging the inside of my thighs and the other cupping my hairy balls. My cock was again rock hard and slowly she sucked on her sugar-sweet until her mouth was full and I began to move slowly forwards and backwards with my hips as she noisily slurped on the huge rod that engorged her mouth. I screamed inwardly as she engulfed me, taking almost all my length sheathed deep in her throat, sucking so sweetly that I was soon forced to whisper that I could no longer hold back. Faster and faster I pumped my prick until she gently squeezed my balls and I exploded inside her mouth, filling it with salty white cream which she licked greedily before swallowing, lapping up my juices, wallowing in the sweet taste of sperm as I moaned out my ecstasy, bathed in that wonderful glow of release that flowed all over every fibre of my body.

This was the most wonderful fucking session but after coming three times in a very short space of time I was quite ready for other players to take the stage! Paul and Lucy had already stripped for action and Lucy was bending over the bed, thrusting her superbly rounded bum cheeks upwards and parting her legs so that we had a marvellous view of her vermilion cunny through which dribblings of love juice were already coursing down her thighs. Paul stood behind her and paused only to give a gentle rub to his long prick which, although not of the thickness of Pelham's or mine, was perhaps an inch or even two longer and it stood stiff as steel with its uncapped red dome reaching his belly-button.

Now he began in earnest. With one hand Paul manipulated Lucy's sensitive cunt lips and clitoris and with the other he moved his long stiff pronger in a gentle in-and-out movement in the little wrinkled arse-hole that beckoned him so invitingly. He increased the tempo and pushed deeper so that soon he was driving full in and Louella and I watched with great enjoyment the long shaft of Paul's tool whizz in and out of Lucy's wriggling bum. She responded with wild, rising cries of joy and it occurred to me that a girl who is well and frequently fucked may be seen by her bright complexion and general merriness to be so.

Paul's cock pistoned in and out and the long thick shaft of my own prick began to swell yet again and Louella rubbed the great rod fervently as at last Lucy reached the zenith of her pleasure and the bubble of passion burst. Paul shot powerful jets of jism into Lucy's bottom-hole as he worked that long prick all round its tight little sheath. His strong young prick spurted with such vigour that Lucy's thighs palpitated like moth wings as she reached the crest of a tremendous orgasm, her bum cheeks rhythmically swelling and tensing.

This had roused Louella to such a state that she could not bear to be bereft of the comfort of a prick in her cunt. She lay back and I moved on top of her and inserted my cock deep into the cunny that wetly enclosed its entire length. Louella gurgled with delight and her heels drummed upon the small of my back as her legs scissored round me.

'Get your cunt right on the shaft, Louella!' I cried, oblivious to the fact that Paul and Lucy were watching with renewed interest and—of even more import—the door of the room had opened and a young servant girl, Elaine, had entered. What a surprise for that sixteen-year-old beauty who had come merely to turn down the sheets of Lucy's bed! The pretty girl stood transfixed as she watched me fuck Louella who writhed around on the floor as I shafted her with long, hard driving strokes of my thick stiff prick.

'Now, Andrew, now!' Louella cried. 'Oh, my sweet love, fill me!'

My teeth were set with the coming of a lust that I could not restrain. I would not have cared if fifty young servant girls had been viewing us. I gripped Louella's hips like a maniac, forcing her even closer to me. Smoothing out every little wrinkle inside her sopping cunny, my cock drove to her soft depths and the great gusts of love pulsed and shot deep into her womb and she too climaxed in a glorious mutual spend. How we panted and threshed around as I pumped spunk into her with Louella's own effusion drenching my pubic hairs.

My cock drained to the last drop of spunk, I then fell full upon her, heaving with passion and exhaustion with my face pressed between her large titties. We looked up at Elaine who must have been astonished to see four naked young people cavorting around Miss Lucy's bedroom! She was an appealing girl of just sixteen with straight brown hair cut just short of her shoulders. Her lively brown eyes illuminated a fair-skinned face with clear, strong lines in nose and chin. The brown hair ended in a short, slanting fringe on her forehead. In her long skirt and blouse she gave a strong hint of having a firm and luscious figure with the contours of womanhood taking shape, especially in her breasts and hips.

'Go away, Elaine!' commanded Lucy. But still the girl stood stock still, saying nothing, but looking at the four of us with wide-open eyes.

'Go away, I said, you naughty girl. How dare you come into my room without first knocking,' said Lucy, her voice rising. 'Now go before I tell the housekeeper, Miss Carlton, who will dismiss you if I complain about your work!'

The girl recovered her senses. 'Oh, don't do that, Miss Lucy,' she said somewhat breathlessly. 'I did knock but you cannot have heard me. Goodness, what a fat prick you have Master Scott, it's even thicker than Fred's!'

I wondered who Fred might be and the girl must have read my thoughts. She said: 'Fred is the gardener's boy, Master Scott, and he loves me to rub his prick up and down until he spurts his white jets of fluid all over my hand. But although I've played with myself and let Fred frig me I still have not experienced that great joy of having a lovely stiff cock throb in my pussy. I don't suppose you would do me the honour, Master Scott?'

'Well, I don't know about that,' I said slowly. 'After all, I don't want to take your virginity.'

'Oh but I'm only a virgin in that I have never had a prick inside me, sir,' she said pleadingly. 'My hymen has gone with all the frigging and all I need now is a stiff prick. Please, please fuck me, I've always thought you the handsomest fellow of all at Nottsgrove!'

I looked around for advice. Paul shrugged his shoulders for this was one question that the scholar did not wish to answer. But the two girls nodded their heads and begged me to oblige the girl who was already unbuttoning her blouse, and even before I could give my assent she pulled off her camisole and unbuttoned her skirt so that she stood only in her stockings. The young minx went about her work without wearing any knickers! She later explained to me that she only did so on hot summer days when she was feeling roused and would go to the gardener's shed for a quick frig with young Fred. She stepped out of her shoes and unrolled her stockings so that she stood absolutely naked in front of me.

I was truly enthralled by the prospect of becoming the possessor of those gorgeous limbs for Elaine was a healthy, well-exercised girl. Her thighs were taut and lightly muscled. From the front I eyed her critically yet could find little fault. I viewed the narrow triangle of bushy brown hair above her cunt which was soon to be at my disposal. Her young belly was still firm and quite flat whilst she was also well-made in the seat. The cheeks of her bottom were nicely filled but without a pinch of surplus fat. I passed my hand round her waist, drawing her close to me, caressing the *rondeurs* of her fleshy bottom. My prick now began to rise majestically upwards, stiffening and swelling against my belly as I raised her chin with my free hand and passed my lips across hers. She quivered with delight and straining upwards rose on tiptoe with my hand now firmly on her bottom crack. I passed my forefinger under her bottom cheeks and instantly felt for the soft warm lips of her delicate little quim which moistened at the touch. The impress of our mouths grew stronger as her lips parted and she received my tongue, as she slipped her hand down to grasp my throbbing cock, gently frigging the shaft as her cunny began to grow damper and damper from her juices that were beginning to flow. Our tongues flashed together in such utter yearning that the moment clearly could no longer be delayed.

'You are sure, really sure that you want to be fucked, Elaine?' I asked anxiously.

'Yes, oh, yes, very, very much—and now!' she assented and we fell together on the floor, though I took care to lay her gently upon her back, so that she would not hurt herself. I knelt before her and firmly thrust her legs apart, raising myself above her whilst I placed my lips against her soft white breasts, washing my tongue over a tiny little titty and settling full down to a lick-flick mouthing until both stood hard and erect as she arched her torso up as if to offer them for further urgent attention. My tongue licked and licked eagerly and moved in swathes over the resilient youthfulness of her breasts. No girl's bosom was ever so thoroughly or lovingly licked and her nipples were now as hard as unripe berries to the touch. My cock was now bursting and I guided the huge uncovered knob to the pouting cunny lips that were ready to receive it. For a split second our hot eyes locked together and then, with an ineffable groan, I inserted some two inches of the meaty shaft and was full on top of her. Our lips collided and meshed together. She wriggled and worked her bottom to obtain a further length of cock inside her and this enabled me to embed more of my throbbing shaft as her cunny magically expanded to receive it. With a passionate jolt of my loins my prick was fully inserted and she cried out in glee as our bottoms began to work together in unison. How tightly her cunt enclasped and sucked upon my prick! We gloried in each giant thrust as her spendings dripped onto my balls as they banged against her arse. She implored me to drive deeper by twirling her tongue in my mouth, and cupped now in my broad palms, her tight bottom-cheeks rotated almost savagely as my tool rammed in and out lustily and she withdrew her mouth from mine, gasping and panting for air. Her kisses now rained upon my neck and I felt the throbbing of her pussy increase apace as she cried out aloud with joy at the stinging excitement of my thick prick driving furiously into her soft depths.

I plunged my face between her breasts and began to suck furiously at her left nipple whilst the friction in her cunt reached new heights as my prick began to move even faster, making us breathless with excitement. All the time she wriggled lasciviously and my tongue now lifted itself from the erect titty and shot into her mouth as she automatically flexed her vaginal muscles to milk the full length of my pulsating cock that was pumping in and out as my balls swished down, banging gently against her bum. Elaine was really finding out what the pleasures of a good fucking could be as her fingers now dug into the flesh of my back and her bucking torso wildly sought more and more of my prick as our pubic hairs crashed together. Alas, I could not contain myself much longer and she screamed with joy as, arching my body upwards, I plunged down hard, crushing her soft body beneath me as her legs flexed and she gurgled with pleasure as my frothy seed poured into her with a spurting gush. Elaine too had spent copiously and I hoped that our love juices would not stain the carpet. I said as much but Elaine quickly reassured me that she could remove any stains with a patent medicine!

'A patent medicine? That is very odd,' said Lucy. 'What on earth is it called?'

'Doctor Hopkins' cough medicine, Miss Lucy,' said Elaine, sitting herself down on the bed and showing no inclination to cover up her naked charms. 'Why, we buy it especially to take the stains out of the sheets in the dormitories when the boys soil them after playing with themselves.'

'Good heavens! I must remember not to buy the mixture for any other reason,' said Paul.

'Doctor White uses it too,' laughed Elaine. 'He says it makes his roses grow!'

We all laughed merrily and cuddled up to one another on Lucy's large bed. 'There is just one matter bothering me,' I said to Elaine. 'I really should have shot my load over your tummy, for the last thing we want is to put you in the family way. This was most thoughtless of me and I do hope that all will be well.'

'Oh, yes, Master Andrew,' she replied gaily. 'I have only just finished my curse days and I am certain that no harm will come to me.'

'We are not foolish,' chimed in Louella. 'We have to take

the risks so we are always as careful as possible, aren't we, ladies? I personally sponge myself afterwards with vinegar and lemon juice, but choosing the safe days is perhaps the best way.'

'I wish there was a medicine we could take to make us completely certain that no harm will come to us,' said Lucy thoughtfully. 'Whoever discovers such a potion will make his fortune.'

'Or perhaps *her* fortune!' corrected Louella. 'I believe there should be female doctors. We are quite capable of learning the art of medicine.'

'I agree with you,' said Paul. 'But don't let us begin a discussion on the rights of women just now. Instead, who knows what Samuel Pepys said about a course of action to take if a man got a swollen belly up.' None of us knew the answer. 'Why,' said Paul triumphantly, 'he said, and I quote: "He that do get a wench with child and marry her afterwards is as if a man should shit in his hat and then clap it on his head!" '

'That's all very well,' said Lucy. 'But hopefully there will be easy, cheap ways made available soon so that society can adopt a more responsible attitude about bringing unwanted children into the world. It is a grave problem and most unfair as women take all the blame and shame of such a situation as Pepys describes, whereas it takes two to make a belly swell.'

We all agreed with her observation but were in no mood for serious talking and soon we were entangled in one heap of bodies rolling around on the bed. Unfortunately, Paul and I have only one prick each so whilst we lay on our backs with Lucy on top of Paul and Louella wriggling her pert bum in front of my face as she lowered her dripping wet pussy on my rampant pole, poor Elaine had to be content with the role of spectator. However, I placed her down between Paul and myself and frigged her hairy little slit with two fingers whilst Paul diddled her titties to an upright stance.

Now Paul professed to be a Socialist and I was (and still am) a staunch Liberal but we agreed upon the unfairness of the distribution of the good things in life. Why should Elaine be deprived of a good fuck whilst Lucy and Louella had almost as many pricks as they could comfortably manage? So to make up for this unhealthy situation, Paul and I spread the lovely sixteen-year-old on the bed and I lay down on her right, lying on my left side, and moved her firm young body to face my own.

'I am now going to fuck you, Elaine,' I declared. 'And at the same time Paul will prod your tight little bum-hole with his prick, thus enabling you to enjoy a double dose of sheer bliss.'

'Will it hurt?' she enquired anxiously. 'I have never had a cock stuffed up my backside before.'

'Not at all, Elaine,' I reassured the trembling girl. 'Just relax completely and Paul will first wet his instrument to allow it free passage.'

'I will help him,' chimed in Lucy, and taking his great tool in her mouth, liberally coated it with spittle.

Without further ado, I reached for Elaine's shoulders and glued my lips to hers, holding my hands firmly upon her shoulders. She reached for my rock-hard cock and I pushed my knob inside those juicy portals, feeling myself buried to the hilt in her throbbing sheath. We began the old heaving and shoving motions and as she thrust her luscious bum cheeks backwards as I plunged into her, I grasped them and opened wide the crack in between, parting the rounded globes so that the tiny, wrinkled little brown bum-hole was fully exposed to the attack of Paul's long cock. Fortunately, the spittle and the fact that his tool was long rather than thick enabled him to push hard from the start. With only a short cry of discomfort he was well placed as Elaine began to wriggle and twist as we jointly rammed in and out. At one stage we both pushed in together so that I could feel my own prick rubbing against Paul's with only the thin divisional membrane running between us. This was simply too much for me to bear and I pumped jet after jet of frothy white jism as Elaine and Paul continued to writhe in new paroxysms of pleasure until, screaming with excitement, they reached the summit of the mountain of love and we three sank back quite sated from this novel experience.

Lucy and Louella were so fired up by our little threesome that they frigged themselves throughout the proceedings. But what a surprise was in store as, calmly as you please, young Elaine suddenly dived down and buried her head in Lucy's blonde muff, licking frantically all over the golden forest until she came to the lovely wet crack, revelling in the depths of Lucy's pussy and licking lasciviously inside her cunny-lips as far as her tongue would go, whilst one of her hands slipped under Lucy's bum and her forefinger invaded her bottom-hole, working in and out in a most exciting way.

Elaine's own bottom wriggled up and down and I jumped behind her and, passing my hand round her narrow waist, handled her luxuriously covered mount quite freely, slipping two fingers inside her juicy quim. Her bottom cheeks wriggled again, so with my free hand, I guided my already stiff cock between them. Paul's spendings had lubricated her arse-hole so my rigid prick slipped in quite easily, deeper and deeper as she rolled around, still keeping her head firmly between Lucy's legs, nibbling away at the swollen clitty as, with a series of sighs, Lucy tried desperately to rub herself off against Elaine's mouth. I had spent so much that day that it was several minutes before the hot squirts of cream shot off into Elaine's bum-hole, in such quantities that I felt completely drained as I withdrew my still extended prick, now red and a tiny bit raw from the little wrinkled home it had found. A final spatter of love juice dribbled down from my dome onto the floor. I adjusted my foreskin and Louella giggled. 'We'll need an extra bottle of Doctor Hopkins' medicine to clean the carpet!' she gasped, and we all burst out laughing merrily.

I was now too exhausted for even one more cockstand, but Louella managed to suck Paul up to a final full erection and Lucy and Elaine took turns to have his long cock in their bum-holes until he shot a full load of sperm into Louella's furry little cunt.

We exchanged our good-nights and crept back to our

beds—Louella having arranged to stay the night with Lucy—
and we none of us needed any potion to drug our senses. As
soon as my head touched the pillow I knew nothing more
until the morning alarm bell awakened me.

All that fucking must have been refreshing for my brain,
even though physically I was quite exhausted, for I remember
distinctly that an essay I composed that next morning on the
foreign policy of Pitt the Younger was awarded an alpha
minus by Doctor White—a rare honour rarely bestowed!

CHAPTER FIVE

DO YOU ever wonder, dear reader, who you are? Do you ever think that Mr Gladstone or the dear Queen ever wonder about who they think they really are? Or the Pope? Or even the editor of this esteemed journal of quality? Obviously they know who they really are but where, I would like to know, do their minds go to during those lazy daydreaming hours?

So far as I am able to ascertain from the study of science, man is the sole animal with this extraordinary ability to while away the time in daydreaming. Occasionally, when on a journey (for my work sometimes takes me to the provinces) I look around at the silent people in my railway carriage and ponder as to where their meditations are taking them, what private thoughts are coursing through their minds and what ideas are really behind those bland, expressionless faces, what lovers both imaginary and real are being wooed, what triumphs and failures are being lived and relived.

We are none of us quite what we appear to be. Running parallel with our physical existence, with our mundane chores and daily habits, is another secret, ghostly character, a private companion forever commenting upon what we see and do, rewriting the manuscript record of our lives in a manner more satisfying to us.

It is this gap between reality and fantasy, between what is and what might be or might have been which I find truly a source of endless fascination.

Will the fucking of a particular girl be an anticlimax, I wonder? Will reality be but a pale imitation of the adventures of the mind? We accept these dreams with hardly any consideration, never questioning for a moment our right to be able to leave our bodies for a while whenever the mood takes us but for some reason, as we progress from childhood to adult life, we become peculiarly embarrassed to admit to this. For the older we become, the less likely we are to admit to the more expansive fantasies, as grown-up, responsible citizens are supposed to have put away this childish habit. This is an impossible task for surely in all of us there are two beings that ride through life as if on a tandem bicycle, steered by the chap in front but commented upon endlessly by the man in the back seat.

I do not discourage daydreaming for it represents perhaps the only time in life when you can be sure of playing the lead role—and in that sense dreams are great levellers. In the vivid play that is acted out in the daydream all manner of wrongs are put right, all kinds of witty ripostes are applauded and the most beautiful of women conquered totally and without resistance.

Throughout my life I have daydreamed. As a child my fantasies were glorious, unblocked by considerations of reality, but adults dream, increasingly as the years slip away, about what might have been had their lives taken other turnings.

I must immediately confess to this kind of post-mortem, especially over the critical decisions which affect us until our dying days. We are all faced with a series of crossroads that are unique to us and we can continually look back and examine the routes that we chose, for better or for worse, that have brought us to the present time.

By and large this is a fruitless and indeed even a totally futile exercise, but then since when was mere futility the servant of common sense?

What brings these musings to mind? I suppose, reader, that were I to be fully truthful, my brain is taking a much needed respite from the hard labours of recall. Oh, do not misunderstand me—I have enjoyed penning these sexual exploits, which are all totally verifiable. If any person wishes to see proof furnished, simply write to me care of the Post Office, Sudbury, Suffolk and I will personally reply to all letters. How pleasant it is to recall that free and easy life we enjoyed as schoolboys at the Nottsgrove Academy for the Sons of Gentlefolk and what wonderful memories I have of that giant amongst mortals, dear old Doctor White, whose wise leadership has since influenced me and all other students to such good effect. What a man! His immense learning and erudition were matched only by his cheery manner and true kindness of heart which was shown to one and all, regardless of their station in life. He was a man who won the respect of both peer and pauper. And it seems that it is but yesterday that I was sitting in his book-lined study, sipping a glass of port and discussing with the old headmaster pertinent questions of social and political affairs which had been brought up in that day's edition of *The Times*.

You will see, then, how my mind has been straying far, far away on a merry trip to the lands of yesteryear whilst my body has been locked here in the admittedly splendidly comfortable present: the warm armchair in the library of my fine old friend Sir Lionel T——, himself of course a scholar and artist of great distinction.

So I have skeltered through this brief period of my adolescent life with great joy; which leads me to suggest that if we sometimes feel prisoners of our present circumstances, this may simply be because we are blocking the escape valves of our imagination. If all adults could play the innocent game of make-believe as do our children, we would, I dare suspect, live out our lives in a fuller, more contented fashion.

Let us now return to the main theme of this narrative, and I crave again the indulgence of the reader for my digression.

I awoke that next morning quite bleary-eyed and indeed I was so tired that I even forwent my usual morning ritual of shrinking my stiff prick by a vigorous tossing off. Today, however, I performed my ablutions as if in a trance and what I consumed at breakfast will forever remain a mystery as I have no recollection whatsoever of even sitting down in the dining hall that morning! Luckily, I could enjoy a free period after breakfast, which I spent taking a refreshing sleep in the library until the mid-morning break bell shattered my slumbers.

After the interval I joined the rest of my sixth form colleagues in the Art Room where Doctor White was due to give his weekly lecture upon matters of culture. I sat down next to Pelham who whispered to me: 'I say, old chap, are you quite well? You look rather tired.'

'I am somewhat sleepy,' I confessed. 'I just could not get to sleep last night.'

'Well, you are not the only one. Look at Paul sitting slumped over his desk. He also looks as pale as a ghost,' said Pelham.

I was pleased that at this point Doctor White swept in and began his dissertation immediately, thus saving me the problem of explaining to Pelham just why Paul and I were so exhausted at a quarter past eleven in the morning!

'My subject today is women in the arts,' rumbled the Doctor. 'Let us look at the status of women in society, and of the current agitation by many females to be freed from the ties of home and hearth.

'Of course, both men and women have always needed a great deal of determination to succeed in their various professions. But historically women have needed more determination and more talent merely to keep in the race for the glittering prizes even though both sexes alike suffer from inequalities of brainpower. Let us take art and politics. This latter subject is perhaps so controversial that we will keep discussion of it until next week's lecture. So let us today look solely at the world of art, a field in which practitioners have often been forced to suffer varying degrees of injustice.

'Every artist suffers in this way, but for women the injustice has always been greater, which goes much of the way to explain why relatively few women artists have surfaced and why so many have failed, or why so many women have made initial headway against male prejudices only to sink back later into obscurity.

'Even an ardent espouser of women's rights such as my niece Lucy will admit that no significant art movement has ever been started by a woman. But, gentlemen, we must ask ourselves why this is so. And the answer is very simple: historically there has always been a lack of educational facilities for girls and, even when they have matured, there has been a taboo against women at meeting places for artists such as bars, clubs or, heavens alive!, a genuine artist's studio! So there has been no real chance availed to them and the female artist has been left in painful solitude.

'There are still far too many obstacles in their path and I propose that we at Nottsgrove here and now symbolically show the way forward.'

On this stirring note he strode to the door and motioned into the room a most attractive young girl of about nineteen or twenty years old. She was slightly taller than the average with a mop of bright auburn curls that set off a cheeky little face, the best features of which were a *retroussé* nose and large grey eyes that sparkled with promise. Her slim, athletic frame was delightfully shown off by a close-fitting dark green costume in the modern style. My tiredness vanished in a trice at the sight of this lovely girl and my eyes gazed longingly at her small but perfectly-formed breasts that jutted out like two firm apples ripe for my mouth . . .

'Gentlemen, I would like to introduce Miss Agnes Carter to you. Miss Carter is a close friend of mine and . . . ' Doctor White looked balefully around the room as some of the fellows tittered at the thought of the headmaster having such a beautiful young female friend. I saw no reason for untoward merriment as Doctor White was certainly no mysogynist. If he was fortunate enough to find such a voluptuous companion, jolly good luck to them both!

'Good morning, boys!' said the young minx with a saucy smile. 'As you heard your headmaster tell you, it is now time for women to be given their fair chance at showing their artistic prowess. Over there you will see that on the raised platform in front of the blackboard I have set up my easel. On the floor lie my pencils and brushes. With your help we shall today show the world that it is the picture that matters and that the sex of the artist is immaterial.'

'I don't think that sex is ever immaterial!' whispered Pelham Forbes-Mackenzie and there was another murmur of laughter.

Doctor White stepped forward with a frown on his face and said: 'Who said that? Was that you, Forbes-Mackenzie? Yes? I thought so. Very well, you have just volunteered to be Miss Carter's model for this morning's lesson. As for you others, I want your words of honour that you will each remain absolutely silent for the rest of this lesson which will not end until luncheon at one o'clock. Have I your words, gentlemen?'

We were abashed and readily volunteered our promise to stay silent.

'Very well,' grunted our dear old pedagogue. 'Pelham, come up here on the dais. The rest of you, stay where you are. I must finish some administrative work this morning so I leave you in the very capable hands of Miss Carter. Boys! I rely on you all not to dishonour me, yourselves and the good old school.' And with that short speech he turned on his heel and left us to the tender mercies of our new young teacher.

'Your name is Pelham?' she enquired. 'Well, I will call you Pelham and you will call me Agnes. Is that satisfactory? Good. Now, Pelham, please remove your clothes and take up the position of—'

'What did you say, Miss Carter?' interrupted Pelham in astonishment.

'You may call me Agnes,' she replied patiently. 'I said take off your clothes and then I will show you in what position I should like you to pose before I begin my work.'

We tried hard not to laugh out loud at poor Pelham's predicament as we had given our sworn word not to break silence and all that could be heard was a muffled, choking laugh from fourteen lusty young throats.

'Come on, Pelham, don't be shy. Look, if it makes you feel any easier, I shall take off my jacket so all I shall be wearing is this blouse and skirt. I am kicking off these rather uncomfortable shoes—do not tell Doctor White, boys, as they were a present from him some few weeks ago on my nineteenth birthday. Now, Pelham, please do as I ask,' pleaded Agnes. Pelham was a ripping sport and he was not that shy, especially since Lucy and I had initiated him into *l'arte de faire l'amour*. So he sat down and removed his shoes and socks, slipped off his jacket and unbuttoned his trousers. He wriggled out of his trousers and under-drawers and stood up, covered just by a flapping white shirt which he pulled off over his head. His thick prick was dangling down but I could see the tip of his foreskin rise just a little and the head of his dome rose up too to give air, so to speak, to the little 'eye' in the centre though the dome itself remained capped by the skin of the shaft. He flexed his muscles and I saw that Agnes was very taken with the handsome young specimen who paraded his naked charms in front of her.

'Yes, that's fine, Pelham. Stand with your back to the blackboard at a slight angle to the class but facing me full on. Oh, yes, that is absolutely perfect, can you hold that position, please? Are you comfortable? Lay your hands on your thighs—good, now please keep completely still.'

Pelham complied with this gentle request and I must say that I admired his fine, manly torso. His muscular chest and flat, white belly were excellently proportioned, but of course the *pièce de résistance* was his thick rod which dangled down with its ruby-coloured head semi-covered; though it was clear that Nature, as ever, could not bear to be denied and that his massive prick was stiffening perceptibly even though his hands remained firmly in place on his thighs.

This fact had not escaped the attention of Agnes, who licked her lips voraciously but said nothing as that massive tool rose higher and higher, uncapping the red-topped dome and swelling up to a full nine inches, standing smartly to attention against his belly.

'My goodness, what a truly magnificent body and such a marvellously proportioned cock. It looks so powerful yet sweet enough to eat. May I be permitted to make a closer inspection?'

She moved across the dais and slipped her little hand round the monstrous shaft. Her long fingers, working as though they possessed a will of their own, began to frig the giant cock slowly, rubbing it up to an even greater height.

'Ah! I really am naughty to do this to you. How silly I am to let myself be excited by this handsome creature and his enormous prick. But oh! oh! I cannot help it! I must! I must!' she muttered as she drew back the skin, making its red head swell and bound in her hand. Pelham, nothing loath, remained silent as instructed by our mentor, but this did not prevent his massaging the firm little breasts that jutted out so provocatively in front of him. With her free hand Agnes unbuttoned her thin blouse to allow Pelham to pull off the offending garment from her and on this fine July day she wore nothing underneath, which gave all the boys the horn as those bouncy breasts with exquisitely swollen nipples were exposed to our view. Still holding on to the fat lollipop of a prick, she managed to unfasten her skirt and step out of it, and Pelham assisted the completion by pulling down her short cotton drawers. We feasted our gaze upon the delicious little triangle of auburn hair into which Pelham plunged his hand as their bodies crushed together in a fierce embrace. I could see his hand working inside her hairy mound, opening the large cunny lips and inserting first one and then two digits inside the moist vaginal entrance. Agnes groaned with passion. 'Stop, Pelham, dear, you must stop. I too made a promise to Doctor White which was that I would not let myself be fucked this morning by any boy in this class.'

She sighed as her frigging hand increased the pace of its motion and Pelham's face was now flushed, yet the stalwart fellow kept his word and not a sound passed his lips even when the sensual rubbing brought him quickly to the inevitable result and he spent copiously, the froth shooting out of his prick all over her hand and sprinkling her mossy mount and belly with spunk. But Pelham was a lively chap and his prick remained firmly upright and the hot, soft head was forcing its way between the love-lips of the naked beauty in his arms.

'Oh, Pelham,' she whispered. 'I must taste that luscious sweetmeat that feels too good merely to hold in my hand.'

She knelt in front of him and slowly nibbled away at the fiery swollen dome and then she opened her mouth and sucked away noisily, massaging her breasts with one hand and plunging her other hand deep inside her own quim.

Pelham's legs became as weak as jelly and luckily there was a chair behind him as he sank backwards. Some of the other chaps could no longer contain themselves and I saw Simon Allingham and John Mitchell free their bursting tools from the confines of their trousers and were busy frigging away. Meanwhile, poor Pelham could no longer hold back and his body racked with convulsions as he shot a series of pulsating emissions straight into Agnes's mouth which was like a suction pump, milking his cock of every last drop of sperm. Still the fiery girl would not release the juicy morsel that lay between her lips and within a trice she had sucked up that thick knob to almost a full erection.

'Now I am going to explain something to you all,' she said to the class, who by some superhuman dint of strength had managed to remain true to the vow of silence sworn to Doctor White. 'I want to be fucked but precious Pelham has already spunked copiously. His sperm tastes very well, too, with just the right salty tang that I crave. But as he must be somewhat tired I shall adapt the sexual position with the female on top so that he does not have to work so hard. You may wish to watch carefully for future reference if your wife or lady partner wants a fuck but you feel too tired to perform as well as you would like to do.'

She motioned to Pelham to lie down on the floor which he did with his noble prick waving like a flagpole, and then she sat astride him, pressing down the lips of her aching slit to the glowing head. She spread her cunny lips apart and directed the tip of his cock to the entrance and slowly sat down, letting Pelham feel the juices of her warm cunny clasp his raging prick. His hands slid across to her bare bottom and Agnes wriggled around to work the hard shaft of prick inside her as far up within her as possible. Agnes bounced merrily away on

Pelham's iron-hard rod and though my own prick was straining unbearably against the material of my trousers I successfully fought to retain my composure—unlike Allingham and Mitchell who were both jetting creamy spurts of white foam all over their hands and trousers (Elaine would need extra bottles of that famous stain-remover that afternoon!).

'Notice how well this so-called female superior position works,' gasped out Agnes. 'I can certainly advocate it for a change in one's regular fucking pattern although I do not recommend it as a steady diet. It is quite exhausting and leaves the girl to do most of the work! Unless she has excellent control of her vaginal muscles, she has to lift herself up and down with her legs in a rather cramped position and this may occasionally—ooh, Pelham, what a superb thick prick you have—this may set up harmonic motions which can spoil the fuck in a most exasperating way.

'Also, too much fucking in this position gives my cunt walls a hard pounding, especially if the boy is as well made as young thick-pricked Pelham. Oooooh, that's good. I think this method works best for me especially when I can sit down like this and grind my arse around whilst I work my cunny muscles—this gives my clitty a good rub as well!'

She worked her bottom from side to side as Pelham jerked his hips up and down, and then she caught his rhythm and lifted herself up and down to meet his upward thrusts with downward pushes of her own.

'You see, boys,' she gasped. 'Oh, Pelham, harder, harder. Ooooh! Oooooh! A man normally enjoys this kind of fuck immensely for all he has to do is lie back and watch although dear Pelham here is a considerate sort of chap who wants to give pleasure—oooh!—as well as simply receive it. There are lazy and self-indulgent types who like this method best, but this means that the girl becomes little more than a frigging post. So this is a good, convenient variant but as a regular way of fucking perhaps—ooh! Pelham, I'm coming, I'm coming!'

And as if by magic I saw the first gush of cream spurt out

of the top of his sinewy cock as they crashed together in a glorious mutual spend. Now Doctor White had commanded silence but surely a round of applause would not be considered amiss and I began to clap heartily which was immediately taken up by the other boys, even the sticky-fingered Allingham and Mitchell, and Agnes and Pelham stood up before us and bowed.

Agnes held up her hand for silence and said: 'Boys, I hope that you have learned an important lesson which perhaps Doctor White has already given the more advanced of you lusty young men. Making love is a partnership. You may eat and drink alone. You may listen to music in solitude or read a book all by yourself. But for a proper fuck you need two people and to make it perfect there must be no holding back. Know what your partner prefers or what he or she dislikes. And you too must be frank and state what are your own preferences. Is that fully understood? Good. Now, Pelham we must return to the original purpose of this lesson. Stand as we agreed and I will draw your body. Class, you are dismissed. Please leave quietly. I am going to finish my work and then we will dress and leave. There will be no more fucking to look at so you may all rest easy!'

At luncheon I sat next to Pelham and he confirmed that Agnes had told the truth. They had not even embraced until the lesson had ended and they said a fond *au revoir*. She was leaving Nottsgrove for London that afternoon but was returning after a duty visit to a sick aunt within a week.

'Jolly good,' I said. 'You will have a marvellous fuck when she comes back.'

'Won't I just!' said Pelham. 'All this exercise has made me ravenous. I'm going for seconds. See you after lunch!'

In fact I would not see Pelham until later in the day, as along with some five other fellows I was due to spend the rest of the afternoon in our music-room. I stopped to have a quick chat with one of the chaps about some later appointment for cricket practice, and then hurried along to the music room where indeed I was the last man to arrive. However Professor Marchiano had not yet arrived (which was strange, as unlike most Italians he was an extremely punctual person) and I sat down with relief.

'I say, Allingham,' said Peter Hodgson, who was captain of cricket. 'I saw you and Mitchell masturbating during the last lesson. You are two dirty beasts.'

'Nonsense!' said Allingham crisply. 'You just could not free your chopper before you came!'

'That's right!' said Mitchell robustly. 'I saw you and Dixon fondling each other's bulges.'

'Come on chaps, lay off!' I cried. 'Professor Marchiano will be here any moment. Indeed, I cannot think what has detained him as he is usually the first here.'

As I spoke the door opened and to my utter amazement in came Agnes Carter! What on earth was she doing here? As if she had read my thoughts she held up her hand to quell the buzz of noise that had erupted and said: 'I know I said goodbye before luncheon but regrettably Professor Marchiano is indisposed. He has a severe cold and Doctor White has asked me to take this lesson as my train does not leave until this evening and my cases are already packed.'

'Welcome again,' I blurted out. 'I am sure that this lesson will be just as stimulating.'

'I hope so, Scott—that is your name is it not? Very well, gentlemen, I believe that Professor Marchiano was about to deliver a lecture upon the great contemporary composer Bedrich Smetana. Would you please make yourselves comfortable and I will deliver his dissertation from the notes he would have used had he been well enough to be here.'

Life is a strange thing, is it not? A drunkard is forever being offered a glass, and for a fervent fucker like myself it seemed that temptation was again being thrown in my way. Still, I settled myself as comfortably as I could with a familiar swelling beginning in my cock as Agnes began her lecture.

'Smetana was born in March, 1824 and he enjoyed a calm and happy childhood in the charming little town of Litomsyl in Eastern Bohemia. He began his studies seriously in Prague but this period was marked by poverty and hardship which was only partially alleviated by giving music lessons to the sons and daughters of noble families. From dance pieces he wrote at this time he proceeded to the responsible and purposeful work of a serious composer. In 1856, to solve his difficult financial problems, he left for the Swedish seaport of Gothenburg where he gave successful concerts and worked as a teacher.

'He returned home although he visited Sweden several times afterwards. His first opera was well received, but his second opera 'The Bartered Bride' won international acclaim, and in 1866 he was appointed Kappelmeister of the Czech Opera, which at least allowed him to eke out a modest subsistence. In the course of the years he created several more operas but his extensive works were curtailed in 1874 when, at the age of fifty, he was suddenly struck by deafness. Nevertheless he continued his music writing despite this tremendous handicap, and soon afterwards composed his symphonic poems which were to be the first parts of his planned six-part cycle 'My Country'. Other operas followed of which my favourite is 'The Kiss' and another opera, 'Viola' sadly remained unfinished at his death three years ago. I am convinced that his work will survive his death and that he will be ranked as one of the most memorable composers of the century.'

We were all most disappointed as she droned on—then suddenly I had a most brilliant idea, and I raised my hand.

'The influence of Smetana upon his country's culture is certain to be—yes, Scott, why do you wish to interrupt me?'

'I do apologise, Miss Carter, only it is most devilishly warm in here. As you know, Doctor White does not allow the windows to be opened in case the sound of music or singing disturbs others. But this means that the room becomes uncomfortably warm. May I have your permission to remove my jacket?'

'Certainly, Scott, please feel free—and this applies to anyone else who wishes to take off a jacket. I myself will take off this cardigan,' she said.

Of course this was a signal for all six chaps to take off their jackets. I remember the scene as if it were only an hour ago.

There were Allingham, Mitchell, Pearce, Foster-Jeffries, Wilkinson and myself, and I must confess that I was the leader in the sport that quickly followed.

'I think I would prefer to loosen my tie,' I said carefully.

'Oh, very well, anyone who wishes to loosen their cravats, please do so now and perhaps we can return to our study of Smetana,' said Agnes rather crossly.

We all took off our ties and as I decided that I could not find an excuse for removing any other garment, I simply proceeded to take off my shoes and socks and began to unbuckle my trouser belt.

'Scott! What on earth do you think you are doing? Stop it, my goodness, stop it immediately or I shall call for assistance,' Agnes cried out in horror as I stepped out of my trousers and pulled off my vest, standing before her in my underdrawers with the knob of my prick clearly visible through the front vent. The other chaps realised that here was a lark indeed and quickly they all threw off all their clothes except for their drawers and we stood in a line facing the shocked girl who blushed furiously as Allingham's large circumcised prick (the poor fellow had suffered from a tight foreskin and had been forced to undergo a painful operation) suddenly stuck out of his white cotton briefs.

'I think you boys would prefer to fuck rather than to hear me talk about Smetana,' she said softly. 'Mind, you are all taking advantage of the fact that I am a new and inexperienced teacher, so I think I will show you that I can give as good as I can take! All right, just let's all get into the mood!'

She was as good as her word. She immediately unbuttoned her blouse and skirt and pulled down her drawers to expose her gorgeous nude body to our view. Five pricks shot up into the air in salute and she responded by rapidly pulling down all our drawers so that we too were all naked. She first went over to Mitchell who possessed a fleshy, medium-sized chopper and she kissed him violently, exploring his mouth with her tongue and putting his hands on her heaving breasts. Nothing loath, he cupped them, squeezed them and rubbed the nipples up to a fine erection. She traced a delicate pattern on his chest with her long fingers and then she swooped down to grasp his straining cock which she began to frig expertly, stroking the shaft and capping and uncapping the swollen knob which bulged quite alarmingly from her fist. Mitchell was obviously raw at this game so I moved over and began to kiss Agnes's large erect titties, and then bent my head down to suck them as I inserted a finger into her wet cunny which was already nicely juicy and ready for a good stiff prick.

'Let me show you how to fuck properly like a gentleman,' I said to Mitchell who stepped aside to let me face Agnes. She slid down onto the floor on her back and I sat forward on my knees, and she rubbed my prick to perfection. I moved forward to tease her outer cunt lips with my swollen knob before forcefully plunging it deep inside her sopping pussy as she instinctively opened her legs to receive me. She drew her legs up either side of my body as I began to fuck her slowly with long, powerful strokes. She gyrated wildly beneath me as if her vagina had never held a cock so big before, and what with the sensation of the fucking, her nipples grazing against my chest and the hot sun beating through the closed windows, I was almost fainting away with pleasure. So to maintain our momentum I quickened my stroke as she wrapped her legs across my back so that I could fuck her even more deeply; and then I was fucking her faster and we were kissing and biting each other in a sexual frenzy as the most indescribable pleasure built up in my balls and then in my shaft, which suddenly exploded into a blistering orgasm that attacked every nerve-end in my body as I spurted jet after jet of white spunk inside the delicious slit.

We spent a couple of seconds getting our breath back and then Agnes whispered: 'Oh, darling, that was marvellous. I came at least twice before you spunked. Now roll off and let someone else have his turn!'

Obediently I disengaged myself and Mitchell got down to join us on the rug. Agnes needed a moment or two to recover so she spent a minute kissing and fondling the handsome boy. I must admit that I was fascinated by the exposed glans of his large circumcised tool and I could see that he too became worked up by pulling her cunt lips apart and watching my sperm trickle down her thighs. He then positioned himself on top of her and slid his prick into her soaking slit, and the mix of Agnes's own love-juices and my coating of spunk enabled his sinewy weapon to slide in and out extremely easily. Agnes lay blissfully with her legs stretched wide and Mitchell's huge glistening cock shafting in and out; but then she whispered something that I could not hear and he withdrew his gleaming cock as Agnes rolled over onto her belly and then lifted herself on all fours so as to present her wrinkled little arse-hole to Mitchell's fat prick. He hesitated only a moment before pushing his cock into the tight, puckered little hole and Agnes drew in her breath. 'Hold on a moment,' I cautioned him. 'First wet your prick with spittle, for you surely have no wish to hurt your partner.'

He did as I advised and pushed ahead gamely whilst I called upon Wilkinson to kneel down in front of Agnes who immediately grabbed his huge, rock-hard cock in a delirious excitement. My work as master of ceremonies was not yet over and I motioned over Pearce to place himself next to Wilkinson. Agnes took hold of his meaty prick in her other hand and began to rub it up and down. She toyed with both the cocks for a moment and then began to rub them hard as Foster-Jeffries obeyed my murmured instruction to put his finely-formed prick, which was not too large but beautifully proportioned, by Agnes's mouth. My reading of Agnes's desires proved to be correct as she opened her mouth and sucked mightily on his lovely cock, a sucking that was accompanied by a delicious squelching noise. I rightly believed her cunt was a little sore from the pounding I had given it, so I took hold of poor Allingham's tool myself and frigged him to emission as there was no other way that he could be satisfied. Almost at once miniature jets of foam spurted out from her fast-moving hands as Wilkinson and Pearce climaxed in a deluge of spunk which left Agnes's hands coated with cream. Young Foster-Jeffries came too in torrents of sperm, most of which she was able to swallow. Mitchell was still valiantly fucking her bottom, and how they panted and threshed as he slewed up and down while her bottom cheeks rose and fell. All was soon over and he pumped his spunk into her, draining his cock of the last drop until he withdrew his shrinking member out of her arse.

We all collapsed in an exhausted heap, lying awhile in the sun regaining our strength and composure, as Agnes licked the last drops of spunk from Foster-Jeffries' prick and with a handkerchief dabbed the dribbles of juice that trickled down her glistening thighs, which were drenched with perspiration.

Soon we all dressed hurriedly, and I made the other chaps promise never to reveal a word as to what had taken place that afternoon.

'You must all appreciate what a jolly sport Agnes has been and she is going to suck off Allingham before she leaves us tonight as he didn't have a fuck or suck himself. Now we have all enjoyed ourselves, haven't we, so we must all protect Agnes's reputation amongst the more prudish members of society. There are many who would, *sub rosa*, have thoroughly enjoyed our delightful afternoon but would look askance at Agnes if what we all did ever came to their attention. Gentlemen, I am sure that Doctor White would want us to swear a vow of secrecy.'

They all readily agreed upon their honour as Nottsgrove scholars, when to our horror Doctor White entered the room.

'Well, boys, how was your lecture on Smetana?' he boomed out, and I noticed a jolly twinkle in his eye.

'I'm afraid we didn't get much further than a brief biographical sketch,' laughed Agnes, and I looked puzzled—surely I had not misjudged the situation?

'They behaved exquisitely,' she went on. 'Young Andrew Scott here was everything you said—a born leader who showed every courtesy to me as well as ensuring that as many boys as possible enjoyed my favours.'

'Excellent,' said Doctor White, stroking his curly beard. 'Boys, I think you deserve an explanation. May I present to you not Miss Agnes Carter but Miss Agnes Wilson, currently of the Alhambra Theatre, Holborn. She enjoys fucking young men and I well knew that none of you would mind helping to satisfy her needs. I further took this opportunity to devise my own test of initiative and I must congratulate you, Andrew, for your performance. Forbes-Mackenzie also deserves credit for his sterling work this morning. Agnes, my dear friend, I hope you are satisfied with our labours?'

'Oh, indeed I am, Doctor. How can I ever thank you? My cunny is rather sore just now but it was well worth the ache to have those iron-hard young rods inside my orifices. To mark this auspicious occasion I have asked my patron, Lord Paddington to donate two hundred guineas for the establishment of a scholarship that will allow boys from poorer homes with the necessary academic qualifications to study here at your wonderful establishment.'

'How very kind of you,' replied the good Doctor.

'Merciful heavens, Doctor White, I do assure you most wholeheartedly that the pleasure was quite a mutual affair. Now I must thank all your wonderful pupils again for a glorious bout of fucking that has afforded me much enjoyment.'

'Is there no way by which we can repay you?'

'Oh, I suppose there is perhaps one favour you may do for me. I would be most grateful if Allingham could be excused from his studies this afternoon as I have promised to suck him off—he has never enjoyed the sensation before now and I have no wish to break my promise, particularly to such a strapping young fellow who has such a fine, upstanding prick!'

Doctor White laughed and said: 'But of course you must not break your word. Allingham, you lucky young pup, you are excused for the rest of this afternoon. Everyone else, back to your labours immediately, please, as we have much work to get through before the end of this term and I don't want anyone falling behind. Agnes, my dear, once again, *au revoir*, and do come back to visit us again as soon as you can.'

I led the chaps in a rousing chorus of 'For She's A Jolly Good Fellow' and we trudged back to the classroom to complete the day's studies—which for us all was a most disappointing anti-climax! Indeed, I can hardly recall what we were studying, but as my mind fetches forth these happy memories from the store of my recollections, I am put in mind of those famous words of the Bard of Avon as so wittily changed by Lord Byron who wrote:

'There is a tide in the affairs of women

Which, when taken at the flood, lead on to God knows where!'

How true, how very true!

CHAPTER SIX

THE NEXT day we were assembled in the classroom listening to Doctor White comment upon the news of the day. The good doctor was always a strong proponent of women's rights, and on that particular day he snorted with fury at a letter written to *The Times* by some 'old fool of a retired colonel' about the proposal for women's suffrage.

'Listen to this idiot,' he snorted, 'I will read you what this misguided misogynist who probably prefers to have boys in his bed has written: "Quite as disagreeable as the bearded chin, the bass voice, flat chest and lean hips of a woman who has failed physically in her rightful development, the unfeminine ways of the wild women of politics and morals are even worse for the world in which they live. Their disdain is for the duties and limitations imposed upon them by nature, their desire as impossible as that of the moth for the star. Marriage, in its old-fashioned aspect as the union of two lives, they repudiate as a one-sided tyranny; and maternity for which, after all, women primarily exist, they regard as degradation.

"Their idea of freedom is their own preponderance, so that they shall do all they wish to do without let or hindrance from outside regulations or the restraints of self-discipline; their idea of morality, that men shall do nothing, they choose to disallow. Their grand aim is to directly influence imperial policies, while they, and those men who uphold them, desire to shake off their own peculiar responsibilities.

"This clamour for political rights is woman's confession of

sexual enmity. Gloss over it as we may, it comes to this in the end. No woman who loves her husband would wish to usurp his province. Unless we are prepared to make of marriage a mere civil partnership, dissoluble at will, it is certain that the normal relationship between husband and wife must be one of control and decision on the husband's side and deference and submission on the wife's. For when two ride on a horse, one must ride behind.

"It is only those whose instincts are inverted or whose anti-sexual vanity is insatiable, who would wish to take the reins from the strong masculine hands which have always held them to give to others—weaker, less capable and wholly unaccustomed.

"To women who love, their 'desire is to their husbands'; and the feeling remains as an echo in the soul when even the master's voice is silent. Amongst our most renowned women are some who say with their whole heart: 'I would rather have been the wife of a great man or the mother of a hero than what I am—famous in my own person.' A woman's own fame is barren. It begins and ends with herself whilst when reflected from her husband or her son, it has in it the glory of immortality—of continuance. Sex is in circumstance as well as in body and in mind. We date from our fathers, not our mothers; and the shield they won for valour counts to us still for honour." '

'Please, Sir,' interrupted Paul. 'Surely the great houses are mostly descended from the whores who pleasured King Charles II who gave his ladies titles of nobility?'

'Of course, my boy,' beamed Doctor White, 'but let me finish this pompous idiot's nonsense. He finishes thus: "The miserable little mannikin who creeps to obscurity, over-shadowed by his wife's glory is as pitiful in history as contemptible in fact. 'The husband of his wife' is no title to honour and the best and sweetest of our famous women take care that this shall not be said of them and theirs.

"My earnest hope is that the political franchise will not be given to women. To give it may be termed 'progress' but this will be progress in the wrong direction," ' he concluded, laying down the newspaper and adding: 'Now who will be the first to comment on this piece?'

Paul Hill-Wallace, by far the brainiest chap at Nottsgrove, was naturally the first to raise his hand and Doctor White nodded at him to begin his speech.

Paul cleared his throat, stood up and began: 'Gentlemen, a woman may never be fitted intellectually to be a Minister of the Crown, an ambassador or even—and this takes an enormous flight of imagination—to become Prime Minister; but with her present rate of progress he would be a rash man who would attempt to predict just how far she will go. But, I submit, this does not affect one way or another her right to vote or the right of the nation to have her opinion recorded. Why should she sit on a School Board, for example, and in that capacity make recommendations to Parliament on the Education Code only to be denied a voice in that august assembly to support its provisions or secure its rejection? It is all quite absurd.

'We cannot afford as a great nation to allow such a potent force for good as that of our women to lie fallow. With our new, vast cities and the ever-increasing complication of interests and industry, our lives are becoming more and more impersonal, and the combination of a strong moral influence of both sexes is vital. Men are going forward so fast, gentlemen, that the rift between the sexes will grow even wider if women are to continue to be stuck in the same rigid pattern and never be allowed to take a step in advance. The choice, then, is not between standing still and going on, it is between retreating and advancing.

'There is no sadder sight in the world than that of a wasted life, yet how wanton is the huge waste continually going on in the lives of thousands of intelligent young women, whose powers, by a long course of trivialities and mental stagnation, are being slowly diminished.'

Pearce rose to question the previous speaker. 'This is all very fine,' he said, 'but I am still not convinced of the necessity for female suffrage.'

There were immediate shouts of 'Boo', 'Shame' and even

'Go suck your cock' from around him, and Doctor White raised his arms in the air for quiet. 'Free speech!' he thundered, and the noise died down immediately. 'Carry on, my boy, we will all listen to you, however misguided your views appear to be.'

'Thank you, sir. My contention is simply that the great danger in giving voting power to women is that those best qualified would hold aloof from those whose distorted views of their social duties would lead them to seek public office, and women's views would be represented by the noisiest and least feminine of their sex.'

'Well argued, Pearce,' said Doctor White. 'Scott, can you speak against him?'

I slowly rose to my feet, thinking how best to phrase my words. 'The fact of the matter is thus,' I said slowly, marshalling my thoughts carefully. 'When women's suffrage does come, as it assuredly must, it will not come as an isolated phenomenon but as a necessary corollary of other radical changes which have been gradually introduced during this century. It will be a political change of relatively little significance alongside the great social, economic and educational changes that will have already taken place. It will have the effect of adjusting the political machinery of the country to the altered social conditions of its inhabitants.

'So the political change will not be a revolution but a public recognition by the State that the lot of women in England is not what it was, say, at the beginning of this century.'

I will not be falsely immodest, and will record that my words were cheered to the echo, not least by Lucy who had entered the room unseen to me as I was speaking. She exchanged a few words with Doctor White who beamed broadly and said to me: 'Scott, would you be so kind as to help my niece with some corrections to the French essays handed in by the fourth form? You are excused the rest of this lesson.'

I needed no second invitation and strode down the corridor with Lucy.

'What essays do you need me to correct, sweetheart? My

French is not nearly up to the standard you have achieved,' I said.

'Now, now, Andrew, you need not be so unforthcoming. We are not discussing equality of the sexes!' she laughed. 'Mind, your French is not as good as mine.'

'My French kissing is top-hole!' I said, grabbing the delectable girl and forcing my lips to hers, inserting my tongue between her rich cherry adornments.

'Not here, Andrew,' she giggled. 'At least wait till we reach my study.'

'Look, we're nearer my room, let's have a quick fuck there!' I begged. 'Why, here we are already, do step inside!'

She giggled again but did not refuse my invitation. I locked the door behind her as I wanted no interruptions and quickly we threw off our clothes. When we were both naked Lucy began to stroke my skin with her fingertips. My cock was already hard but the touch of her warm hands made it even more erect. She kissed me lightly on my cheek and then her lips travelled down onto my neck and shoulders and down my body, until she was on her knees and her hands were encircling my giant prick which stood high in the air flat against my belly. Her tongue flicked out and teased the end of my knob which was oozing a drop of semen. Instinctively I reached out and pulled her head towards me and she opened her mouth wide to swallow as much of the shaft that I pushed into her.

Her mouth was like a cave of fire which warmed but did not burn as her tongue circled my knob, savouring the juices which were dribbling from the end. Her teeth scraped the sensitive dome of my glans as she drew me in between those luscious lips, sucking hard, as though she wanted to suck me right off.

I let myself gently to the ground, and without loosening her mouth's grip upon my throbbing cock, she edged round until her cunt was above my head and the delicate slit opened and closed as she moved her thighs. Drops of love-juice pattered upon my face and I pulled her down until that lovely crack was upon my mouth. My tongue now was put to good use as it slid up and down the warm slit, savouring the taste and aroma. I heard Lucy gasp with delight as I probed between her love-lips and thrust deep into her vagina. Then I found her erect little clitty and began to roll it between my lips and suck it into my mouth as she moaned with pleasure and tried to excite herself even more by rubbing herself off against my mouth. I could feel her bite on my prick, but as I pushed in and out of her sopping mouth I felt only pure ecstasy as I felt my balls hardening, and I shouted that I was going to come.

'Pump into me, darling,' she cried, letting my cock out of her mouth. We quickly changed positions so my staff rammed into her velvety cunny and its spongy gripping was accentuated by Lucy waggling her bottom. I knew that my spunking could not be held back much longer. There was nothing I could now do but let go, and the semen boiled up in my shaft to squirt thickly out of my prick as I pushed hard to ram my tool full inside her sopping pussy, which was now awash with her own juices. She screamed with happiness as the hot, creamy sperm flooded into her and at once I felt her shuddering through a tremendous orgasm as she drained the last drops of spunk from my pulsating prick. We kept glued together until my cock, which had exercised itself quite magnificently that day, fell out from the juicy folds of its nest.

I covered my darling with burning kisses and we rolled about on my bed until my cock swelled up again and, as the poet Dryden has it:

'Thus every creature, and of every kind,
 The sweet joys of sweet coition find.'

Reader, you will know that first love can be idyllic or it can be unmitigated disaster. How fortunate was I to have Lucy as my loving tutor, to find a girl who took trouble to understand and cater for my every need, so making the act of sexual union so superb an experience for us both.

I kissed her large titties and her nips stood up like twin rosebuds; below, her white belly was set off at the bottom by the golden haired pubic mound. My hand still tweaking the nipple of her right breast, I slid my other arm further down and two of my questing fingers glissaded down into the inviting wetness of her cleft. She quivered all over and softly moaned as she opened her legs and took hold of my straining cock. Still playing inside her cunny lips I sucked on her rosy nipple until she begged me to insert my rod inside her. She guided my prick with her hands and I buried my cock in her sopping slit. Oh, ye Gods! how tight did her cunny clasp my prick, and what luscious suction was created by the juicy folds of her cunt as my piston shoved in and out of its sheath. How gloriously she met all my thrusts by the most energetic heaves and oh! how her fiery kisses were lavished upon my cheeks and lips as I pressed her to my bosom. To fully enjoy the pleasures of love, it is necessary to cast away all mental restraints, for man was made for woman and woman for man —and we revelled in our voluptuous delights with the utmost vigour.

Lucy was expert in the use of her vaginal muscles to contract and relax her cunny, and she made the passage tight as I slowly drew out my cock until only the dome remained inside, causing so great a suction that it sent a thrill of pleasure through my whole body. We played at this three or four times; I would slowly draw my prick out and then dart it in again to stretch and engorge the deliciously tight cunt that held me like a soft, moist hand. I worked away for as long as I could hold back and she spent twice more until the sensitive contractions of her clever little cunt milked my cock of a flood of boiling spunk that lubricated her innermost passages.

We sank back exhausted and fell to sleep, quite forgetting that we had Doctor White's work still hanging over our heads. I woke first after about an hour and watched my love who was still deep in the arms of Morpheus. Lucy goes to sleep the way you would close the door of a cupboard. So many times have I seen her lovely body squirm a moment as though she were fitting herself into a cocoon. She sighs once and at the end of it her eyes close and her lips, untroubled, fall into that wise and remote smile of the ancient Greek gods.

She smiles in her sleep, her breath purrs in her throat, not a snore but a kitten's purr. She insists that she does not dream yet she must, of course—simply, her dreams do not trouble her so she forgets them before awakening from her slumbers. Lucy loves to sleep and sleep welcomes her.

I gently shook her shoulder and she smiled sweetly at me. 'Don't worry, Andrew,' she said. 'In fact, I have finished all the marking by myself. I only wanted to drag you out of your class because I wanted you to fuck me.'

Her candid and truthful manner warmed my heart even more towards my beloved girl. I kissed her lovely lips and she responded by waggling her little tongue in my mouth, but then pulled away.

'We will fuck a little later, darling boy,' she said. 'Let us talk awhile. I rarely have the opportunity of speaking with you. We never engage in serious conversation but as soon as we come together my blood is so fired all I want to do is possess your lovely prick!'

I laughed aloud and replied: 'Very well, my dearest Lucy. Let us not coop ourselves up here in the study, for it is a perfectly lovely afternoon. The air is exquisite so let us get dressed and go out for a walk on Arkley Common. Then we can lie on the grass and discuss Irish Home Rule!'

'For the first part, yes my dear, but let us simply take our walk and forgo lying in the grass. Nature has good intentions but, as Aristotle once said, she cannot carry them out. Grass is hard and lumpy and damp and is often full of dreadful black insects.'

I laughed again and agreed to her demand, so we soon dressed ourselves and set out for the pleasant little green. I remembered that Rosalie, the girl who cleaned my study, was eighteen years old later in the week, and I resolved to buy her some trifle. I purchased some ribbons from the village shop, which was kept by a grumpy old curmudgeon by the name of Corney who lived with his wife and pretty young daughter, Danielle, who assisted him there.

'You know, dearest,' said Lucy, after I had made my purchase, 'old Mr Corney puts himself forward as the

112

champion of respectability in conduct, of puritanism in life, and of morality in art.'

'Is he one of the killjoys?' I said absently. 'They can be very silly sometimes.'

'I think, indeed, that such people are sinister,' replied Lucy. 'It is their very certainty that disturbs me. They are so sure of their righteousness that they can never see even a morsel of justice in the argument put forward by an opponent. For me, *voila ou mènent les mauvais chemins . . .*'

'The paths of evil lead here,' I translated, to show Lucy that my French was up to the mark.

'Precisely, Andrew,' she added. 'I am always cautious of people who are so certain of the correctness of all their actions, for it can often lead to an opposite effect to that which was originally desired.'

'Are you thinking of something specific, my love?' I enquired.

'I am, dearest, but if I confide in you, may I have your assurance that what I say will be kept in the strictest confidence?'

'I give you my word as a Nottsgrovian,' I said and this oath was of course good enough for Lucy to share her secret with me.

'Very well, then, I shall entrust my secret with you. Some few weeks back you may recall that Doctor White was suffering with a summer chill. I decided to buy him some more handkerchiefs and I walked down to the village shop where I was served by Danielle, Mr Corney's daughter, who is only sixteen years of age.

'I could not fail to observe that she walked rather ungainly and I thought that I detected a strange bulge in the front of her dress. I asked her if she was well and to my horror she burst out crying and told me that her father had taken it into his head that she had been free with her sexual favours with the local youth. The truth is, Andrew, that she is *a virgo intact* and she has only been kissed by Arthur Greystokes, that fair-haired boy who runs errands and works as an apprentice to his father, the cobbler. I made so bold as to ask her if she had

113

ever been threaded and she swore to me that the furthest she had allowed Arthur to travel was to fondle her breasts through her clothing and she had rubbed his prick through the cloth of his trousers. But be that as it may, old Corney decided to make his daughter a chastity belt!'

'A chastity belt! In this enlightened day and age?' I cried out.

'I assure you that he has done so. She called me upstairs into her room as her parents were out and stripped to the skin. She has a lovely body, I must tell you, with firm young breasts and a very pattable bottom. But around her hips is a tight but flexible wire to which is attached a loincloth of leather which runs between her legs and is pulled up snugly between her bottom cheeks so that any attempts to reach her bum-hole will also be foiled. A wire mesh covers her cunny so that she can relieve herself but each morning her loving father locks his daughter up and unlocks it at night . . . .

'Now chastity belts date back to medieval times and perhaps were a result of the Crusades. When the knights knew that they would be away from their castles for many months, or even years, they did not trust their wives to remain cockless. I shudder to think what wearing this belt will do to this poor girl in these modern times.'

'Can you not talk to her mother?' I put in with some anxiety.

'Alas, she is completely dominated by her husband. I promised Danielle that I would not mention this to a soul but I have broken my word as I feel that someone should help the poor girl. Unfortunately, they have no close friends or relations to whom she can turn, which is why she told me about this dreadful garment.'

'How about the Vicar?' I suggested. 'The Reverend Ferningham is a most liberal gentleman who surely would not countenance such a barbarity?'

'Well, he has some goodness, I suppose,' said Lucy stiffly. 'But I cannot very well speak to him just now as we had a furious argument over dinner when he came over to the school last week. He was pontificating about the dignity of manual labour and I said that there was nothing necessarily dignified about manual labour at all and that most of it was absolutely degrading. He argued that men would become demoralised if they had no work and I countered by saying that many forms of labour are quite pleasureless activities and must be regarded as such. To sweep a slushy crossing, for example, for eight hours, especially when the wind is blowing, is a particularly disgusting occupation, and to sweep it with dignity or joy is impossible.'

I had no mind to argue the point but attempted to put Lucy back in a good humour by reciting a verse I had heard the village layabouts recite after a pint or two of ale.

'There was an old vicar named Ferningham
Who assaulted young girls whilst confirming 'em
Midst thunderous applause
He pulled down their drawers
And injected episcopal sperm in 'em!

'Rather a jolly poem, don't you think?' I said lightly.

'If you like limericks,' said Lucy. 'At least the filthy ones are funnier than those of Lear which I find extremely tedious.'

'Why, I know some jolly ones,' I said. 'Shall I tell you another one?'

'If you must,' she smiled.

'Alright; there's just time because we are almost at the Vicarage. Here goes:—

There once was a jolly old bloke
Who took a girl to his rooms for a poke
But she said that his prong
Was too thick and too long
So he shit in her shoes for a joke!'

Despite her attempting to put on a cross face, Lucy could not help giving a little giggle.

'Hush now, Andrew, no more poetry in front of the Vicar!' she admonished me, tapping me lightly on the nose with her forefinger.

I rang the bell of the front door of the vicarage but there was no reply. The Vicarage was surrounded by a quarter acre of what could best be called mature garden, as the previous incumbent, Reverend Guy, had not bothered himself with keeping the lawns and flowerbeds in a tidy state. Reverend Ferningham, though, was a younger man, some thirty-five years old. Though of a slim build, he was strong and wiry and he liked nothing better than to amuse himself in his garden. Doctor White, as you will recall my mentioning very early in this narrative, was also a keen horticulturalist, and they spent many a pleasant afternoon in the Vicarage grounds.

To go behind the house required only the opening of a wooden gate and I suggested to Lucy that perhaps our quarry was busying himself there, so we went round the back. But again there was no sign of the vicar.

'He must be out,' said Lucy.

'Hold on a moment,' I said, looking towards the uncurtained windows of the drawing room. 'I do believe that I saw some movement inside the house. Let us take a closer look.'

Well, we did take a closer-look—and what a shock we had as we gazed through the open windows. For there on the couch, stark naked, was the Reverend Colin Ferningham and next to him, also stark naked, was Rosalie, the girl who cleaned my study and for whose eighteenth birthday I had purchased a present in the village shop. She was a pretty girl, a fact I had genuinely not noticed before now, full bodied and yet not run to fat, but firm and curvaceous everywhere, and she presented in her nudity, as tasty a sight of feminine pulchritude as ever I had seen.

Now they were kissing, and as his hand cupped one large breast I saw that his thick prick was standing stiff between his thighs and that Rosalie had taken the shaft of his tool between her long fingers. Her own nipples seemed to grow before my eyes and they stabbed at his palm as he fondled each lovely large breast in turn. Then, suddenly rising, he caught her in his arms, pulled her straight up and then placed her down on her back on the rich, red carpet which set off her white skin most fetchingly. He knelt between her parted legs and she pulled his head to her bosom and he turned his lips from side to side, kissing each bubbie as he encountered its warm, rounded sides and whilst doing so his right arm reached down so that his hand was set between her legs and his fingers played with the thick brush of dark hair that covered her mound. He parted the rolled lips of her cunny, pale pink as they were, protruding enchantingly through the nest of black curls and she twisted with desire, rolling her belly silkily on his stiff cock.

As he continued to suck hard on those raised-up little nipples, she threw back her head and moaned with joy. Ever so lightly, his fingertips traced the open, wet slit of her cunny, flicking the erect little clitty that was peeping out. Then the cunny lips were forced apart as he took hold of his own rigid pole and thrust the red crown between the pouting lips of the juicy pussy, and Rosalie moaned again with delight as he propelled in inch after inch until their pubic hair was matted together. The Vicar pulled right back, and then drove the powerful length of his shaft full depth inside the lovely girl again and again as she urged him on, closing her feet together at the small of his back to try and force even more of that throbbing tool inside her. Then he gave a series of little jerks and withdrew his glistening cock and pumped spurts of white spunk onto her belly.

'No, don't say a word. I know, my dear, that you haven't come,' said the Vicar. 'So let us continue.'

'I have, Vicar, honestly, I've come,' said Rosalie earnestly.

'That is very kind of you, my sweet girl, but a man can sense when his partner has achieved full satisfaction. Now you just go over to the settee and open up for me, there's a good girl.'

She did as she was told, sitting, however, with her legs dangling wide apart over the side of the settee. He clambered up and then sank down again, gazing at the open vagina and giving Lucy and I full view of the pink inner lips.

'It is so lovely, I must suck and kiss it and pay homage to that unique womanly scent,' said the Vicar, kissing her open cunt with his tongue running the full length of its parted lips. Rosalie shuddered as his tongue found her hardened clitty that I saw sticking out like a miniature cock and he gave it his full attention. Side to side, up and down, she began to jerk wildly. 'Oh, Vicar, more, more, I'm coming, I'm coming.' His hands gripped her hips as she moaned and writhed around making it difficult for him to keep his mouth on her clit. He took his face away from between her legs and began rubbing and pinching her clitty with his thumb and forefinger.

Now Rosalie was twisting from side to side as her love-juices began to flow again and her hands went to her breasts as she played with her own titties, roughly massaging those elongated nips.

'Rub it, oh, rub it, harder, please. Ooooh, Oooooh!' she cried as her gyrations increased as she twisted and writhed, heaved and humped; until with a shriek she achieved a full climax and imprisoned the hand between her legs, wrapping it tightly between her jerking thighs as she slowly subsided. The Vicar stood before her, the red knob of his prick still visible as it stood semi-erect in front of her.

'I have been naughty,' said Rosalie softly. 'I'm such a naughty girl.'

'Yes, you were naughty, weren't you?' said the Vicar, sitting down beside her. 'And you know what happens to naughty girls, don't you?'

There was a slight pause.

'You do know, don't you?' he said again.

'They get their bottoms slapped,' said Rosalie.

'Well then?' he queried and she rose and draped herself over his knees.

'Open your legs wider, that's right, you naughty girl, for I want to ensure that your cunny feels the edge of my slaps too.'

She was now fully bent over his knees and his left hand reached under to fondle her hanging breasts and his right hand ran gently over her fat, slack bottom cheeks. Then he brought both hands up to explore the intricacies of her bum, opening the cheeks then pushing them tightly together again. Then he started, lightly at first, a few rapid slaps which made her wriggle.

'Your bum cheeks are beginning to change colour now, Rosalie,' he said, delighted with his handiwork as he quickened the pace and increased the force of the slaps, which really must have stung Rosalie's bum as she jerked and winced under her 'punishment'.

'Now then, Rosalie, you have been naughty and you must get slapped like all naughty girls. Besides, I like to see your fat bum cheeks change colour for they should always be a little red just as they are now. Also, I like the way your cheeks jiggle when I slap them!'

He must have slapped her thirty times on the rump before she got up and stood with her back to him so that he could survey his handiwork. His cock was now standing stiffly upwards, slightly curving, but the skin was pulled back to show an almost purple knob, which twitched away as she turned back and sank to her knees in front of it.

'Would you like me to suck you?' she enquired.

'Oh yes, yes, I would love that very much if you would be so kind,' said the Vicar as she kissed the purple dome and licked her way round the rim.

'You do that magnificently, Rosalie. But I do not want to force you to do this. It is of your own free choice?' he said.

She nodded as she opened her wide mouth and slipped in the knob, enclosing her lips around it as tightly as she could and working on the tip with her tongue. She eased her lips forward, taking in a little more as her hands circled the base of his cock. She worked the loose skin up and down the shaft at the same time as she began to bob her head up and down, and his hands went to the back of her head, pushing her further down on his swollen prick. Somehow she managed to swallow even more of the shaft, and soon I saw that the Vicar could contain himself no longer as he thrust his hips upward and the sperm spurted into her mouth in powerful jets. She tried hard to swallow all the creamy emission but some of the flood dripped from her lips onto the carpet, a fact that was immediately noticed by Lucy, who whispered to me: 'This means another job for Doctor Hopkins' cough mixture which Elaine told us removes any stains.'

I could not contain my mirth at her merry jest and burst out laughing noisily. Naturally, I was heard by the lovers inside the lounge and they looked up, startled, towards the window.

'Do not concern yourselves,' Lucy called out. 'It is only Lucy Essex and Andrew Scott. We must apologise for disturbing you and for not making our presence known earlier.' We stepped through the French doors as the Vicar and Rosalie hastily pulled on their clothes.

'Master Andrew, you won't shop me, will you?' said Rosalie anxiously.

'Of course not, Rosalie! I hope you enjoyed yourself. Just don't get yourself in the family way!' I said, looking hard towards Reverend Ferningham.

'No I won't do that, sir. The Vicar never comes inside me except near my bleeding times and I always give myself a douche afterwards,' said Rosalie.

'That is very sensible,' said Lucy. 'I am all for enjoying a good fucking but it is us poor ladies who have to pay for any mistakes.'

'There we are in total agreement, Miss Essex,' said the Vicar, buttoning his shirt. 'Ah, I hope that our rather unnecessarily heated words of a few days ago will not lead to any unfortunate consequences regarding what you have just seen.'

'Oh, no, I am no sneak. But I must say that I am curious, to say the least, how a man of the cloth can fornicate like this even though it is true that neither of you are married persons,' said Lucy, somewhat stiffly.

'That is not an unfair observation,' I added as the Vicar looked a little worried.

'No, it is not unfair and I think you deserve an explanation. Will you wait a moment, however, whilst I say goodbye to Rosalie?'

'Of course we will,' I replied, and at his invitation we sat down whilst he whispered a few words to Rosalie, who wished us good-day as she left to go back to Nottsgrove.

The Vicar came back and offered us some refreshment. We

accepted a glass of wine and he settled himself back in his chair to explain the unusual happenings we had witnessed.

'Perhaps you do not know that before I entered the Church I studied medicine with some of the most learned professors in Europe,' he said. 'Indeed, after my graduation I spent two years in Paris with Doctor Kleiman and Doctor Bagell who are the foremost specialists in female nervous disorders.'

'Doctor Kleiman has developed a simple, though highly original, method of curing these disorders. I won't bother you with his theories on the origin of what he calls latent neuroses except to say that all women possess a sexual feeling which either develops or vanishes to frigidity in abnormal cases.

'As might be expected, these disorders develop most easily in young women who have been brought up extremely strictly and become virtual prisoners of their own education. They cannot bring themselves to express their sexual needs by taking lovers, and even inside bonds of marriage they cannot achieve any sexual pleasure or release. Yes, indeed, as the French writer, Dumas, has said, the bonds of wedlock are so heavy that it takes two to carry them—or even three.

'Now Doctor Kleiman has dared to suggest a cure which will rid the patient of her inhibitions and enable her to enjoy sexual intercourse, and thus enable her body to achieve the satisfaction it needs in order to maintain good health—and one must remember that this is all a question of health rather than strict morality in the conventional sense of the phrase.

'To begin with, the girl who is being helped is sent to a strange house, preferably away from her own home. Usually, she stays alone with her servants although occasionally two patients go together so that they may enjoy each other's company. Then after a few days, a gentleman comes along and takes the patient out for walks during the day, on rambles, on picnics or what have you. He then arrives for dinner on one day, and sees even more of the girl until—well, I think you understand the picture, don't you?'

Lucy was fascinated by his little lecture. 'That is very interesting, Vicar, but surely you are not saying that the male visitor has to have sexual relations with the patient for a cure to be effected?' she asked.

'Oh, yes, very often this follows naturally; and it is precisely because the girls meet men of experience, vigour and, dare I say, wisdom and discretion which forms the basis of the cure. The doctor cannot place his patient in weak or clumsy hands. What may surprise you is that the majority of women go back to their husbands refreshed and invigorated, and both partners will thus have benefited from this treatment. It is true that unfortunately some women, a very few, have wished to divorce their husbands and marry their instructors. This has actually happened, but more usually a patient simply continues to use the services of her, ah, lover after she goes home. This liaison is not encouraged and usually this affair terminates of its own accord within a few months and again the woman and her husband are fully reconciled and fully enjoying life.'

'This is quite extraordinary,' I said. 'But surely, Rosalie is not married and needs no help in freeing herself from the confines of a nervous disorder.'

'That is not entirely true,' replied the Vicar. 'She is unmarried, as you rightly say, but she does suffer from a sexual disorder that I believe required treatment. I do not think that either of you will repeat what I say so I will tell you of her problem.'

'Just a moment,' Lucy interrupted. 'Are you still a doctor?'

'In the sense that I am a qualified practitioner, although after a disturbing personal experience that I do not wish to relate, I left medicine and entered the Church. My father, as perhaps you know, was Rector of Grantham in Lincolnshire and so I have followed his footsteps into the ministry. I do still keep up with the world of medicine and subscribe to all the learned journals. Some day, perhaps, I shall return to it but this work keeps me occupied and thanks to my aunt, who left me a most generous annuity, I have no financial cares and so I may freely choose to do with my life whatever may take my fancy.'

'Nevertheless, it surely is a most heavy responsibility,' I said.

'It most certainly is, and is not one to be undertaken lightly or immorally. This is why instructors have to be chosen with great discretion. I am afraid that you, for example, would be considered too young for such onerous work.'

'That may be,' said Lucy. 'Certainly, I would not want to act as a female teacher for any man who had such difficulties, although I do agree with what you are trying to do. However, you said that Rosalie had been suffering from a disorder.'

'That is correct,' he said. 'Would you like me to relate the full story? You would? Let me first pour you another glass of wine, perhaps. There, now I will tell you how all this came about.

'It began earlier this summer when Rosalie came to me in some distress. She had been walking out with young Arthur Greystokes, the youngest son of old Greystokes the cobbler, and he had asked her to marry him. I would have counselled against the nuptials as she is far too young, though that is not strictly relevant here.'

'I would have counselled against it too,' I said grimly, remembering what Danielle Corney had told Lucy about young Master Greystokes.

'Anyhow, like all courting couples they had indulged in some cuddling and kissing, and indeed they had progressed right up to the point of sexual union but then Rosalie's mind would not obey the dictates of her body and she could not enjoy herself further than the gates of the mansion, so to speak.

'Perhaps you know that she is an educated girl who comes from a most respectable family. Her father was a chief clerk at a City Office until he was tragically injured by a gang of hooligans as he was walking home one night after work. He never fully recovered, and died not long after, leaving the family almost destitute. Fortunately, a wealthy relative in America now knows of their plight and has offered to bring them all out to his home in New York. They will leave in

October. Until then Rosalie, her brother, and her two sisters are working even at menial jobs to scrape together enough money to enable her eldest brother to continue his studies at medical school in London. This is how I knew Rosalie, as one of her brother's lecturers is a friend of mine.

'Of course, when she first mentioned her problem to me, I counselled against partaking of forbidden fruits, as sexual intercourse should take place inside the bounds of holy matrimony; although this narrow interpretation of the Scriptures is now being challenged by many people.

'I was firm about this until I was completely convinced that she was going to have sexual intercourse regardless of what I said, and of course that she knew when to abstain from the activity to avoid an unwanted parturient condition.

'She assured me that she was fully aware of everything I had said and to prove her point she handed me her diary out of which I will now read a relevant passage. This is what happened to Rosalie a few months ago on her day off . . .

Rosalie's Diary
It was a gloriously hot morning and the sun was high overhead, sending down great shafts of golden light, warming the earth and sparkling in the still dew-wet grass.

I was walking barefoot in the lush green meadow, my long thin dress hanging loosely on my otherwise naked body, my hair falling on my shoulders and moving slightly in the gentle breeze, filling me with a sense of freedom and carelessness that urged me to throw off my dress and run totally naked and uninhibited until I reached some distant land of erotic pleasure. I sat down on a hummock of earth which pressed into my cunny and sent an exciting, shivering sensation right through me. I leaned back against a huge tree trunk which stood behind me, opening my legs wide so that the sun struck warmly on my pussy, making its curly dark hair shine and glisten in the light. I closed my eyes, allowing the warmth to seep through me, filling me with an acute and sensuous awareness of my own physical being. I moved my hand lazily to my thigh and ran my fingertips along its smooth surface.

My hand moved down and began to fondle the lips of my cunt, rubbing up and down until I could feel the moisture beginning to form and dampen my fingertips. It filled me with an intense feeling of wholeness, and with a realisation that I could so easily fulfil my own physical needs.

Suddenly, I heard a crackling of dry leaves behind me and I didn't turn round or cease rubbing my moist pussy although I was aware that someone could be watching me from a close distance. I heard nothing more for a moment, and then who should it be but dear Arthur who walked out from behind a clump of bushes. He came towards me and stopped not a foot from where I was propped up against the tree. How tall he looked, and how I loved the mass of fair curling hair which fell forward over his face. He had a strong body, and the lump which protruded forward from his trousers looked as firm as ever. His acute blue eyes roamed all over my body but stopped at my open pussy and he smiled as he sat down, facing me but still not speaking.

'Were you looking for me?' I asked.

'Might have been, might have been looking for someone else!' he replied laconically.

'I came out here to feel sensual,' I said, 'but as you are now here—'

'Let's fuck, then,' he said quickly.

'Oh, Arthur, you cannot just undress, jump on and fuck and then simply go away leaving me wondering what on earth has happened. You must seduce me like the sun and breeze do.'

'You are over-romantic, Rosalie, and anyway the sun and the breeze cannot fuck you like my prick can,' he retorted.

'But the sun can make me feel sexual and I can do the rest by myself,' I said.

'That is not nearly so satisfying, especially when you know that you care for me,' he said. 'I will show you how good fucking can really be.'

'Oh, Arthur, will you really?'

Without replying he slid down so that he was lying beside me. I stretched my legs out in front of me leaving them wide apart. My dress was lying in a cotton pile just above my pussy and his hand came to rest on my neck and he twisted his fingers through my hair. His face moved closer to mine and his moist lips touched my neck and gently moved up so that I could hear and feel his soft breathing in my ear. He took my dress in both hands and lifted it up and over my head so that now I lay totally naked before him. His fingers brushed my breasts lightly and my nipples immediately jumped to attention.

'You have really fantastic bubbies,' he muttered softly. 'Let me suck you.'

His mouth came down to meet the soft flesh, his hands gently pushing my titties together as his tongue came forward and circled round my roused nipples. Then his mouth opened and drew in the soft flesh, his tongue constantly moving, sending wild vibrations through my whole body. Then he let go my breasts and ran his hand down and over my belly until his fingers were caressing my pubic bush. My cunt throbbed, pulsing my juice from me in a hot sticky wetness. His mouth was now on my titties again, his tongue reaching out to slide around my nipples. His hand moved in and out of my now thoroughly wet cunny until he was sliding his wicked fingers around my pulsating clitty, pressing it and releasing it in a throbbing movement and my juices were now flowing freely as he inserted first one, then two and then three fingers up and into me. I moved my own hand to the bulge in front of his trousers, which he had unbuttoned, and I pushed my fingers down to feel the proud stiffness of his thick cock. He helped me pull down his trousers and drawers and his naked prick stood out hard before me. I moved forward and brought my lips down onto it. My tongue ran the length of the shaft and ran back to the dome to catch a hot sticky drip of spend that had formed at the 'eye' of the knob. I ran my lips around the tip of his noble cock and then I opened my mouth to accept its entrance. In one single movement he forced at least three inches into my mouth and my body jerked violently from the utter force of it. He retracted slightly so that it lay motionless, though throbbing on my tongue. I closed my lips around the monster sweetmeat and moved my tongue across its width. I sucked greedily on his prick as Arthur twisted himself down so that his face was pushed into my love pit, and my head almost swam with delight as his tongue began to circle around my dripping crack.

Arthur's mouth closed in on my cunt as I continued to suck his throbbing cock. His own soft tongue ran along my slit in moist, teasing strokes and I moved my cunt up and down as Arthur rolled his hips to move his cock in and out of my yearning mouth. I squeezed his balls gently, and then like liquid fire he shot jets of hot, creamy spunk which poured down my throat in a frenzy of salty froth, and I swallowed it to the last burning drops.

Meanwhile, his tongue continued to quiver across my frantic clitty as I swayed my body in harmony with his hard-working tongue. At last I felt my body rocket to the heights of ecstatic madness and I moaned and tossed my head from side to side with the sheer unashamed glory of my long-awaited climax. I fell silent, shuddering quietly as each exhausted throb of relief echoed within my numbed clitty.

Arthur lifted his head from my sopping bush and he twisted back again so that his body was on top of mine and I could feel his prick stiffening up again against my cunt. Now my own body stiffened and for no reason I can give, I sat up and stared at him, all the time feeling the heat of my passion draining from me.

'What is the matter?' Arthur said, looking up at me.

'I don't know,' I said truthfully, although I somehow knew that he would not really understand.

'You've frozen up again just when I was going to fuck you,' he shouted. 'You told me to seduce you and I did but it's always the same story. Anyone would think that you were offering me Aladdin's Lamp! I am tired of all this nonsense!'

Then he pushed me down again and threw himself on top of me. His hands roamed all over my body in hurried clumsy movements. Suddenly he relaxed and leaning himself up on his elbows, he looked down into my face.

*'Oh come on, Rosalie,' he said. 'You know that I cannot
fuck you if you just freeze up like a block of ice. Come on,
relax.'*

*But try as I would, I just could not let him fuck me and he
stormed off in a rage saying that he wanted to break the
arrangement we had and that he could find plenty of other
girls who would happily let him fuck them all day and all
night if he wanted.*

The Vicar concluded this extract from Rosalie's diary and
sipped at his glass of wine.

'That is most interesting,' said Lucy. 'But the question
now of course is what caused her to be so frightened of letting
Arthur fuck her. Was she a virgin, may I ask?'

'No, she had some limited experience in *l'art de faire
l'amour*,' he replied, 'but only with one boy, and she had not
enjoyed the experience as much as she might.'

'And because she did not enjoy the experience she was
frightened to try again,' I said triumphantly.

'This is partly true. But another part of the cause was
young Arthur himself who was a selfish brute and concerned
only with his own pleasure. A few gentle words coupled with
understanding patience might have solved the problem. If he
had known better he could have purchased some cold cream
although a favourite remedy for many couples is to slip a
pillow in between the buttocks. This helps enormously to
open out the cunny lips and make insertion easier.'

'Perhaps she was afraid of the size of his weapon,'
suggested Lucy.

'I don't think so, although I am sure you will agree, my
dear, that some foolish men seem to expect their girls to
swoon with pleasure at the very sight of an outsize prick.'

'Yes, they do and they are very silly,' said Lucy warmly.
'Some men are sufficiently conceited to believe that a huge
prick will immediately reduce the recipient to quivering
ecstasy. Now I have sampled men of surprising variance of
size, and neither of the two ten-inch partners I have had
seemed to care a button about the finer points of the game.

On each occasion with both these men, their assurances that they would be careful were forgotten during their final throes, resulting in my experiencing in a severe, stabbing pain which led to the complete inability on my part to reach orgasm.

'The average or even smaller-than-average man, on the other hand, is more aware that he cannot rely solely on sheer dimension to bring pleasure and is generally more careful to make the act more interesting by bringing a sense of variety and purpose to his love-making.'

'I do so agree with you,' said the Vicar. 'Unusual length and girth may look quite splendid, but although they might afford an initial advantage, occasionally an oversized member can be a hazard to enjoyable sport and indeed in general size is totally unimportant. What a man needs most of all is the ability to exercise his imagination, consideration and patience.'

'I could not express these sentiments better,' cried Lucy. 'Why, I must confess to you that while Andrew's prick is of good size and he has the ability to use it well, I have been transported out of this world by the manipulation of two skilfully wielded fingers! It is a man's attitude that makes him a good lover, like Andrew here, rather than the size or shape of his equipment.'

'Thank you very much,' I said rather indignantly. 'Are you saying that my cock is too small for you?'

'Oh no, my dearest,' she laughed. 'It is just the right size and it possesses the best owner in all the world. All the Vicar and I are saying is that even the smallest tool can be like a paintbrush in the hands of an artist and that an overgrown prick can never even match a smaller one if the possessor of the large instrument does not know how to play the right melody!'

'Indeed this is so,' said the Vicar. 'Anyhow, I was telling you about Rosalie. She came to me for advice about how to solve this problem and I concluded that Arthur was far too immature a youth for her. And as we talked I must allow that I became somewhat infatuated with this pretty young girl.

'One fine day we were walking hand in hand across that

very same meadow where she had experienced her problem with Arthur and we nestled down by that very same tree trunk. I knelt down by her side and took her right hand and placed it on my cheek. Slowly her fingertips moved across my face, exploring my cheeks, my nose and my mouth and I then took hold of her hand and imprisoned it gently in my own. "I am ready now," she whispered but I hesitated—for surely she did not want me to complete the union she once desired with Arthur. "Please, please take me," she murmured, "I do so want you to make love to me." I resolved to see whether she really wanted me as opposed to the wretched boy, so I silenced her pleadings with a kiss which startled her, although she did not try to draw away. And then, as I gently forced open her lips with my tongue, she responded and clasped me round the neck. My hands held her shoulders lightly and then slid down, delving into her dress, breaking open the tiny buttons until her wriggling pulled her full firm young breasts out into the open air. I kissed her passionately again with my hand cupping those gorgeous breasts, and to my astonishment the sweet young girl moved her hand downwards to grasp my swollen tool and rubbed the shaft through the material of my trousers with her palm.

'Then to my astonishment and delight she moved away, and pulled up her frock over her head and cast it off, her raised arms momentarily muffled by it. Then her alabaster white nudity was there in front of me, her slender legs, her uptilted, pointed breasts, her flat belly below which her curly-haired love mound seemed to glint in the warm sunshine. I took her in my arms, and with my mouth on hers started to caress her thighs, and then my mouth slid down her perfect pulsating body, planting kisses on each raised nipple, then her navel until, now using both hands, I prised apart her legs and buried my face between her unresisting thighs. I licked the juice round her cunt lips and she lifted her bottom as my hands clasped her bum cheeks to lift them nearer to me. Her pussy seemed to open wide as I slipped my tongue through the pink lips and licked away between the inner grooves in long thrusting strokes. Her cunny was now gushing love-juice, and each time I tongued her the little clitty stiffened even more eagerly. I tasted her sweetness, rousing her to new peaks of delight, and her hands began to caress my hair and my cheeks, pressing on my temples as if to direct my onslaught. She exploded once, twice and yet still was not satisfied as I continued my caresses and her hips and her bottom moved in synchronised rhythm with my mouth. Her body was jerking away and my face rubbed against her thick curly bush as she screamed again with delight, and I worked my tongue until my jaw ached. Heaving violently the lovely girl managed to achieve the heights of bliss again as she gently pushed my face away from her juicy slit. "Fuck me, oh, you must fuck me now!" she gasped, and I could not deny either her or my body as chills of lust ran up and down my spine.

'My eyes were on the full flow of breasts, waist, hips and thighs as I quickly peeled off my garments and my tool sprang up fierce and free as the sweet girl kissed the uncapped red dome. She clutched at my cock and brought it to her mouth as I lay over her. She rolled her tongue round the swollen knob, and I could feel the loving playful bite of her pearly teeth. She sucked hard on my shaft and I felt my prick swell even nearer to bursting point, and I spurted a creamy emission into her tight yet luscious little mouth which was engorged with my swollen prick. She eagerly sucked every drop of my sperm and despite my copious spend, my prick was still ramrod stiff as I slowly withdrew it from her pouting lips. First wetting my finger in her juicy crack, I easily inserted it in her beautifully wrinkled brown bum-hole and I worked her up to such a state of desire that she grabbed my prick and pushed the head just slightly between the outer lips of her cunny.

'Then, throwing her arms around my neck, she drew my lips to hers, as she thrust her tongue into my mouth with all the wild abandon of love, and shoved up her bottom to meet my charge. I had placed one hand under her buttocks, while with the other I kept my cock straight to the mark and plunged into her, stretching the resilient opening of her young cunny. She spread her legs and bent her knees so that her

131

heels rested lightly on the small of my back. I pressed in and out gently and slowly, and the sensations produced on my swollen cock by her tight little cunt were almost unendurable. I knew that soon I would have to come, but I wanted to make this last for both our sakes. Unbelievably, I found the control I sought so desperately, and began to move a little more quickly. Rosalie was immediately responsive and twining her legs now about my waist she asked me to put my hands under her hips and lift her. I did as instructed and then thrust my full length inside her. As I kept my prick deep inside she began to rub her clitty hard against my rigid shaft, and I began to pump wildly feeling my balls slapping against her bottom as her sighs turned to moans and then a shriek as she reached the heights of ecstasy; and I flooded her cunny with jets of hot sperm so powerful that the love juices oozed out of her luscious nest to trickle slowly down her thighs. A few frenetic quiverings more and I slowly took out my now turgid cock and we lay in each other's arms, while over us the summer sky stretched like a giant blue tent and the smell of the crushed grasses beneath us mingled with our perspiration. The dance of butterflies, disturbed by our advent, reformed its fluttering patterns above our heads.'

We sat silently for a moment or two as the Vicar concluded his moving tale of love and passion.

'You obviously feel much love for this sweet girl,' commented Lucy. 'Do you wish to make your liaison a permanent one or do you plan to love and leave her?'

'Oh no, if she will do me the honour of becoming my wife I would be the happiest man in the world, but I fear that she will not have me because the difference in our ages is too great,' he said.

'Has she told you this?'

'No, she is the dearest soul and would not dream of hurting my feelings but I am sure that she feels this way.'

'I will speak to her and advise her not to be so silly—if indeed she does believe such foolishness,' said Lucy. 'I know that there is a gap of some eighteen years between you but this is not such a high barrier that it cannot be surmounted. As soon as I know what Rosalie really feels I will communicate those feelings to you.'

'You are most kind, my dear Lucy, how can I ever repay you?'

'There is a matter upon which I would welcome your aid,' she said, remembering the original purpose of our visit. 'I have come about poor Danielle Corney.'

The Vicar held up his hands. 'Say no more, I am sure that I know what you are going to ask. Is this about that dreadful belt that she wears? Am I correct? Yes, I thought so. Well, I can assure you that I have tried very hard to persuade old Corney to take off the stupid contraption but he will not listen to reason. What makes him so adamant is that ignoble fear that his daughter will take after his wife's example. As you may know, Mrs Corney is half French and she has a most passionate nature. It has come to my ears that she is, shall we say, somewhat free with her favours as her husband suffers somewhat from drinking too much ale and cannot always satisfy his wife in the marital pleasures.'

'So he takes out his worries on his poor daughter,' I said.

'Yes, I am afraid so, but there is nothing you or I can do about it as she is still under his care. By all means try and reason with him but I think you will find him to be a most stubborn old man. But having said that I have just remembered that my old mentor Doctor Kleiman of Vienna is coming to stay with me for a few days and is arriving in the morning. If you can persuade Mr Corney to come and see the doctor I am sure we can sort this whole sorry business out once and for all.'

'That seems a marvellous suggestion, Vicar,' beamed Lucy. 'Andrew and I will go and see Mr Corney now.'

'You will find him in Oaklands Lane,' called out the Vicar as we turned to leave. 'I know that he makes his deliveries there this afternoon to the big houses with his pony and cart.'

It was only a matter of a few minutes walk to Oaklands Lane, where we soon spotted the old red cart that Mr Corney used for making deliveries to the neighbourhood 'swells'. The pony was munching his way through a nosebag that Mr Corney had thoughtfully placed round the animal's neck.

'That is a little strange,' I said quietly to Lucy. 'I would have thought that Mr Corney only spent a minute or two in each house. Surely it would have made more sense to give the pony his meal after his deliveries had been made.'

'Well, let us wait here for him to come out of that fine new mansion on the corner,' said Lucy.

We sat down on a bank of dry grass for about ten minutes but there was still no sign of the missing shopkeeper.

'He must be inside that new house,' said Lucy firmly. 'Let us go round the back as we did at the Vicarage and see what he is up to.'

So we walked round the side to the tradesmen's entrance which was barred only by an unlatched door, and I was about to ring the back doorbell when Lucy pulled urgently at my sleeve.

'Andrew,' she whispered softly. 'I can hardly believe my eyes. Look there, in the garden. Is there something in the well water here in Arkley which makes people behave like this?'

Reader, I know well that you will hardly credit what we saw but for the second time in the space of an hour or two at the most, we saw yet another couple both quite naked, heaving merrily away on a large towel that had been draped on the back lawn! At first I could not make out who the two participants in this frenzied bout of fucking might be, but as we noiselessly approached it was clear that the owner of the fat bottom which wobbled up and down as he plunged his prick into the squelchy cunny below was none other than old Mr Corney himself! We took cover behind a huge clump of bushes, as with a final great shudder Corney discharged his seed over the belly of the well-proportioned girl underneath him. With a cry, she too finished her spending and he rolled off her, panting like a great whale for he must have weighed at least fifteen stone. He was a large man, over six feet tall and well-proportioned except for a large belly which flopped around with folds of fat as he went on his knees to wipe his wet prick with the edge of the towel. I stared at the extremely attractive girl who was dabbing at her cunt with a large handkerchief.

'Her name is Angela Anglethorpe,' whispered Lucy. 'She is the daughter of Sir Graeme and Lady Vera Anglethorpe whose residence this is, and she is only nineteen years old.'

My eyes took in more of this beautiful creature. Her hair was of a deep brown colour and she wore it long and loose so that as she sat up it hung down behind her back almost to her bottom. Her cheeks were rosy-red and her full lips were like ripe cherries while her teeth, as white as the snow of winter, were even and firm. I noted her graceful neck, her small but superbly formed uptilted young breasts each crowned with a tiny button of a pink nipple, the slender waist and there at the base of her belly was perhaps the most exquisite cunt I have ever been privileged to see.

Her splendid mount was covered with glossy brown hair, and the serrated lips of her cunny were slightly parted. From them there projected quite three inches a stiff fleshy clitoris as big as a man's thumb. She idly parted the lips with her long tapering fingers and my prick sprang to attention as I imagined passing my tongue lasciviously about those most sensitive parts, taking that glorious clitty in my mouth, rolling my tongue around it and playfully biting it with my teeth; and from Lucy's heavy breathing I knew full well that similar thoughts were passing through her mind.

Before I could say anything, Lucy stepped boldly out and approached Angela who gave a little gasp of surprise. 'Lucy,' she squawked, 'what on earth brings you here?' As for Mr Corney, he looked on dumbfounded.

'Never mind that now,' said Lucy sweetly. 'Is this a game for only two players or may a third party join in?'

'I have no objection,' said Angela. 'I don't know about my friend here.'

'You must forgive me. I am too tired to play any more, ma'am,' said the shopkeeper regretfully.

'Never mind,' said Angela. 'You may stay there and watch us!'

In a flash Lucy had pulled off her clothes and her fair,

golden hair pleasantly contrasted with the dark brown of her companion. The two girls were now entwined in each other's arms and were kissing each other, fastening their open mouths together and running their hands over each other's luscious curves. Then Angela rolled Lucy over on her back and leaning over her first kissed her face and throat. She then progressed downwards kissing her erect little titties and mouthing the little darlings as Lucy wriggled with sensuous joy.

'Lie still my precious and I will give you the most delightful thrills with my tongue,' cried Angela.

Lucy did as she was bidden, and Angela slid her hand up and down her back, gently patting the firm flesh of her bottom. She glued her lips back to Lucy's and her left hand slipped between Lucy's firm buttocks and began to frig her wrinkled little bottom-hole, while her head moved down to nestle in that glossy bush of brown curls as she kissed and tongued the mount of love in a frenzy of delight. Circling Lucy's hips now with her free right arm, she fastened her mouth to Lucy's slit, and as the darling girl's thighs fell loosely apart Lucy grasped her head between her hands as she drove her tongue deep into the juicy crack.

'Oh, that is heavenly,' gasped Lucy. 'More, more, you are making me come, darling!' And with a cry she gave a huge shudder and I could see the love-juice trickle down her thighs as Angela sucked furiously until Lucy pulled her head back and gently forced her away.

'Now it is my turn,' said Lucy as she pushed Angela's head back and cupped her partner's bottom-cheeks. Angela was nothing loath and wriggled up so that she was sitting astride Lucy with her thickly-haired slit just an inch or so away from Lucy's upturned face, and she began to rub against and between her hungry lips. Lucy's tongue revelled in slipping in and out of her partner's sopping muff, out of which that superb three inch clitty was already projecting between the pouting lips.

'Oh, I must have some cock to fully satisfy me!' shouted Angela but Mr Corney was still unable to urge his flaccid tool into a state of erection. I, of course, needed not to be asked twice when such sport was at hand and it took only seconds to pull off my clothes. I ran across with my prick in my hand as I caressed it to its full height, and the swollen purple dome rammed up against my belly-button. I sank down behind Angela and carefully pointed my rod at the wrinkled brown bum-hole that wriggled so deliciously before me. There was no cold cream handy, of course, but I wet the head of my thick prick well with spittle and drove into her bottom with fury. She nipped and squeezed my stiff cock so thoroughly that I spent almost at once but my rod stayed ramrod stiff and our mutual spend made my movements blissfully pleasurable. A perfect frenzy of lust racked my body as I withdrew from the narrowest gate of Paradise to attack Lucy's gaping cunt which was well primed for the head of my tool. I moved Angela's body slightly to the side so that I could insert my full nine inches of iron-hard rammer into the womb of my only true love. She made her cunny nip and contract as I engorged her crack to repletion as she spent, sighing with delight before I could make a move, continuing throughout to greedily gobble at Angela's soaking clitty as the girl wriggled around lasciviously. Lucy heaved up her bottom to meet my manly thrusts and then raised her legs so that her feet met together behind my calves.

I stretched forward putting my face on the inside of Angela's thighs as I endeavoured to push the last fraction of my length into my lovely girl's heated cunny. We all three tried hard to keep still to enjoy the mutual sensations of repletion and possession so delightful to the participators, but I could feel my love juice gathering in my shaft, and I commenced working my cock in and out of its juicy sheath. These soul-stirring movements worked our heated desires to that state of frenzied madness which can only be allayed by the divinely beneficient ecstasy of spending, and I shot a tremendous warm flood of creamy white seed into her belly.

Do not ask me, reader, from where I summoned the strength but my cock would still not relax into flaccidity, but remained stiff in the folds of Lucy's cunny as I gently pulled away and pushed back, pulled away and pushed back, my tool almost swimming in a sea of spend. Angela moved off to sit on one side as, after lying over my girl for a few moments, I began to heave my bottom again to give Lucy the benefit of a second fucking without taking out my prick.

'My, my, my, you are so strong, Andrew!' smiled Lucy lovingly as Mr Corney stooped over us and said: 'Oh, what it is to be so powerful! I wish I could fuck as well as you two.' Lucy smiled and stretching out her hand took hold of his prick which was still soft and hanging down. I decided to carry on and slowly drove my own hard rod in and out of the delicious crack.

Now Mr Corney's prick began to stand and he pushed it towards her face as she stroked back the foreskin to uncap the fiery red dome, and she opened her mouth wide and sucked lustily away as he heaved his great heavy bum and worked his prick in and out of her mouth. With increasing vigour I drove my cock in and out of her cunt. She heaved up and down with excitement, while the sight of his tool darting in and out of her slurping lips soon made my balls harden and I gushed a creamy libation of sperm into her cunt as she drained me of every last drop of love juice, pumping my fluids out into her dark, secret warmth.

I was now as exhausted as Mr Corney, but who dares say that the female is the weaker of the sexes? As we two men lay panting from our labours, Angela jumped down between Lucy's thighs, and pushing her face down into the golden moss of blonde hair she kissed and sucked at that delicious slit, still damp with my frothy emission, as her tongue sought out the love cleft and without hesitation she drove the point of her tongue between those luscious lips and wriggled it.

'Oh, how lovely! Do it more! More!' gasped Lucy, and her bottom jerked and wriggled as Angela's tongue began to work back and forth. Lifting her legs by instinct, she placed them on Lucy's shoulders and so hid nothing of her charms. Her cunny lips became even damper as Angela's tongue prodded through to nip her clitty, licking and sucking her juices, moving quickly along the velvety grooves of her pussy as with each stroke Lucy arched her body in ecstasy, pressing her fully erect clitty against her flickering tongue.

'Aaaaahhhh!' moaned Lucy and then let out a little scream of happiness as the flames of passion crackled along her nerve fibres. By this time Angela's mouth was soaked in love juice and from the thrilling movements of her rounded bottom, she herself would have loved nothing better than to be receiving a good, stiff prick up her crack at the same time. But not only were we mere males *hors de combat*, the time was passing and though I felt some slight growth in my somewhat sore cock, I let the moment pass.

'Lucy, we must both be back at Nottsgrove shortly,' I said.

'Yes, you are right, Andrew, we had better get dressed quickly.'

'But we must speak to Mr Corney about his daughter.'

'Your daughter?' said Angela accusingly to her paramour. 'Surely you have not been guilty of the heinous crime of—'

'Certainly not,' said Mr Corney indignantly. 'Far from that, I have fixed upon her a device that will stop her playing around with the frisky lads of Arkley.'

'Yes, quite so,' said Lucy. 'But whilst I do not question your right to instruct your daughter, I most certainly do doubt your wisdom in fitting her with a barbaric device from the Middle Ages!'

'Good heavens!' said Angela. 'What on earth are you talking about, Lucy? Surely you cannot mean a chastity belt?'

'I most certainly do,' said Lucy. 'Can you actually credit such a foolishness?'

There was a short period of quiet whilst we finished dressing. Then Mr Corney, who no doubt felt abashed by our complete condemnation, said: 'Perhaps I have gone too far, but Danielle is a headstrong girl and I know that she has been seen with that rascal Arthur Greystokes, who has boasted he has poked every girl between fifteen and twenty-five in this village. You know that my wife is half-French and I am afraid that Danielle has more than her share of hot blood and I don't want to see her shamed by a villain such as young

Arthur! I shudder to think about what might become of her if she is left to run wild without my guidance!'

'You must trust your daughter,' said Angela sternly. 'You must also warn her of the consequences of her actions, and if she is determined to have a lover she must know all about the ways to prevent an unwanted conception.'

'That's all very well, but women must not be allowed such freedom!'

Oh, merciful heavens! I just prayed that Lucy would not strike this foolish man!

'My dear,' Lucy said sweetly to me, 'I hope you are not in too much of a hurry?'

'No, no,' I replied with resignation. 'Do say your piece, my dearest. I hope Mr Corney will listen willingly to your instruction and maybe gain the rudiments of wisdom.'

Lucy said: 'Just sit down a moment, Mr Corney. You think perhaps that women enjoy an easy time? That it is easier to be a daughter than a son?

'Let us just look at the life of the average daughter. She must arrange the flowers, help with the housework, pay the family calls, entertain the family visitors, always be at hand, well-dressed, cheerful and smiling, like household angels—which they are often called—without any personal preferences or pursuits, ready to meet every call and to contribute to everyone's pleasures except their own.

'All this is true, and an essential part of the duty belonging to an unmarried daughter at home; but it is only a part. The tyranny of it comes when it is considered to be all. It is the fact that she must always be "on tap", if I may use the expression, that makes life so hard and dull for her.

'Under such circumstances the girl can never sit down to read or write without fear of being disturbed; she can never undertake any definite pursuit however harmless lest it might interfere with some of these unceasing claims. She has, in truth, never an hour that she can call absolutely her own, free from the dangers of interruption.

'There is always something wanted by somebody, and a girl of average conscientiousness would feel very selfish

140

indeed should she refuse to meet these unceasing claims, even though many of them may be trivial and though she herself may have on hand at that moment some quite important work of her own.

'If she has a brother, who perhaps is reading at home during his vacation from school or college, he of course must never be disturbed. That is because he is reading for some examinations which will later affect his career—but the girl, who is so often refused leave to study and never expected to do any great things, she has no need to be allowed some definite time for study and improvement except for some outside philanthropic work, perhaps either in our home slums or for some benighted heathen folks overseas!

'The suffering endured by many a young woman under these circumstances has never really been fully told, perhaps because men do not wish to hear it, or know of it!'

'Hear, hear!' cried Angela. 'No one could have described our plight better, Lucy, my dear friend. Let us face the fact, that in the usual case, possessing no money in her own right and obliged to beg, too often from an unwilling father (though I must admit that this is not an adjective I would use with regard to my own Papa), a girl of character as she grows into maturity, living as a woman in her father's house, suffers a bitter, frustrating sense of sheer humiliation that no-one who has not experienced it can fully understand.

'Many young women under these circumstances would gladly engage in honourable labour, however menial, that would enable them to be independent and to own themselves. But this of course is a notion "not to be thought about for a moment" by the fathers.'

'Such an idea frightens the fathers,' chipped in Lucy. 'Could the parents of these girls, who have been instructed not to think of themselves as independent beings but only as mere appendages of their parents, created for the sole purpose of ministering to their pleasures, and waiting upon their fancies—could these parents for one single moment get a glimpse into the hearts of their quiet, uncomplaining daughters, they would be astonished and even, I would hope, horrified. They might ask what their daughters want now? They have a good home and if money is in abundance, every known comfort and the society of their parents' friends and relations; perhaps even in the upper regions of Society a carriage to drive in and a horse to ride. What more can they possibly desire?'

'I know what I would reply,' said Angela. 'To such parents I would say, your daughter wants only herself. She belongs to you now and can only walk in your paths, enjoy your pleasures and live your life. She only wants now to belong to herself. She has paths of her own she longs to walk in, and purposes of her own she is eager to carry out, for she is an independent being created by God for the development of her own talent and capabilities and for the use of her own time.

'Her capacities were not given to her parents but to herself; her life is not their possession, but her own; and to herself she must make a full account of the use she makes of it. Put yourself in her place, Nicholas Corney, and ask yourself how *you* would like to have no true independence of your own, but be obliged always to live someone else's life and carry out only someone else's purpose. You have had aims and purposes in your life and have been free, in part, to carry them out bound only by your financial position and the vagaries of fortune. Can you dare, then, to lay hands upon the life of your daughter and say that she must live not as she pleases to do but solely as you please? There can be no objection to laying down guidelines of sensible reason and exercising the wise judgement of mature parental control, and no-one is suggesting that parents should not guide and lay down rules for their children, both sons and daughters alike.

'But if the daughters yield to your demands it can only be at the expense of a truly grievous waste of energies and capabilities. Alas, this is an aspect of the question that far too few realise—though Andrew, through the sagacious teaching of Doctor White, is an exception to the rule.'

Lucy concluded the lesson by saying: 'There is no sadder sight in the world than that of a wasted life. And when this waste is the result of carelessness or selfishness on the part of the strong towards the weak, it becomes no less a tragedy even though it may be done in the name of parental love. Such tragedies are not fiction as may be read in the three-volume novel, but the very occurrence of everyday life around us. How wanton is the waste continually going on in the lives of thousands of women, whose powers, by a long course of trivialities and mental starvation, deteriorate year after year until they themselves and all their friends suffer incalculable loss!'

The strictures of the two girls evidently made a real impression on Mr Corney who heaved a sigh and said that he supposed that they had made a good point of debate.

'I will take off the belt but I would remind both of you that Danielle is still only sixteen years old and I maintain that this is still somewhat too young an age to be prick'd!'

'Perhaps it is,' said Lucy firmly, 'but she is of an age to be allowed, if she so wishes, to at least taste the fruits even if she does not at this early stage take part in the fullest expression of sexual passion. Certainly, Mr Corney, by forbidding her totally you are encouraging the very thing you do not want! I have a fine idea. Suppose this situation if you please. If you promise to release Danielle from her hideous belt, I will speak with her sensibly about country matters and advise her to keep her hymen until she is older and certain in her mind that she wishes to lose her virginity. Is this not a good plan?'

He looked doubtful for a moment and then said: 'I hope you know what you are doing. But her mother is just not capable of advising her and I suppose it would be a great weight off my mind.'

'Very well then. Send Danielle round to Nottsgrove at noon tomorrow and I will see to it.'

We took our goodbyes and Lucy and I strolled back to the old *alma mater*, and I smiled as I realised that Lucy was in danger of becoming a nurse, so to speak, for all the girls in the village.

'What is so funny?' she asked as we strode back briskly.

'You will soon be qualified as a professor of intimate affairs,' I replied. 'You have sworn to tell Rosalie about not

143

worrying overmuch about the age difference between her and the Vicar and now you have promised to instruct young Danielle Corney in *l'art de faire l'amour*.'

'Rosalie's dilemma is an easy problem to solve, but I must give great care to the words which I shall say to Danielle. After all, I don't want to put her off the sweet joys of fucking for life! Anyhow, shall we meet for lunch tomorrow? It is a half day and I could pack a picnic box and we could eat *al fresco* in Morrison's meadow if the weather is kind. You know where I mean, just where you and Louella . . . '

'Yes, yes, I know well enough,' I interrupted irritably. 'Shall we say one o'clock or just a few moments after in case Doctor White detains us for a little extra tuition?' I was somewhat short-tempered as I was not a little embarrassed about Lucy bringing up an incident that I would have preferred to keep secret from her.

I looked forward to the picnic with relish, though that evening I was pleasantly surprised to be invited to dinner with the headmaster along with some other members of the sixth form. Other guests dining that night were the Vicar and Doctor Kleiman of Vienna, and a splendid meal was enjoyed by all, especially as the headmaster opened six bottles of his Mouton Rothschild, '75.

Well, dear readers, I have excited myself so much by this recitation of times past that I must now put down my pen and repair to Leicester Square and seek a companion for this evening who may be able to rekindle my ardour. I have no apology to make in putting this to paper as my own dear wife passed on some three and a half years ago, and though I no longer possess the enormous procreative powers of my youth, I can still manage a stand once a week after a cup of refreshing beef-tea!

CHAPTER SEVEN

WE DINED that evening with the headmaster and his select party, and a most pleasant evening was enjoyed by all fourteen persons who sat down at the superb Georgian mahogany table that graced the large dining room. I must confess that my knowledge of the German language is at best rudimentary, and I was most relieved to find out that Doctor Kleiman spoke almost perfect English with only the slightest trace of a foreign accent. He was a middle-aged man of just under average height who had lost most of his hair, yet who still effused a spirit of youthfulness and a touch of devilment by his twinkling blue eyes and general agreeable manner. He still retained his vital manly functions, I was sure, for although he complained to me how he had damaged his ankle while climbing some stairs to give a lecture at the Sorbonne in Paris, it appeared to me that his injured foot sneaked out towards Lucy's legs, and more than once I thought I detected a look of surprise on her pretty face before she retired with the other ladies to leave us with the port and cigars.

Be that as it may, the next day Lucy and I made our way to the agreed location for our outdoor feast. We each carried a basket of comestibles prepared by Mrs Harris, our school cook, who was not averse to earning the odd ten shillings by preparing special repasts for the sixth formers. Again we were most fortunate as regards the weather, as the heatwave showed little sign of abatement and the sun shone down as brightly as ever—though, pleasingly, the heat was tempered by a light southerly breeze as we walked slowly down to Morrison's meadow.

We struck across a half-made road, and tussocks of feathery grass covered the rough surface of the ground and out of these the larks soared into the haze of sunshine. On the far horizon over a countless succession of fields and hedges rose a line of downs, and in a silver streak to the right of us could be seen the line of the stream. Almost from our feet stretched the tall, thick grass that dipped into a small copse beyond, and I suggested that the copse would be the ideal place to partake of our repast. Lucy nodded her head and I perceived that there was a matter that was troubling her, for she had been very quiet since we had met and had hardly uttered a word to me.

I asked her if there was anything amiss and she blushed, turned to me and said: 'You are as perceptive as ever, Andrew. I can never hope to deceive you even if I were of the inclination to attempt such an unkind commission.'

'I know, Lucy, that you are the very essence of honesty,' I said gallantly. 'Lighten your heart and tell me what is of concern. You know the old saying, a trouble shared is a trouble halved.'

'You are so kind to me,' she said, her lips trembling. 'I am so ashamed about my behaviour but I can see that I must tell you all. Andrew, the fact of the matter is that I let Doctor Kleiman fuck me last night!'

I was stunned by this revelation. 'I see,' I said slowly. 'Well, I am rather surprised to hear such a confession, though I am unable to condemn you for your actions. After all, look what happened between me and Louella a few days ago.'

'You are the dearest, dearest boy to be so understanding. Later, after we have eaten, I will show my appreciation by sucking you off and then when you have recovered I will ride a St George upon your marvellous prick.'

'I would like to know exactly what happened last night,' I said as we put down the baskets and sat down on the warm earth.

'Do you really want to know? Then I will confess all to

you. As I think you noticed, Alfred, Doctor Kleiman that is, was spooning with me throughout dinner. He kept rubbing his leg against mine and once or twice caught hold of my hand and stroked it gently.

'After the party broke up, you had to retire at once to your study but Alfred offered to escort me back to my rooms. My blood had been fired by the rich food and the deliciously cool wine and I was feeling somewhat light-headed and gay. When we reached my door I asked him whether he wished to have a glass of brandy as a nightcap and he accepted with no little alacrity. I can remember very little after that except that I found myself lying on the bed with Alfred who was busily unbuttoning my dress and unhooking the catches. With a quick movement he pulled down the frock and my breasts burst forth from their confines. His hasty hands pulled off my shoes and stockings and in a trice my drawers were off and I was lying totally naked. He tore off his own clothes and lay down beside me. We kissed and I could feel his throbbing tool banging against me. He began squeezing my breasts, and my titties hardened up to his touch to two little pink peaks of perfection.

'I reached down for that rock-hard cock and began rubbing my hand up and down his bulging tentpole. I must tell you, my dear, that Alfred has the most delightful prick. Like many Continentals he was circumcised when he was an infant, and I really enjoyed rubbing that purple shaft up and down to the bulbous, swollen head with no foreskin to get in the way. My little cunny was sopping wet as Alfred eased his hand between my unprotesting legs and ruffled the soft down of my silky muff. His wicked fingers gradually opened my juicy slit and he slipped one and then two fingers in and out of my cunt, thrilling me with his gentle yet firm touch, and electrifying my whole body with a most delicious sensation. His pulsating tentpole of a prick was standing high and mighty above a bush of black hair and I grasped the monster just underneath its swollen rosy head and gently moved my hand up and down. "Faster, faster!" he cried, and I worked my fingers up and down as his own hand slid in and out of my sopping cunny which was pumping love juices that already were dribbling down my thighs. I jerked my hand up and down even quicker along his smooth prick until all too soon the white froth gushed out of the top of the purple-domed head like a miniature fountain. At almost the same instant I found myself climaxing beautifully as a shuddering spasm of pleasure ran through every inch of my body.

'We lay back, temporarily exhausted, with Alfred's fingers still entwined around my love nest and my hand still resting on his still hard prick. I moved over and kneeling beside him I began gently to lift his velvety tool to my lips. I kissed the top and tickled his hairy balls and I felt his prick swell on my lips as I licked all round the glans as he groaned with delight. I swung over and pushed my firm young bum cheeks almost in his face and drew up my legs so that Alfred could see the outline of my hairy crack.

'His shaft was now swollen to bursting point and the head felt even harder in my mouth. I began to suck at this great lollipop and my tongue travelled slowly from the base to the top again and again. My movement became faster and faster, and judging from Alfred's expression and his uncontrollable twitching, his first sucking off by an English girl would be an experience he would remember all his life. His eyes remained closed but he grunted away with the pure pleasure of it. His prick tightened and he began to push upwards as if he wanted to fuck my throat. I had to resist him or I would have choked and ruined everything.

'He bucked wildly as his massive prick slurped in and out of my hungry mouth. Any moment now and he will spunk, I thought, and I began to swallow in anticipation. I was soon to be proved right—a few early shoots of salty spunk and crash! My mouth was filled with lovely gushing foam as his cock throbbed wildly as I held it lightly between my teeth. My own supreme pleasure flowed from my own cunny as I sucked and sucked the spurts pouring out of his magnificent prick.

'Then I felt that gorgeous spongy tool soften as I rolled my lips around the dome. Alfred's movements ceased and he lay spent as I nibbled away at that funny round bulb with its tiny

148

hole until at last he struggled to rise to a sitting position. 'My dear Lucy,' he said. 'You are the best lover I have had the pleasure of fucking for many a long month. I wonder if I could interest you in work as a helper at my clinic?' I thanked him for his kind offer, but of course I had no interest in accepting the work even though it was very well paid indeed. For as you know, although I enjoy a good fuck, it must always be on my terms, when and where and with whom I desire it and not just on a cold, formal basis.

'Anyhow, I have told you all, Andrew. Alfred left my room shortly afterwards and I slept alone. I do hope all this has not distressed you too much.'

Had I not played the goat with Louella I might have been more upset, but in truth her story had fired my blood and my prick was bursting within the confines of my trousers. Lucy could see the uncomfortable way I was wriggling around, and with a deft movement of her hands she unbuttoned my trousers and took out my naked prick and ran her pink little tongue up and down the shaft. Her moist tonguing and her nibbling at the tip with her pearly teeth coupled with the exciting adventure I had just heard was all far too much for me to bear and in a trice I was pumping all my cock in and out of her mouth, jetting a gush of spunk that spurted almost straight into her throat. She sucked greedily on my tool, milking every lingering drop of sperm.

'Ah, Andrew, I do enjoy sucking a good thick prick. I know that some other girls do not enjoy it but I could happily suck your prick for hours. It never lasts that long, of course, and like all men you squirt off in just a few minutes. I think swallowing the froth is just as nice for nothing tastes so clean and fine. And there is the additional benefit of knowing that I can enjoy myself without any fear of getting in the family way!'

'Whatever activity you try in bed, the essential core of enjoyment lies in choosing an understanding and tender partner,' I said, stroking her fine locks of golden hair.

Lucy did not wish to fuck until later that evening so I buttoned myself up and we began to spread out our delicacies

149

on the tablecloth that Mrs Harris had thoughtfully provided. To our surprise we saw a girl coming across the meadow to our little copse and we wondered who this could be as we had told no-one where we were going to partake of our outdoor meal. The stranger turned out to be Louella and we bid her a cheery good-day and she asked us what we were doing here. We explained and she said: 'How jolly! May I join you?'

'Of course you may,' I said gallantly. 'There is more than enough food and drink here and we would be pleased to enjoy the pleasure of your company.'

'Thank you, Andrew. You are a true gentleman which is more than can be said for one of your headmaster's guests!'

'My goodness, I had forgotten that you and your father dined with us last night. Pray who has offended you?'

'I see no reason why I should not confide in you. The wretch I refer to is that horrid Doctor Kleiman of Vienna!'

'Doctor Kleiman?' exclaimed Lucy. 'I thought he was a very interesting gentleman.'

'Yes, so did I! So much so that I invited him to visit me in my bedroom after we broke up the dinner party. But he arrived in my room so late and so tired that he could only fuck me once and then he fell fast asleep. Is that right?' cried Louella.

'What exactly happened?' I asked trying hard not to smile.

'Well, he did arrive where I was waiting at our back door, though far later than I expected. I had performed my ablutions and was more than ready when he finally came and tapped at the window. We undressed quickly and I must say that I did admire his physique. He may not be in the prime of youth but he has kept himself in trim, and what a fine looking prick swung between his legs. His foreskin has been cut away and I do not mind admitting that the thought of this rod, once swollen, surging into me heightened my appetite.

'In a matter of seconds we were on the bed and we kissed each other with tender, deep thrusts of our tongues in each other's mouths. I felt his prick swell against my pussy mound and the smell of his manliness aroused me even further. My fingers travelled down his back whilst I opened my legs even further to feel his large balls against my thighs. I reached down and rubbed his cock up to a full hardness, and he slightly raised himself on to his hands and then thrust his flagpole of a prick firmly into my juicy pussy. The lunge and thrust was nigh perfect and my cunt seemed to burst open like a water lily as the fiery red head plunged into me, and our hairy triangles mingled as he pumped that great thick cock in and out of my soaking pussy. The lips of my cunny parted before his tool, wet and willing as I rocked beneath him awaiting the peak of pleasure which we were both climbing rapidly. His rampant cock pumped up and down at a steady pace until he sensed by my shuddering that I was ready to achieve the highest point of excitement. He then increased the tempo of his jerking prick until I was frantic with desire. "Now!" I whispered fiercely, as I could not scream for fear of waking others in the house. "Now!" and Alfred shot a heavy load of creamy white spunk into me as our pubic mounds crashed together; and we writhed happily on my bed as my hips gyrated forwards and backwards to enclose every piece of that darling pole that had driven me to such heights of ecstasy.'

'I cannot see why you have cause for complaint,' I said, 'Doctor Kleiman seems to have performed well enough according to this account.'

'That may be, but immediately afterwards I wanted to fuck again as my breasts were still tingling and my cunny was aching for another bout of good stiff prick pushing in and out of it. But even though I took the head of his cock in my mouth and rolled my tongue all around it, Doctor Kleiman just groaned and fell asleep and I could not rouse him until dawn. Luckily he managed to escape from the house without anyone seeing him and no doubt he is making up some strange story to tell his friend, Reverend Bernard Ferningham, as to why his bed was not slept in last night,' said Louella with some annoyance.

'I am sure that your secret is safe with Doctor Kleiman,' said Lucy in a small voice.

'How can you be so sure?' Louella demanded.

'I just know that he would not divulge details of his sexual encounters to another man. Andrew, will you bear me out here?'

'Most certainly, my dear Lucy, I am quite sure that you are correct.'

Louella still looked grim and said she hoped that we were not being too optimistic, as her opinion of Doctor Kleiman had been lowered enormously by what she considered to be extremely rude behaviour. Of course, neither Lucy nor I could enlighten her as to why Doctor Kleiman had been so weary, and indeed I made a mental note to congratulate him upon his strength; for at his age to fuck two girls after a heavy dinner was no mean feat. But Lucy was clearly embarrassed by the whole business and began to change the subject of our conversation; and at the risk of relating a somewhat tedious narrative I shall record her thoughts. Naturally, being connected with Nottsgrove Academy she enthusiastically espoused the Liberal and even Socialist ideas whilst Louella, being a farmer's daughter, was much more inclined to the philosophy of Conservatism. Lucy argued for radical changes in society and Louella argued passionately with her while I lay down and drank a glass of refreshing lemonade.

'I am as distressed as you at the condition of the poor,' said Louella, 'but I maintain that the position of the working man with regard to his own condition is pretty much that suggested by Sydney Smith. He is perfectly contented to go without things which he has never used. The working man may read about the richer man's luxurious dinners and fine cigars. Yet the humble smoker of the pipe and the diner off roast mutton is not in the least discontented, for these are unrealities which the instant needs of work and sleep and his own amusements give him very little time to bother about. The working classes are only unhappy with their lot when they are egged on by foolish agitators such as the Socialists and the Anarchists.'

'So you would deny, perhaps, that the lower classes deserve the franchise?' said Lucy in some anger.

'I am certain that those hard-working men in the rural

villages such as ours at best have little desire above working, eating, drinking and sleeping, and are content to let their more favoured superiors think for them, make laws for them, and administer those laws. What are your views on the question, Andrew?'

This put me on the spot, as although I agreed wholeheartedly with Lucy, I had no desire to offend Louella, especially as I had designs upon her large, heaving breasts which I longed to cup and squeeze until her little nipples stood up like two hard little bullets.

'I think we must look at this matter dispassionately,' I said carefully. 'I do not really believe that the farm labourers, for example, are such animal-like clods as you describe them, Louella. For years they have campaigned against their unenfranchised state and their position in life during past years has been such as has to a very great extent prevented them from making their grievances known beyond themselves.

'A public meeting in a rural village ten years ago would have caused considerable alarm among well-to-do people. The vicar and the maiden ladies would have wondered at the audacity of the rustics who would dare disturb the stagnant pool of social life. But all is *not* well with our peasantry. As Doctor White remarked over dinner last night, the depopulation of the countryside is a serious matter. If the men are happy here why do they run away in shoals from homes in the peaceful tranquillity of an English country village? The answer is simply that they run away from the odious thought of living and dying in a squalid hovel with a clay floor and two dark cabins under the rafters, reached by a rickety ladder. Yes! People do run away from a life like that, leaving it behind them as a dreadful past which they remember solely with indignation, or rebelling against the prospect of it as a future too hideous to be entertained except with scorn. And I, for one, do not blame them!' I concluded.

'I do not contradict you when you speak of some areas where there is abject poverty which is worse in the big cities. I only wish there were a way in which we could show sympathy with those deserving poor who have been brought to misfortune and to relieve their distress in a manner that will give no encouragement to idleness and vice,' said Louella.

'Oh, heavens alive!' exclaimed Lucy. 'Surely, you are not one of those foolish people who in detestation of possible roguery forget that by a wholesale condemnation of charity, they risk driving the honest man to despair, and threaten to turn him into the very rogue of whom they desire so ardently to be quit.'

'I must agree with you here,' I said. 'Such hesitation to show charity only plays into the hands of the Socialists, Louella. Distress among the working classes has been very general and very severe, and many have been thrown upon their own inadequate resources and not infrequently reduced to destitution by no fault of their own.'

'Quite so, Andrew. Rich people with tender hearts have been having a hard time of it lately in many ways as well,' said Lucy sarcastically. 'Never, surely, never before were so many harrowing appeals made every day to their delicate feelings on behalf of sufferers of every description. The sufferings of the poor in sickness and in poverty-stricken old age, our neglected half-starved children, hard times, strikes, workhouses, crowded alleys, fever-nests, polluted water supplies, smallpox, pauperism, all haunt our thoughts by day if not our dreams by night. Schemes for alleviations and reforms meet us at every turn. But in our fevered minds we always have this fearful concern that by helping those in need we may inadvertently demoralise the recipients. This is almost as hard a load to bear as that distress which we seek to ameliorate!'

'There is no need to speak with such heavy irony, Lucy,' said Louella stiffly. 'I am just as concerned as you that our social problems be solved.'

'I do not doubt this for an instant,' cried Lucy. 'I just wish that you would ignore the cold economic dictates of your head and let the warm, loving impulses of your heart take precedence. I know you to be a true and loving friend. Come, let us not quarrel!'

'Quite right, Lucy. I would like to see you two girls kiss

and make up your disagreements. Let us all be the very best of friends now and forever!' I said warmly.

The girls agreed, and to put them in a mood to kiss and be friends with each other I decided to read them another passage from the master of seventeenth-century gallant literature, Mr John Cleland. It also crossed my mind that the reading would quicken their pulses and lead to some fun and games! I sat them down next to each other, leaning on each other's shoulders and I began my recitation from the book that I had thoughtfully brought with me with the avowed intention of putting Lucy in a frisky mood—but there was no reason why three should not play the game that I had envisaged for just two players! I began to read:

'The girl who fell to my share either had not thrown off all, or else prudently affected some sense of modesty. Leaving the liquorish band to their rowdy devices, Jenny (for that was her name) and I stole to a small chamber furnished with a large bed and the French cabinet named an armoire.

'Jenny began to draw her pins and as she had no stays to unloose, was swiftly naked of all but her shift. For my part, my breeches were as swiftly off, my shirt collar unfastened, when Jenny, reclining amongst the soft pillows, let out a gasp. I followed the direction of her eyes with my own and saw that my rod, long absent from the pleasures of the flesh, had swollen to a fearful size. It sprang from the thicket of hairs that nestled at its root; its head was too much for the breadth of one hand; Jenny had need to encircle the demon with both hands extended to their fullest reach. As I stepped forward towards the pleasure pallet, Jenny spread her fulsome thighs to their utmost, and I discovered there with my bold eyes the erect mark of her sex, the crimson-centred cleft of flesh whose lips, blushing ever more red, led inward to the waiting pleasure channel.

'My passion, long pent, could not wait a moment more. I lay down beside the wench, kissing her moistly, making free with my hands, playing over her plump breasts with their hardened nipples, licking them furiously, arousing her to ever-higher fevers of excitation.

155

'Wasting no time in the niceties of the preliminaries, I thrust my throbbing member roughly into the delicate channel. So large had my engine distended that she gasped again at the ferocity of my thrust. But I gave the girl no surcease from the vigorous onslaughts effected by my fearful member. I reached my hands beneath her luscious bottom, thus positioning her more advantageously for the thrusts of my rod. I reached down within the sweet cleft and felt with my hands the strength of my shaft as I coupled with her wide-spread nether-lips. Our hairs mingled; our most sensitive parts were entirely conjoined.

'Oh, What adorable bliss! What heavenly rapture! What sweetness sublime! So long had I been without the soothment of her sex that the honey liquid burst from my vessel in a tidal wave of boiling fury. It washed down her thighs and its colour was tinged pinkish by the blood my huge machine had torn from the miniature entrance of the poor girl.

'I lay back for the moment, drained of all strength. But the minx's fires burned high still and her little tongue slipped its humid way through the tufts of hair round my own nipples. It followed its route down towards my birth knot and ever down towards my listless member. But rogue that he was! In no time he stood up again, as firm and as strong and as large and as monstrous as if he had never been tall before.

'Jenny held him by the shaft with both her firm hands and circled the vermilion head of that impish demon with her pointed, slightly rough tongue. I had to clench my jaw to stop from spraying her again with the juices of passion. At length she left her lubricious tonguing of my private parts and stretched herself out on the bed. This time resolved not to be so hot in my quest, I tongued her mouth, exploring the warm, dark wetness of it with growing languor and heat.

'I moved next to her ripe, full breasts, first licking at the erect, long nipples then biting them ever and ever more fiercely so that the poor girl cried out despite her pleasure. I sucked their sweetness, leaving bruises around the nipples where the pressure of my mouth had drawn blood to the surface. My attention next was placed on that very summit of

156

pleasure and I spread her knees with my hands, kissing her inner thighs so that the dear creature squealed time and time again with delight. I next mouthed the golden soft curls that sheltered the central joys of her sex. My spittle wetted and matted that fine moss and I soon found my tongue wandering round the outer portion of that pink shell. The resistant texture of the hair, that smooth resilience of the pearly flesh—such were delights to offer kings. I circled smaller and smaller with my searching tongue till it probed that very centre of sensual enjoyment.

'Her secret orifice opened to the probing of my ardent tongue. Her rounded bottom began to move in rhythm with the explorations of my own. Sensing that it was time to leave off this occupation, pleasurable though it was, I retraced my steps, kissing again the delicate outer lips, the still-wet moss, the bluish-white skin of her inner thighs, and concentrated myself upon the main enjoyments. Inch by inch, I impaled her with my sturdy rod, now grown to even greater dimensions by preceding excitations. This time with her mount of pleasure fully receptive to the aggressions of my member, she did not gasp with pain but moaned with pleasure.

'I thrust; she answers; I stroke, she heaves; our rhythms join and our passions grew. I push so deep into her that I think I must rend the wench in twain but her sole response is yet another moan, this low in the throat as our breathing deepens to a growl, then, in unison, to a roar. The bed shudders with the weight and fury of our entwined violence. Then with a shriek she adds her juices to my own and I discharge in an enormity of passion, my juices boiling over, searing her deepest vitals.

'When we had recovered ourselves, I asked if I might call again upon her. Oh, indeed, Sir, she replied. She promised then to show me the Italian delight of which I had so oft heard but which in truth, I had not ever experienced.'

I ended my reading and sipped slowly at my glass of cool lemonade. The passionate words of Mr Cleland had certainly achieved the desired effect. Louella and Lucy were entwined in a passionate embrace and their mouths met as Lucy's hands examined the large breasts of the dark-haired Louella who unbuttoned her blouse to let Lucy enjoy free play with her plump bubbies. She continued to play with those magnificent breasts while Louella's hands were under Lucy's skirts doing all kinds of things to her clitty. Louella eased down her partner's underdrawers and Lucy's rounded bottom cheeks were naked to my eyes, which feasted upon them as Louella's hands probed the cleft between them, making the blonde girl gasp with joy.

Without further ado, they pulled off their clothes and lay naked together until Lucy stood up and Louella sank to her knees between her strong thighs and began to lick and kiss her tribade who guided her head with her long, tapering fingers. Louella pushed those long white legs apart and nuzzled her full lips around that curly bush of blonde hair, clasping Lucy's bottom cheeks as the pussy lips opened wide and Louella's tongue flashed around the damp hair as Lucy pushed her head further down and she slipped her tongue through the pink lips, licking between the inner grooves of Lucy's cunny in long, thrusting strokes. Lucy's pussy was now gushing love juice, and I stole behind Louella and tore off my clothes. I first slipped a hand round to her hairy dark mound and slipped a finger into her now sopping pussy and rubbed harder and harder until her little clitty turned as hard as my own cock to my touch.

Lucy now lay down and spread her legs wide and as Louella bent forward to suck noisily at the soaking bush in front of her, I positioned my iron-hard tool at the base of her bottom cheeks. I opened the lips wide with my fingers, and as Louella's tongue lashed juicily around Lucy's bush and in and out of her crack, my trusty prick thrust from behind into Louella's dripping slit. I banged my cock in and out as I threw my hands around her, squeezing and pinching those gorgeous, heavy breasts, tickling the nipples up to their fullest erection. I soon exploded fierce jets of hot sperm, coating Louella's cunt with love juice as her frenzied sucking brought Lucy off to a tremendous climax.

Now fair is fair, and I knew that Lucy harboured egalitarian sentiments so I whispered to Louella: 'Would you like to sit and watch while I fuck Lucy?' She assented readily and Lucy, who guessed at my intent, lay there on the ground stretching her arms out to me as I gently eased myself on top of her, my prick already standing up to my belly like a rod of iron. I slid the head of my cock into the crimson gap between her thighs which was already soaking wet from Louella's tonguing and Lucy's own copious emission of love-juices. Her head rolled from side to side in an ecstasy of delight, little moans escaped from her lips, and her hips began working as I drove my proud cock deep into the glistening slit; while her legs came up and wrapped themselves around my back and her arms encircled my neck as we swayed backwards and forwards. I fucked her with long, powerful strokes and Lucy stretched and squeezed beautifully, nipping and tickling my prick in her firm clasp. She twisted and squirmed as we went off together, our mutual spends filling her cunny, and for some moments neither of us moved as we just lay there soaking in bliss.

I rolled off her but as I lay on my back there was Louella, still quite naked, stooping over me, her heavy breasts dangling down as she kissed and sucked my prick. My eyes feasted upon those full, red lips and those rosy nipples, so firm and erect looking for all the world like two tiny strawberries.

'How handsome your prick looks, Andrew,' said Louella softly. 'Dear Lucy won't mind if I have just one suck at this delicious sweetmeat as we are such close friends!'

She worked her hand up and down the now erect shaft, kissing and sucking until with a downwards lunge with her open lips she plunged my shaft far into her mouth, sucking away with all her might. Her mass of dark hair bobbed up and down as she sucked mightily away and I slipped my hand round to her bum and frigged her bottom as I felt the sperm build up inside me. With my other hand I clutched her head and pulled it down so that my shaft was fully in her mouth and throat and I thought that she would attempt to swallow my balls as well! I shot my load of froth into her eager mouth and she greedily swallowed every drop of my boiling seed.

Ah, reader! Such joys did we experience that truly, as the poet writes:

What peaceful hours I once enjoyed!
How sweet their memory still!
But they have left an aching void,
The world can never fill.

However, let us return to the story. Into view now came the figure of the man who had been at the epicentre of our previous discussion, the one and only Doctor Alfred Kleiman. He had not spotted our party, so we hastily dressed ourselves and the girls began to lay a cloth down on the grass. Sure enough, he walked briskly towards us until we caught his eye and he waved a greeting. It was only politeness and a sense of duty that made me return his salute, which I did with a grudging heart, and the girls were somewhat displeased when he evidently decided to join our party.

'Good morning, everybody! What an extremely pleasant day. We are most fortunate to enjoy such sunshine. I declare that this reminds me of Southern France. Ladies, take care not to let the sun burn too brightly upon your faces or your beautiful white complexions may be spoiled.'

We acknowledged his greeting and Lucy politely asked if he wished to share our repast.

'I would be glad of a glass of wine,' he said. 'I am quite exhausted from my walk—but I must be frank and say that the three of you must also have walked at a brisk pace to be here. You all look quite worn out!'

I could not forbear a smile and Louella and Lucy giggled as they laid out the knives and forks.

'Oh dear! Have I said something wrong? What is so amusing?' said Doctor Kleiman good-naturedly.

'Actually, Alfred, we are all tired from having a marvellous mutual fuck,' said Louella impudently. 'Such a shame that you did not arrive some twenty minutes ago for then you could have participated.'

160

'Most certainly,' said Lucy, catching on to Louella's little game of teasing our visitor.

'How wonderful it would have been to suck your great cock whilst Andrew was pumping his trusty tool in and out of my crack and I was slipping my fingers in and out of Louella's hairy muff.'

'I would have then wanted to ride a St George upon your prick,' said Louella.

'And I would have made love to your bum-hole, Louella,' I chipped in, noticing that Doctor Kleiman had turned quite pale. 'Still, I am sure that after your nocturnal exertions, this would have been far too onerous a chore for you to undertake.'

To be fair, he took the jest in good part and said little as we continued to regale him with lurid accounts of what delights he might have sampled if only he had arrived just a short time before.

He drank his lemonade and indeed joined us for a light meal afterwards. As we lay back, reclining on the warm earth, Louella suddenly said: 'Alfred, I have a question concerning intimate matters. You are a noted specialist in these areas and I wonder if you would be kind enough to answer my question frankly, even though it is a query born out of an idle curiosity.'

'Of course, my dear girl, it would give me the greatest of pleasure—and this also applies to any query you other two may wish to put to me!'

'Very well, Alfred, my question is simply this,' said Louella. 'What do you say of the old country saying that a girl can gauge the size of a man's prick from the size of his nose and that a girl's mouth size will give a fair estimate of the size of her cunny?'

'I have heard that said too,' added Lucy. 'And is it true that the dome is the most sensitive part of the prick?'

'Yes, this is true,' said Doctor Kleiman. 'The head of the penis, the soft and sensitive dome, is known as the glans, and it remains soft and sponge-like even when the penis is erect, acting as a buffer to the hard, rigid shaft. The very thin outer tissue layer is crowded with highly sensitive nerve endings called genital corpuscles so that friction of any kind during sexual arousal produces exquisite pleasure, a pleasure which if prolonged culminates in the throwing-out of sperm.

'The natural principle is paradoxical in that pain and pleasure can be mixed—insomuch as any pressure on the glans for some moments after spunking can be most discomforting. It is considered by some people that the glans is more sensitive when the prick has been circumcised and the covering foreskin has been removed. Certainly, the removal means that it is easier to keep the area clean, but I do not think that the case has been proved either one way or the other.

'As to your query on sizes, I must tell you that this is pure poppycock! You may always have a private laugh about how large or small a man's prick might be, but the fact of the matter is simply that total size, height or bone-structure can never be any indication whatsoever of the dimensions of a cock or a cunt.

'A huge man may well possess a small prick while a small woman can often accommodate a very big prick in her vagina; whereas the same prick might prove to fit in very snugly in the cunny of a big woman. I hope this answers your question satisfactorily.'

'It does, Alfred, most certainly, and thank you. Now tell me, is there any truth in the potency of this mixture known as Spanish Fly?' asked Louella.

Doctor Kleiman cleared his throat and said: 'First of all, Louella, I want to tell you and your friends that there is no known chemical or substance of any kind that could be considered to be a *bona fide* aphrodisiac.

'On the other hand, there is a noxious poison known by the name of Spanish Fly which, although it might promote the sexual urge temporarily, is more likely to cause severe medical complications that often lead to a most painful death.

'My advice to anyone is to stay away from all potions and simply try to relax with a glass of wine, loose clothing and above all, a willing and patient partner. There are some men who for one reason or another fear that their potency may be lost. It can occur occasionally that just when the head of the prick enters the vagina it loses its hardness.

'The most important concern here is to realise that constantly worrying about this temporary problem will make matters one thousand times worse! There can be many reasons for the loss of power—too much to drink, too much to eat or straightforward old-fashioned weariness. Or perhaps the man needs some new stimulation in his loveplay. Of this I am sure, once he has cleared his mind about this naturally disturbing phenomenon, the problem will disappear as if by magic!'

'It will just disappear?' I said, as I had expected a technical medical discourse.

'Absolutely, my boy, the problem will simply vanish,' affirmed Doctor Kleiman.

Lucy giggled and said: 'That reminds me of a joke Doctor White told me a few weeks ago.'

'Well, do tell us,' we chorused.

'Very well, if you want me to. It seems that during the age of chivalry a powerful baron rode off to the Crusades leaving only a handful of knights to guard his wife, his castle and his lands.

'His wife was a most attractive lady of only twenty years, so as a precautionary measure he called in the village smithy and arranged for his wife to have fitted a special chastity belt with a secret little mini-guillotine fitted within the mechanism.

'Six months later he returned home, weary and war-stained from his labours, but as he entered the castle the very first command he gave was for his trusty knights to line up in front of him. He ordered them to remove their clothes and, as he had feared, all but one had suffered the pain of having the knobs of their pricks cut off. "Hang them all high from the old oak tree!" he bellowed, and turning to the one remaining knight he said: "Sir Lancelot, at least I still have one true knight who served me faithfully. How did you manage to stay pure?" Sir Lancelot said nothing. "Well, tell me," urged the baron, but Sir Lancelot remained silent. "Come

163

now, there is nothing to be ashamed of; indeed, you should be proud of yourself. What do you have to say about all this?'' Sir Lancelot still said nothing and looked extremely nervous as his squire interrupted to say: "My Lord, I regret that my master is unable to speak. Somehow, he has lost his tongue!" '

We laughed heartily at this jest, and as the ladies did not seem at all offended by this rather ribald tale I ventured to tell the company another merry one.

'There was once a most religious gentleman of the Romish persuasion, who in the prime of life was stricken down by a severe attack of influenza. Happily he made a full recovery but the experience made him think upon the after-life and what might happen to his soul after it finally departed his mortal body.

'So he contacted his parish priest and informed him that he wished to do penance to ensure that he would not descend into the fiery depths. So what should he do? The priest thought for a moment and said: "My son, you must ensure entrance to the gates of St Peter by total abstinence from the pleasures of the flesh for six months. Not a drop of intoxicating liquor must pass your lips, nor a morsel of anything but the plainest of foods; and you must sleep apart from your good lady and refrain from any sort of marital relationship for the period of penance." The gentleman looked staggered, but he thanked the priest and resolved to undertake his punishment; for when all is said and done, what is six months set beside eternity? So he returned home and gave away the contents of his well-stocked cellar, instructed the domestic staff to prepare only the plainest of meals and informed his wife of the words of their religious mentor. As the wife, too, was a deeply religious person, she fully understood and uttered no word of reproof.

'After three months, however, there was a knock on the priest's door and the gentleman stood before him. The priest invited him in and asked if there was any matter that was troubling his mind. "Indeed there is," said the man. "I have tried to do as you instructed me so that I may go to heaven when I pass on, and I have not touched a single thimbleful of any liquid except water, milk or tea. I have only eaten the simplest of meals and have not faltered from the path.'' The priest smiled and said: ''This is marvellous, your soul is heaven-bound.'' But the man looked agitated and said: ''Oh, Father, I must confess the truth to you. While I tried to abstain fully from relations with my wife and indeed any merriment with members of the opposite sex, every time I saw my wife in her tight riding trousers, my penis shot up to a great stiffness, and if she leaned over to pick up anything, I just could not refrain from unbuttoning my trousers and practising the sin of Onan!'' At this the priest looked shocked. ''My son, my son,'' he exclaimed. ''You must desist this or you will be barred from the gates of heaven.''

'And to the priest's horror, the man smiled wanly and said: ''Perhaps I will, Father, and meanwhile it has also barred me from the gates of Captain Jorrocks' Riding Academy!'' '

My audience roared with mirth and Doctor Kleiman said: 'I was told a story which at first I did not find amusing as I did not fully understand your English idioms and collo-quialisms, but I think you will enjoy it.

'This story concerns two gentlemen drinking an afternoon glass of wine at their club when one turns to the other and says: ''Dash it all, Archie, old fellow, I quite forgot to tell you but I am going to marry Lady F——; she is a widow with nine children.''

'His companion looked astounded, but being a gentleman of breeding he had no wish to offend so he simply murmured: ''Douglas, old chap, I hope you have not put your foot in it!'' And to this his friend retorted: ''Oh no, old boy. But I could if I wanted to!'' To which his friend gave no reply but simply puffed on his cigar and stared out of the window!'

'May we be serious again for a moment?' asked Lucy. 'While you are here, Alfred, perhaps there are some other problems that you could solve for us and our friends. This would be of great service. We have no money but Louella and I could find a way to repay you for your time and trouble, I am sure.'

'My dear young ladies, the pleasure is all mine,' said Doctor Kleiman gallantly. 'I would never be averse to feeling a delicious young girl's breasts or fondling the cheeks of her rounded bottom, but never would I expect to be given these or even greater liberties just for my expounding some medical theories to a few young friends.'

'Well, we shall see,' I said. 'Tell me now, why is it that many girls of our age, in their late adolescence and early adult years, prefer older men? I do not mean this in any personal manner, of course.'

'This question has been asked many times. My own belief is that the answer is simple. Many young girls prefer older men because these men are more patient, understanding, experienced, sexually skilled—or frankly, because they have more money to spend upon their companions. On the other hand, many older women prefer younger men for their sexual vigour and more direct and powerful performances in the bedroom.

'I always say to young men who put this question as to how they can compete—once you have found a girl you like, work at developing traits that she finds attractive. In other words, woo her! If this does not succeed, forget her and concentrate upon girls who like you just as you are, which is probably an even more sensible attitude to take.'

'May I ask you to treat this in confidence?' said Louella quietly. 'I will name no names but a group of boys from Nottsgrove have taken to spending their Wednesday afternoon half-holiday in a field on my father's land. They sit down on the grass and each then unbuttons his trousers and they play with themselves. They watch each other and see who can either be first to jet out his sperm or who can rub his prick for the longest without coming. Should this practice be stopped?'

Doctor Kleiman stroked his chin. 'I do not think that they should be stopped except that a way might be found to tell them that their antics have been noticed by strangers. I do not think this is too worrisome, though there are some English colleagues who would disagree violently with me. I am sure that these boys will grow out of this childish behaviour, but there is, I suppose, a problem. This group is perhaps basically shy about girls and hesitant about joining the chase for them. It would be tragic if this led to a lifelong habit of sexual withdrawal which might lead to unnatural desires.

'My speculation would be that they will tire of all this, especially when a member is fortunate enough to find a girl who would show him that instead of being alone on the grass, it is far more fun for two to roll in the hay! This is the correct expression is it not, Andrew?'

'One last query, Alfred,' said Lucy, who like us all had been greatly impressed by Doctor Kleiman's wise words. 'I know that old Walker, the gardener, is no longer enjoying relations with his wife since she gave birth to their fourth child. Although his tool is only of average dimensions, her cunny is far too loose at the moment for either of them to obtain very much joy out of having a good fuck. Now, is there anything you can suggest that might help them out of this awkward predicament?'

He pursed his lips thoughtfully and then replied: 'H'mm, in such a case I think I would recommend a regular programme of tightening of the vaginal muscles. As you know, dear friends, the major lips of the vagina are really muscles and they are quite capable of gripping a prick quite firmly without any problem.'

Louella nodded her pretty little head. 'Oh yes, this is very true. I sometimes use a dildo to keep my cunny in trim for the fray. One has to insert it gently, squeeze and relax, squeeze and relax and then after a while one finds it very easy to grip a cock as one will want to do.

'For instance, when Andrew here was fucking me, as soon as he inserted his lovely dome, I gripped him just under the rim of his prick-head and we had some marvellous fun. A kind of tug-of-war ensued with Andrew trying to get his cock out whilst I tried to stop him. Of course, with my legs closed, it was even easier and felt nicer.'

'I like to grip a cock at the base,' said Lucy. 'Then I can feel it swell up inside me.'

'Yes, I think you have proved that my suggestion is on the correct course,' said Doctor Kleiman. 'I suggest that the lady in question should try to exercise herself some ten times every day, and in a month or so I would think that there will be some genuine improvement in her condition.

'On the other hand, of course, it may be that during childbirth she suffered a small vaginal tear and a simple operation can right this very effectively,' he added.

The girls had a few further questions to put to our guest from overseas but I will not bore my readers with these delicate affairs. Suffice it to say that all this talk about *les affaires d'amour* made us all feel rather active; but my role, alas, was to be only that of a spectator as the attention of both girls was focused solely on Doctor Kleiman who, aided and abetted by Louella, quickly slipped off his clothes and he lay on his back with his large prick as stiff and ready as possible.

Lucy was first to attack that red-headed monster, and whispered something I could not make out to Louella, who was now herself quite naked and was carefully rolling her clothes into a neat pile. Lucy swung herself over his face so that her luscious pussy was directly over his mouth and as the good doctor frigged her moist hairy crack with his tongue, Louella jumped over his stiff prick and began riding up and down upon that huge weapon.

After this, each of them sucked his cock and balls by turn till he mounted Lucy and plunged his prick deep inside her whilst Louella fondled his large balls and worked a finger in his bum-hole to excite him to the very utmost.

I must admit that Doctor Kleiman was in a fine physical state, for even this did not exhaust him for he gamahuched them in turn and buried his great bursting cock one more time in Louella's bottom-hole and jetted a profuse emission inside her.

All this raised my own lustful feelings to an unbearable degree and in a fever of lust I hastily unbuttoned my trousers and brought out my raging prick, which was standing ramrod stiff and fairly bursting as I slipped my hand round the shaft.

And within a moment of rubbing the monster, a huge emission of white froth spurted out of the knob. Such was the force of the jet of sperm that most of the liquid splattered over the bald pate of Doctor Kleiman who was still finishing off plugging Louella's tight little arse-hole. His prick drove in and out and I admired Louella's loins which were moving in spasmodic little jerks. How they rotated! How the cheeks of her well-formed bottom opened and closed! My own cock swelled up again and Lucy sidled across to raise her cherry-red lips to mine and now our tongues mingled and we twined our bodies together as her hand stole down to cap and uncap the ruby head of my cock. For my part, I slipped my hand into her fully exposed thatch of curly hair and rubbed between the lips that opened at my touch.

We sank down to the soft earth and I rolled on top of the lovely girl who took hold of my prick, and ensuring that the foreskin was fully drawn back, inserted the uncapped dome between the lips of her aching cunny. Lucy possessed this extraordinary gift of contracting her pussy so that it took hold of my cock like a delicately soft hand making a frigging motion, and she wriggled and met my energetic thrusts as I grasped and moulded her firm breasts with both hands, inclining my neck to kiss and suck at the erect little titties. Meanwhile, Louella was busy sucking her beloved Alfred Kleiman's tool to a fine stiffness; while he concerned himself with frigging her bum-hole, which made her sigh with delight. Our lustful propensities were engaged to the utmost and we fucked with ever-increasing vigour. Lucy's legs came up and about my back while her arms circled my neck, and with a firm, forward thrust I drove my hard prick deep inside my lover, lifting her thighs to my shoulders, wrapping my arms about her hips. She was moaning with pleasure now as she stiffened, gave a startled little cry: 'Oh, oh, oh, now, Andrew, now!' as my cock explored the inner cavities of her cunt, driving deeper and deeper into the glistening crack until my balls banged against her bum. We tried hard to hold back the peak of pleasure for as long as we could but all too soon the old familiar tingling came upon me and I crashed great shoots of love-cream into my lovely girl's pulsating cunny.

What more is there to tell of this encounter? She sucked me back to erection and then sucked and swallowed my copious emission until we were sated. We dressed ourselves after an hour or so as the sun suddenly hid behind a bank of white cloud and the temperature dropped quite sharply. But as Ovid reminds us, *tempus edax rerum*. Mention of the poet reminds me that as Doctor Kleiman and I walked back to Nottsgrove together (the girls deciding to take a trip together to the village), I asked him whether we had been right to behave as we had.

'Well, my boy,' said Doctor Kleiman thoughtfully, 'you learn Latin at your college do you not? You may well recall the words of Publius Ovidus Naso who commented, *Quae dant, quaeque negant, gaudent tamen esse rogatæ!*'

I should have been able to construe but the physical exertions had tired my brain and my new friend translated for me: 'Whether they give or refuse, women are glad to have been asked!' I have kept in contact with Doctor Kleiman who is now, alas, retired from his noble profession and indeed from the equally noble sport of fucking since he has not achieved a stand for the last three years.

Eh bien, j'y suis, j'y reste!

CHAPTER EIGHT

WHEN ONCE the itch of literature comes over a man, nothing can cure it but the scratching of a pen. So let us now, dear readers, switch the scene from the gentle, rural life at Nottsgrove to the hustle and bustle of metropolitan existence.

I may have neglected to mention in this narrative that Doctor White's brother Edmund was a noted artist whose landscape scenes had attracted much critical comment—so favourable, indeed, that his work was eagerly sought by discerning collectors even while he lived! Most unfortunately Edmund was seriously injured in a railway accident in 1871, and though he still lives in quiet retirement with his wife, Lady Victoria (the third daughter of Lord W——), he was never able to paint again as his hands were both crushed when his carriage overturned. Many of you may remember the dreadful business which occurred that day when a fast train from Euston left the rails just before the approach to Wembley Station, and ploughed into a goods train that was stationary on an adjoining track. Several passengers were fatally injured and many more were hurt, including Edmund White who was never able to hold a paintbrush in his hands again after otherwise making a full recovery from his ordeal.

However, to return to a happier time before this event, Edmund had submitted some works to the Royal Academy and Doctor White, Lucy and I were invited by our great artist to the annual dinner at the Academy in London. As you will know, this is a great event and we were all terribly excited and looked forward to the event with much joy. We arranged to take a train from Barnet into London, and as usual the little country locomotive came hissing and spluttering into Barnet

Station exactly on time. The first-class compartments were empty and we sat down in comfort as the train pulled slowly away.

'You know, my children,' said Doctor White, 'in such a universe as this it is a great gain to lay hold of some one thing that has permanence—something that we can confidently count on reappearing as the years come round, something to which to cling amid the whirl and confusion of continual change.

'And in one particular world we find this blessing in the dinner of the Royal Academy! Were we to judge only by the pictures that hang upon the walls, we might sometimes be tempted to despair of English art. Exhibition after exhibition is unfolded before our eyes, and we look continually in vain for evidence of new genius coming to the front or of established genius holding its own.

'But the younger men become more mannered and the older men show more plainly that once a man enters the Academy, he becomes too contented with himself to care to do anything that he has not done before. My dear brother, I hope, will be an exception to this rule when he is elected to membership of that august assembly.

'If we let the ear rather than the eye guide us, we shall feel no uneasiness on this score. For the language of Art may vary—it may have been expressive yesterday and be mere commonplace today; but the language of compliment never varies. As each summer comes round, speaker after speaker rises to congratulate the President on the splendid works which look down on the guests as they consume their excellent dinners—and long habit has taught even the Hanging Committee to feign total belief in the words they hear!'

We laughed politely at this rather ironic observation as Doctor White brought out his battered old cigar case.

'Uncle Simon,' said Lucy. 'Would you mind very much smoking your cigar in another compartment, or indeed if you so prefer, I will move but I am suffering from a slight sore throat and the aroma from your cigar will make me ill.'

'Oh, I am so sorry,' said Doctor White genially. 'I will go to another compartment—in any case I have yet to finish my copy of *The Times* so I will leave you two young people to your own devices.'

He got up and strode down the corridor. I turned to Lucy and said: 'I am distressed that you are not feeling up to the mark. I do hope that you will be able to go to the dinner this evening.'

'Oh, yes,' she replied. 'It is only but a very minor ailment. The truth is that I don't really like the smell of any tobacco but as my uncle enjoys his cigars so much I did not wish him to forgo the pleasure on my account.'

'That is most thoughtful of you, dear Lucy,' I said. 'It is just like you always to be thinking of the happiness of others. Now to make my day, how about sucking my prick until we arrive in London?'

'Don't be silly,' said Lucy crossly. 'Someone else might come into the carriage and then where shall we be?'

'Very well, then, I surrender. Tell me, though, I have never met Edmund before. Is he a charming man?'

'An extremely charming and gifted gentleman,' said Lucy. 'I first met him some eighteen months ago when he visited my parents' home in London. You remember the house we rented in Green Street? We were there for four months before Papa was made chief of staff or whatever the position is called at our Embassy in Greece.

'Anyhow, Edmund's wife was unwell and he called upon us unexpectedly for tea. My parents and the rest of the family were out and I received him in our sitting room. I must admit to you, Andrew, that I was rather attracted to him.

'We began talking in a more familiar fashion after a time, for we were hardly strangers as he is my uncle, and he began telling me of the figure studies he had made of pretty girls. I asked him where he found the girls and he said that often they were friends, girls he met at parties and receptions, ordinary, attractive girls like me, and even though his fame was that of a landscape painter, he often preferred to make figure studies for his own pleasure. I guessed that he required his models to

173

pose in the nude but this did not worry me as I was vain enough to want Edmund to sketch me, and even if this meant letting him fuck me, well I had not enjoyed a good fuck for at least four weeks so I was feeling somewhat deprived! I crossed and uncrossed my legs, and as I stood up Edmund said: "I would love to see you quite naked as nature intended." I moved towards him and he unbuttoned my blouse, quite slowly and deliberately. He peeled the back off my shoulders and pulled down my undergarments and my breasts just tumbled into his hands. He cupped them in his palms and my nipples popped up like bullets so I could hardly pretend a false modesty. Then he helped me unbutton my skirt and in a flash I was naked except for my stockings, which he pulled off as I lay on the floor. I opened my legs with a feeling of almost total abandonment as he sat back, a movement which emphasised the huge bulge that had risen between his legs.

'A few moments later I had his stiff naked cock in my hand and I began rubbing it slowly back and forth as he slipped his fingers between my legs and started gently stroking my pussy lips. I gasped with excitement as he knelt down and began nuzzling me, running his tongue very lightly along the edge of my slit which made my insides turn to liquid. He was marvellous with his tongue and I wriggled madly as his tongue darted in and out of me so fast that I thought he was actually fucking me properly! As he increased the speed of his tongue, I started to rub his cock faster too, and soon afterwards I felt the thick cream spill out over my hand as he spent his load and his tongue worked even more furiously, making me weak with excitement as he brought me off.

'Then he raised himself to tear off his clothes and for one dreadful moment I thought he had gone but he slipped back on top of me and I felt his warm body crush me down. I reached down to guide his slick red prick and wrapped my fingers round the base of his cock. I eased him onto his back and brought my mouth down to kiss the purple uncovered dome. I opened my lips wide and then my mouth closed over the swollen head. With my other hand massaging his balls, I slid my lips up and down his shaft, taking as much as I could into my mouth and sucking juicily until he began to thrust upwards in and out in time with my own movements.

'Soon I felt his balls pulsate in my hand and I knew that he was about to come. In a moment a stream of warm spunk spurted into my mouth and his prick bucked uncontrollably as I held it lightly between my teeth. My own supreme pleasure flowed over me as I sucked and sucked the jets of sperm that poured out of his magnificent cock. Then all too soon they drained away and I felt that gorgeous spongy-textured tool soften as I rolled my lips around it. Edmund's movements ceased as he lay sated and I nibbled away at that funny little round bulb with the tiny hole until he struggled to rise into a sitting position. We kissed but although I desperately wanted a good fuck, Edmund was just not up to it so we dressed and he made his farewells. I still felt frustrated and by now my cunny was on fire.'

'You should have made him fuck you first before sucking him off,' I said coldly.

'Quite right,' sighed Lucy. 'I should have taken that stiff prick straightaway. *Carpe diem, quam minimum credula postero!*'

'Seize the present day, trusting the morrow as little as you can,' I construed rather sourly, for it gave me little joy to hear of Lucy's adventures whilst my own prick was stiff as a board and in urgent need of female ministrations!

'I do believe that you are jealous, Andrew,' said Lucy, smiling at me, 'but Edmund never had his wicked way with me, you know, not then nor indeed has he ever done so since that time.'

I still looked miserable but Lucy kissed my lips and whispered that we would be able to have a long uninterrupted fucking session that night after dinner so I should not indulge myself too much at table.

We were almost at the end of our journey and Doctor White came back to our compartment.

'Come along now, you two,' said Doctor White as he came in. 'We must find a porter and then look out for the carriage

175

that Alfred Kleiman has sent to the station to take us back to his house.'

'We are staying with Alfred Kleiman?' I asked, noting that Lucy too was surprised. On the rare occasions that we stayed in London we always took accommodation in a small private hotel in Shepherd's Market.

'Did I forget to tell you? Yes, Alfred and Edmund are great friends. Alfred is a noted connoisseur especially in that field in which Edmund specialises.'

'In sucking pussies!' I said quietly.

'In landscape pictures!' said Lucy firmly, trying hard to suppress a giggle.

In fact, Alfred himself had come to meet us, and was on the platform to greet our party. His coachman helped the porter unload our luggage, and soon we were off to his house in Golden Square which, although enjoying a most central location, was becoming far too noisy for his liking.

'The social life of the city has been revolutionised by the gas lamps and now by electricity,' said Doctor White. 'People are going out far more often at night and staying out later. This new underground railway system will also bring more and more people into town.'

'Yes, I believe you are right there,' said Alfred. 'Fortunately I have sold my house, as I am going to live in America for the next few years. Lucy, is your father still with the British Embassy in Washington?'

'No, he has moved on to Greece. I think my parents will make a permanent home in Athens as they are terribly fond of life there,' said Lucy, smiling at our host.

'I can quite believe it,' said Alfred. 'Athens is a most beautiful city and I am hardly surprised at your parents' decision. However, Greece is the country of the ancient past, and the United States of America is the country of the immediate future, do you not agree, my dear Simon?'

'Absolutely so,' boomed Doctor White. 'Our imperial power is now at its peak but I expect it to decline gradually as the colonial countries loosen the bonds that at present tie us so tightly together. Much of our wealth comes from South

Africa, India, and Australasia but I would not be surprised if at least one, if not two, of these countries leaves the Empire in the next twenty years or so.'

'You cannot mean India,' said Lucy. 'How could the natives govern themselves?'

'Pretty well, Lucy,' said Doctor White. 'They may lack our technological prowess but the Indians have their own Eastern style of life to which they can easily return if we leave. The Mutiny was but a taste, alas, of what awaits us. For however benign a rule of one people over another may be, in the end, the oppressed people will rise up and throw off the yoke of occupation.'

We continued this interesting topic until the carriage reached Golden Square. Alfred Kleiman had obviously either inherited a great fortune or made a great deal of money from his medical expertise for it was a fine house in the very heart of the Metropolis. We each had separate bedrooms and a full staff of servants was on hand to wait upon us hand and foot.

After we had unpacked, we sat down for some light refreshments, but the two doctors soon retired to Alfred Kleiman's small but extremely well-stocked library. Lucy and I were left alone, but soon she too begged to be excused.

'Have you a previous engagement?' I inquired for our Academy dinner was set for eight o'clock.

'Not exactly an engagement, but I must leave you for an hour, Andrew. I will be ready at half past seven so perhaps you would be kind enough to knock on the door of my room at that time and escort me to the festivities this evening,' she replied.

I thought nothing of her request at the time but I dressed carefully, and exactly at the time requested knocked smartly on Lucy's door. She opened it herself, her maid having left the room by then, and she looked absolutely enchanting. Her dress was an exquisite Paris creation by Messrs Axelrod, a low-cut gown in light blue satin which set off her blonde colouring quite beautifully. She added to the effect by her own appearance, for she looked the very picture of health despite a complaint earlier in the day of feeling somewhat out of sorts, and this effect had not been procured by the liberal use of any artificial aids.

'My goodness, you look stunning, my darling,' I said.

'That is very good of you, Andrew. You look quite marvellous yourself,' she replied and leaned forward to kiss me on the lips.

'I am glad that your earlier indisposition has now cleared,' I said. 'You look now as if you are on top of the world.'

Lucy smiled and I thought that I detected a slightly wicked look to her grin.

'Hold on a moment,' I said sternly. 'I believe that there may be another factor to all this. Where were you earlier this evening? And do not attempt to deceive me with a falsehood, for you know that I can always tell when you are not telling me the truth!'

Lucy sighed and shook her pretty head. 'Oh dear, I suppose I must tell all. But are you sure you want to know, Andrew?'

I nodded and motioned her to sit down on the bed whilst I drew up a chair to listen to her explanations.

She smiled again and said: 'Well, if you must know, Doctor Kleiman, Alfred that is, asked me to help cure one of his patients. I wasn't interested at first but when he told me that the young gentleman concerned was none other than Lord W—— I just had to agree.

'You may have seen Lord W——'s photograph, but I can assure you that he is a most handsome young man of nineteen. He has suffered for some years, however, from a condition known to medical science as premature ejaculation. It seems that as soon as his prick swells up he cannot prevent himself from coming so that neither he nor his partner can achieve a satisfactory pleasure. As he is soon to be engaged to Lady Helen L——, this frightful condition must be cured as soon as possible. Do think on it, what a scandal if this caused a problem after he was married!

'Anyhow, Alfred asked me to help, so he arranged for me to meet Lord W——, or Alan as I now know him, this evening to see if I could be of any assistance. I went up to my room after I left you at tea-time, and changed into a pair of tight riding trousers. Alan was waiting for me in Doctor Kleiman's bedroom and as instructed he was wearing only a bathrobe and was totally naked underneath. He knew that I was a lady and rose to greet me as I entered. We chatted away for a few minutes about mutual friends then I pretended to see a coin on the floor and leaving him sitting on the bed, I bent down to pick it up, and my bottom, encased in its tight riding trousers, was revealed in its glory to his interested gaze. I laughed and said that I must have been mistaken but then affected to trip and fell across him on the bed.

'I then took his hand and pressed it to my breasts. After a brief period during which he looked very startled, he began to respond and we were soon engaged in the most delicious kiss, our tongues flicking away in each other's mouths and his hands running all over me. I grasped his naked cock which was sticking up between the folds of his robe and though not of a great size, it was very hard when I took the knob in my mouth and sucked on it as I ran my fingernails gently up and down the shaft.

'But straightaway I felt his prick twitch, and before we could begin to really enjoy ourselves, he shot a wad of spunk into my mouth. I swallowed his come and moved over on the bed. I removed his robe leaving his slim, handsome body quite naked. I then slid off the bed and slowly removed my clothes. When I too was absolutely nude, I stood in front of him, opened my legs wide and began to stroke my cunny through my bushy growth of pubic hair. I slipped a finger inside my moist slit and began to rub myself off. Alan looked on with delight and soon his prick began to stiffen. I stopped the show and went over to lie beside him, kissing his nipples and then working my way down to his rising cock. With one sudden gulp I had his balls in my mouth and I massaged his cock up to full attention while I licked and sucked on his heavy balls.

'We moved round again so that my cunt was above his head, and as I lowered myself down he wiggled his tongue all around my crack. Before long I was moaning with genuine pleasure and Alan moved round and over on top of me. I took his throbbing cock in my hands and guided him into my longing pussy.

'This time he did not come so quickly and we fucked very nicely for at least three minutes until we shuddered to a marvellous climax together and he shot a mighty spurt of spunk deep into my moist, eager crack. Oh, Andrew, it was blissful helping him over his hurdle. I am sure that he will be perfectly alright now.

'Mind, he cannot fuck as well as you,' she added hastily for she could see that I was a little miffed by hearing about this adventure. Mind, my prick was not offended by all this and was bulging out uncomfortably at the front of my trousers. Lucy saw my discomfort and slowly undid my buttons until my bursting cock was freed from its confines. She massaged the shaft slowly, capping and uncapping the purple dome and then she went down on her knees, and opening her pretty mouth as wide as possible, swallowed as much of the thick shaft as she could and began to suck noisily on my delighted tool. I pushed in and out as she held my cock in her hands as she sucked firmly, sliding her lips up and down the iron-hard shaft. Normally I would have attempted to delay the grand *finale* but time was pressing and I did not wish us to be disturbed. So I let my mind relax and very soon I gushed a creamy jet of white love-juice into her mouth, as she eagerly milked my prick of every last drop of spunk.

I would have preferred to miss the food and have some fucking instead but we could hardly excuse ourselves at this late stage. We walked slowly downstairs in absolute decorum even though we were somewhat flushed of face, as would be expected of two people who had just indulged themselves in the partaking of the most delicious pleasure known to our species. Alfred Kleiman, our genial host, and Doctor White were ready and waiting and we were ushered out into the warm evening air where Alfred's carriage awaited us.

There was a great deal of traffic in the area and we were obliged to wait until our coachman could force a way through

—though fortunately we had left sufficient time, so we were not late for the great occasion.

'London needs a Haussmann to plan a new centre for the great city,' I said, as we sat in the mêlée of coaches, hansoms and other vehicles that made up Piccadilly's highway.

'Perhaps so,' riposted my headmaster. 'But it needs to be a careful reconstruction unlike a number which have ruined so many places.'

'Certainly,' said Lucy. 'And there should be a plan that benefits all classes of the population. So often we have heard of people being driven out of their homes in the name of hygiene or of progress, but they have left their long-familiar surroundings usually for the enrichment of contractors, town councillors and speculators of every kind.'

'I agree with you,' said Alfred. 'It is most definitely the case that in an old street say in Paris or in Rome, you will almost certainly find a delight for the eye in archway and ogive, in lintel and casement, in the wallflowers rooted in the steps, in the capsicum which has seeded itself between the stones. But the modern street with its monotony, the high and long blank spaces, the even surfaces where not a seed can cling or a bird can build, what does this street say to the eyes and the heart?'

Before any of us could respond to his question, the coach slowed to a stationary position and we alighted. Dear reader, I must excuse myself from recounting the full details of the grand affair for seeing Edmund there, being fêted by the most distinguished folk, made me so angry that my appetite both for food and drink as well as for convivial company was quite taken away. Suffice it to say that I pleaded tiredness and a most uncomfortable headache, hoping of course that Lucy would accompany me back to Golden Square. Alas, though she later explained that she would have dearly loved to do so, she felt it would be too impolite to leave with me, so I took a hansom cab back to the house on my own.

Alfred had instructed his butler, Mr Newman, to wait up for the return of our party so he was on hand to open the front door for me.

'Are you well, sir? I did not expect you back so soon,' he enquired.

'I left early as I feel somewhat unwell. I shall go to bed now as I have a terrible headache,' I replied.

'One of the young house parlourmaids, Clara, could bring you up a hot drink, if you would like one, sir,' he said.

'I think I would rather have a whisky and soda to ensure that I have a good night's sleep,' I replied.

'Very good, sir. I will instruct Clara to bring up your nightcap in about ten minutes.'

I bade him goodnight and retired to my room and undressed myself, as unlike my headmaster and Doctor Kleiman, I did not have the services of a valet. I put on a soft purple bathrobe that had been thoughtfully provided for me and I debated as to whether I should in fact change into some casual evening clothes and wait up downstairs for Lucy and the rest of the party (for truth to tell, the trifling headache that had bothered me somewhat earlier on had by now disappeared), or whether I should simply go straight to bed.

A knock on the door disturbed my thoughts upon the matter and I called out for the person concerned to enter. As I expected, it was the maid with my nightcap—but I was staggered to behold not a mumping old Betty but the most ravishing beauty, who came into my room bearing whisky and soda on a silver tray. She could have been no more than twenty, a most beautiful creature, rather above medium height, with dark auburn hair, fresh colour and sparkling blue eyes that were set off by a merry smile and the most exquisite pearly white little teeth. Furthermore, this apparition wore not the severe black and white of a maid but a low-cut dark blue silk dress that revealed much of the splendours of her full-rounded breasts. I could hardly keep the surprise out of my voice as I said: 'Pardon me, but I was expected to believe that Clara, the house-parlourmaid, was going to bring me a nightcap.'

She giggled deliciously and said: 'I am Clara, sir. Please forgive my attire but I have been out this evening with my gentleman friend without Mr Newman, the butler's knowledge and I slipped in without his seeing me. Cook gave me the message to bring this tray to your room. I do hope you will keep my secret.'

'Of course I will, Clara,' I said. 'But you really did surprise me. You look far more like the ladies I have just seen at the Royal Academy dinner than a servant.'

She giggled again and said: 'Well, it is amusing that you should say that, sir, for indeed that is just where I have come from. You see, my gentleman friend is an artist who indeed may be known to you. Like yourself I left early so as not to embarrass my friend.'

'Good heavens, don't tell me that your friend is Edmund White?'

'Yes, that is his name. He is a very kind man, and as you can see he buys me the most exquisite clothes so that no-one knows that I am but a mere servant. He introduces me to his friends as Lady Clara Cuthbertson! That is my full name, after all.'

'My goodness gracious. This is quite fascinating. Tell me, is Edmund a decent sort of chap? I ask this as although I am barely acquainted with him, his brother is my headmaster and we do have a mutual friend.'

She looked at me and smiled, her blue eyes dancing as she said: 'I don't know, Andrew—I may call you Andrew, may I not? Do you really want me to stay?'

'I most certainly do!' I said warmly and jumped up and closed the door that had been left very slightly ajar.

'H'mm. Well, Andrew, after the most careful consideration, I have decided that I will stay just a little if you like.'

I poured out two large whisky and sodas and we toasted each other. We sat down on my bed and I said: 'Let us make ourselves more comfortable.'

I gently unbuttoned the top of her gown, freeing her large breasts which swelled enticingly. I let my fingers flick gently across them, feeling the hard nipples, and Clara swallowed as if her throat had suddenly gone dry. She finished her whisky, set down the glass on the carpet and went into my arms without further preamble.

Our bodies fastened against one another. Clara kept one hand curled around the back of my head whilst the other investigated the front of my robe as she slipped her hand inside, encountering my stiff cock. She squeezed my prick and gave a little sigh as I fussed with her buttons. But I was clumsy and she stepped back.

'Damn bloomers and the man who invented them!' I said, as I tore off my robe and noticed her eyes gleam with pleasure at the sight of my naked cock standing stiffly to attention against my belly. She was naked now and I moved forward and embraced her. I manoeuvred her towards the bed until the back of her legs touched the edge, and she went over backwards with a squeal of delight. I was now on top of her and our lips crushed together as she ran her hand slowly down my belly, rubbing her fingers through my pubic hair until they closed round the throbbing shaft of my prick. I cupped her superb breasts and sucked on a hard little nipple as she fondled my knob, making the foreskin slide slowly up and down. She kissed my ear and darted her tongue wetly inside, then slid her mouth gradually back towards my lips. The sensation of her palm closing over my prick-head was very exciting and my cock swelled and throbbed, giving off a little trickle of juice which seeped onto her hand. This seemed to please her for she continued to squeeze and fondle my knob, making sensual, squelching noises as she did so.

'Licence my roving hands, and let them go
Behind, before, above, between, below.'

I took John Donne's words to heart as I buried three fingers into her juicy pussy. I then rubbed the lips with my other hand until they opened up and soon I was able to reach her clitty which was standing up like a little soldier. She heaved her body backwards and forwards on my fingers and soon I felt sure that I could insert my whole hand inside her crack if I felt so inclined. Her clitty was incredibly hard and running with juice as I continued to tease it. Suddenly she arched her back and shudaered to a powerful climax. Keeping my fingers buried inside her cunt, I could feel the vibrating heat and the sticky goo of her honey as, thrusting her hips upwards, she willed me to jab my fingers as far as I could get them inside her slit.

Clara's hands were still pushing my foreskin up and down over my prick at an even faster rate and before I could stop myself I spurted a stream of warm spunk over her hand. This excited her more as she moaned with pleasure, twisting and jerking as she reached a peak of shuddering release. Oddly enough, despite the alcohol I had consumed that night, I did not completely lose my stiffness. Although we both calmed down, we never stopped fondling one another and she refused to release my prick and seemed to enjoy smearing my white love-juice all over her belly. 'Oh, yes,' she murmured. 'Oh, yes, oh, yes. Very good.' Her hand moved and she started to rub my wilted prick, squeezing and kneading it gently and rhythmically between her long fingers.

I felt my tool harden and the exquisite sensations began once again until very shortly it was fully erect and raring to go to its resting place in Clara's juicy cunny. I felt myself being pushed down upon my back as Clara climbed on top of me, bending forward so as to kiss my lips as I grasped those luscious breasts which I rolled around my hands, feeling the rock-hard little nipples against my palms. Her soft, oily pussy was just touching the tip of my throbbing prick, and she moved her hips so that her cunny lips slid over it, thrilling me with the sensation of their juicy wetness. Then she lowered herself gently so that the tip of my bursting rod was just inside her inner lips, poking at the entrance to her vagina.

'There, that is nice, isn't it?' cooed the little minx.

'Perfectly splendid, Clara!' I gasped as she lowered herself firmly downwards, pushing hard on my throbbing tool. I felt my cock slip into her, pushing against the slight resistance of her vaginal muscles. Then suddenly I was deep inside her, surrounded by warm, wet flesh—the sensations were so delicious that my head swam with delight as she positioned herself for the forthcoming action.

She groaned as she started to move her strong young body up and down, using her thighs to ride me, bobbing up and down so that my prick was thrusting in and out of her. She began to move faster, panting heavily with the exertion, and her interior muscles began to milk my prick exquisitely as it slid in and out, her buttocks slapping against my thighs with every descent. She heaved herself up and down upon my throbbing length, taking every last inch of the shaft deep into her cunt, and the continuous nipping and contractions of her pussy soon brought me to the climax. I tried at first to hold back but I could feel my hot sperm boiling up inside me, and I crashed powerful jets of love-juice up into her cunt as she moved her hips faster and faster. The feel of her beautifully-formed young body rocking to and fro kept my cock hard even though I jetted spurt after spurt of spunk, filling her pussy with my cream.

Despite her urgings, I could not perform again at once, and I rolled Clara over onto her back—for not even in those days, when I was at the very height of my physical powers, could I fuck three times after a heavy meal and after partaking of alcoholic refreshment. Wine has always affected my prowess, unlike some men such as Sir Lionel T——, who I have known to down a bottle of champagne and then proceed to fuck three girls one after another. Mind, this was when this gentleman was in his prime.

I lay exhausted for some twenty minutes until Clara sucked my prick up to a new fine state of erection and I could see that she was eager for a repetition of the pleasure. She again climbed up to ride a St George upon me and had just commenced to bounce up and down when to my horror the door opened and who should be standing there but my host for the duration, Alfred Kleiman, who looked amazed and somewhat pale as Clara turned her pretty head round and said: 'Oh come in, sir, if you are staying. I know full well that you have wanted to fuck me since I took up service with you. Oooh, that's good, Andrew, push your bottom up as I push down, that's better. Do join us if you've a mind to or please withdraw and close the door behind you.'

She was certainly a cool little miss, but Alfred needed no second invitation. He tore off his clothes with an amazing rapidity and in an instant he was on the bed with us, his cock as hard as iron and eager to get in somewhere. So kneeling up behind Clara he tried to insert his prick in her cunt alongside mine but found this impossible to achieve. Then the charming wrinkled orifice of her bum-hole caught his attention and wetting the knob of his great cock, he inserted himself between the cheeks of her buttocks. Soon his cock was wet with our spendings and his vigorous shoves quickly gained an entrance as Clara wriggled deliciously. We all three rested a moment and enjoyed the sensation of feeling where we were, our two pricks throbbing against each other in a most delicious manner, with only the thin membrane of the anal canal between them. We both spent almost immediately to Clara's huge delight as she at once pleaded with us to go on.

The smooth round dome of Alfred's huge knob was now burrowed well inside Clara's bottom. Clamping his knees on either side of her waist, Alfred held her firmly until some seven inches of his thick shaft were sheathed. Clara moaned with delight and wriggled her *derrière* to each in-and-out motion of Alfred's prick. I too began to jerk my frame up and down until we ran our course, uttering the most abandoned cries. I came first, injecting the gorgeous girl with jets of bubbling spunk, and moments after Alfred pumped his prick forwards and backwards until he too discharged gushes of juice into Clara's bum. She then allowed him to withdraw his cock slowly to the sound of a faint plop! as the gleaming cock emerged and Alfred sank down beside us.

I gently moved Clara between us and asked my guests if they would like a drink, as there was still at least half a bottle of whisky on the tray Clara had brought in. I smiled as I spoke, as the thought crossed my mind that the whisky after all belonged to our kind host, so here I was offering Alfred his own drink! They declined, and not wishing to drink alone I came back to the bed.

'Tell me, Clara,' said Alfred. 'You are obviously experienced in the noble arts of *l'amour*. I wish I had known this before but Mrs Shirley the housekeeper led me to believe that you were not very keen on men.'

'Not keen on men?' laughed Clara. 'That is far from true.

However, I think this is because Mrs Shirley knows that I have visited the Lady Mumford club in Soho which is a haunt of well-known ladies who prefer the company of their own sex.'

'There is no need to mince matters,' said Alfred. 'The inhabitants of that club keep the dildo-makers in business, is this not so?'

'I suppose you could say so,' said Clara seriously. 'Other girls I know have never tried it, but I must say that while females have never formed the main part of my bedroom affairs, truth to tell they have always been in the background.

'Their bodies attract me by their soft smoothness and I enjoy turning to a girl after having a good fuck like tonight's. I was at the club only last night, where I met my good friend Patricia whose preference is definitely for the gentle sex. She asked me how I could go to bed with a man and I replied that I enjoyed tremendously the ecstasy experienced as when you, Andrew, shoved your iron-hard young cock up my pussy.

'Patricia moved closer to me on the settee and asked me if I were really sure about this. We were in her private room at the club and I looked at her pretty face and told her that I enjoyed the bodies of both men and women.

'She began kissing my face very tenderly and I could feel her other hand hovering over my breasts as she felt for the buttons of my dress. Then her fingers slipped inside the opening and her warm hands began to caress my breasts. At first I was too tensed-up to be fully aware, but gradually I felt my tenseness flow away. Patricia turned her face towards mine as she gently tweaked one of my nipples between her fingers. The delicate touch of her lips and fingers is so different from those of a man. She started slipping her tongue into my mouth and I met it halfway with my own, stroking it softly against hers and then licking around the outside of her mouth and tasting the sweet flavour of her light make-up.

'I undid the buttons on her blouse and pressed my hands cautiously onto the smooth firm flesh of her small but beautifully-proportioned breasts. I felt her nipples stiffen as I stroked across them, which was just as exciting a sensation as having my own fondled. She rested her other hand on my tummy, slowly moving it further down till she was stroking my mound through the material of my dress. I could feel a warm wetness gathering between my thighs, and I raised my bottom slightly so that Patricia could pull my dress up as she rubbed me. Then she took her hand away from my breasts and putting them both underneath my dress, began to pull down my drawers.

'It took only a minute before we had pulled off all our clothes, and we both lay naked on the settee entwined in each other's arms. Patricia was like a sleek, pampered kitten, stretching out her legs and arching her back as she silently urged me to explore between her legs. I proceeded to rub the flat of her belly then let my fingers stray to the neat little triangle of mossy black hair. I tingled all over as the warm, ripe lips of her cunt opened magically under my probing fingertips. The skin of her pussy was marvellously soft and wet—I was amazed at how easily my forefinger slid into the slit and how smoothly it could work in and out.

'Still frigging slowly into her, I began to kiss passionately at the firm curve of her pubis, slithering my lips gradually downwards until they were directly over her quim. I could taste the rich juices and I could see the glistening dew on my fingers as they plunged in and out of her soaking cunny.

'Patricia was now so aroused that it was no surprise to find the tips of her fingers starting to stroke lightly round the rim of my own pussy, and with one hand around her waist and the other fondling her titties, I kissed her more urgently, sliding my tongue deep into her mouth, as at the same moment I felt one of her fingers begin to sink in between my cunt lips. Patricia rubbed her knuckles into my crotch as she penetrated further inside my crack. I soon began to get so breathless with excitement that I was forced to stop kissing her. When I took my mouth away from hers, she bent her head and pressed her soft lips against my engorged titties.

'My nipples were already aroused but when she began to lick and suck them she made my titties feel even more sensitive and excited. My whole body ached with passion as her fingers plunged deeper into my slit and her tongue stretched one of my nipples as she sucked it into her mouth. She moved her fingers so expertly in my cunny, rubbing in, out and around with simply fabulous pleasure and speed.

'Then her other hand pressed upon my mound as she slid one of her fingers through my pussy hair and into the crease that covered my clitty, I felt my excitement reach new peaks.

'She found my little button and began to stroke it gently, and it took very little time before she brought me to the most delicious orgasm—and it somehow felt different to any other I had ever experienced.

'Afterwards, I did feel a little bit guilty. Not because of what Patricia had done, you must understand, but because I had acted selfishly—like so many men, if you will forgive my saying so, Andrew. Oh, how often does a man discharge his squirts of juice and then simply lie back, exhausted to the world and unable to offer his eager partner any further delights. And now here was I guilty of such thoughtlessness, for I had neglected to ensure that my delightful partner enjoyed the very fullness of pleasures afforded by our actions.

'I began to fondle and caress her naked body and she moved herself across me so that her hairy motte brushed against my lips. I now knew what she had in mind and I started to kiss the insides of her thighs and moved my lips up until her hairy mound stroked again at my mouth.'

'*De gustibus non est disputandum*,' I muttered softly.

'No, there is no accounting for tastes,' she continued sweetly. 'Then I felt Patricia's mouth flick across the wet grooves of my own cunt, setting off a lovely tingling glow throughout my body. I then pressed my lips firmly against her pussy, feeling a new thrill as I kissed and licked the wet fleshy cunny lips. I eased my tongue into the raw centre of her red, slippery cunt, lapping swiftly against her clitoris and pressing my titties urgently down on the curves of her belly.

'I was itching wildly now, forcing my cunt against her mouth and jerking my hips, I pushed forward until she was comfortably sucking away at my cunny. My own hands went to her thighs, my fingers sinking fiercely into the soft underside of her legs while my lips worked quite feverishly on her pussy and my tongue kept darting across her ultra-sensitive little clitty. She was now enjoying the highest pleasures, as I could tell by the spasms that racked her beautiful young body as she writhed beneath me; but she would not neglect my pleasures even at the climax of her own delights. All the time her mouth continued to suck greedily at my cunny lips, her tongue lapping non-stop inside my crack until I was brought shuddering to new, previously unscaled peaks of joy.

'But yet more was to come as she continued to writhe against my mouth for I could feel her clitty pulsing with excitement as I probed in and out of her juicy quim. While I sank my tongue in as far as I could I heard Patricia mumble something about her handbag, but I was too far involved to pay much attention. I was briefly aware of Patricia fiddling about with her bag until the next thing I knew there was something nudging against my cunt lips, and it was more substantial than a girl's tongue!

'Yes, it was a superbly fashioned wooden dildo. Made from the finest rosewood, it was even thicker than Alfred's cock, which by the by is the thickest I have ever seen—and I will give it a good sucking once I have finished telling my story. It was at least seven or eight inches long. This was the very first time I had ever experienced such an instrument and I had always dismissed them as mere substitutes for the real thing. However, used by an expert, a dildo can be great fun; although in my experience it has stimulated rather than diminished my needs for a regular dosage of strong, hot cock!

'As she inserted the dildo into my receptive cunny my excitement accelerated faster to a pace almost unbearable and very soon I was again coming ccpiously, discharging love-juice down my thighs. The joys of it made me tremble with delight and I tongued Patricia's pussy really frantically as this wonderful little instrument brought me off time and time again. Even when she finally removed it I could still seem to feel those wonderful sensations pulsing through me like a series of tiny echoes.

'Afterwards I used the dildo on Patricia and in spite of my previous exertions I was still able to thoroughly enjoy watching her squirm with excitement just as I had done.'

By now both our pricks were standing stiffly and smartly to attention and Clara inspected them critically. She was a quite delightful girl but goodness how she loved to chatter away. She commenced again to talk when all Alfred and I wanted, so help us, was some relief from our bursting pricks!

'M'mm, two fine cocks, I must admit. Yours is not so big, Andrew, but nevertheless size is not at all important as I am sure Doctor Kleiman must have told you. So many men consider the size of their cocks to be inadequate but really the problem is purely of their own making. Five inches is probably the average size prick and in my experience and the experience of my friends, a nine-inch cock is about the biggest we have ever come across.

'You are just as capable of fully satisfying a girl, for it is not mere size but the ability to pleasure a girl through sheer technique that makes all the difference. Sex is, after all, an art and if the sexual act is carried out in an artistic manner, thinking not so much of how many inches of prick you can shove into a crack but rather how you can use the whole of your mind and body to satisfy your girl, well, that is everything.'

And with a smile she swooped down, clamping her luscious lips round the dome of my prick whilst she grasped Alfred's throbbing shaft at its rigid base and began to rub the massive rod as she sucked and nibbled away at my uncapped vermilion dome. I moaned and pressed her pretty head downwards until her lips enclosed almost all my stiff shaft, and she rose and fell with a regular steady motion that sent me into realms of ecstasy. As she continued to rub Alfred's tool, I saw his hand snake out and reach for her damp pussy, and Clara gasped as he nudged his fingers against her cunny lips, parting them slowly and gently. He pushed first one and then two long fingers deeper inside her cunt as she raised her hips up, panting breathlessly as he began to move in rhythm. Her head continued to bob up and down over my prick until I felt a shudder of pleasure run through me and I shot a stream of sperm into her receptive mouth, and Clara milked my prick expertly, sucking every drain of juice out of me while Alfred continued to play with her juicy cunny as she gripped his hand between her thighs and squeezed it hard against her motte.

She must have realised from the throbbing of his prick that his time would soon come if she did not resist rubbing his tool, so she let go the throbbing shaft and he raised up his body, and Clara parted her thighs enabling him to press his knob against her cunt lips.

I took hold of his giant cock and guided it home between her aching cunny lips, and he sank into her with a grateful sigh. I was now unnecessary to the performance so I leaned back to watch them fuck.

Directly every inch of his huge prick was snugly inside her quim she closed her thighs, making Alfred open his own legs and lie astride her with his tool well and truly trapped inside Clara's pussy. She loved to do this, she told me later, as the sensation is most pleasing to both partners. Alfred could scarcely fuck in and out as the muscles of her cunt were gripping him so tightly, but then Clara began to grind her hips round, massaging his cock as it throbbed powerfully inside her juicy cunny, which was dribbling love juice down her thighs. He sank his fingers into the cheeks of her arse, inserting a finger into her bottom-hole which made her squeal and wriggle with delight. She shifted her thighs now and as the pressure around his prick eased, he began to drive wildly in and out, fucking at such an intense speed that I could not see how he could hold back the jets of spunk.

Meanwhile Clara was being brought off all the time, building herself to a magnificent climax as the fierce momentum made her pussy fairly run with love juice. She brought her legs up against the small of his back, humping the lower half of her body upwards to meet the violent strokes of his raging cock.

He bore down on her yet again, his body now soaked with perspiration, fucking harder and harder, the rippling movement of his cock playing lustily against the velvety skin of her cunt. Suddenly I saw him tense his frame and then he crashed down upon the girl, his cock jetting spasms of spunk inside her as Clara quickly squeezed her thighs together again, milking every last drop from his spurting length, not releasing him until she was sure that he had completely finished. Alfred climaxed beautifully reminding me of the words of one Mr Emerson, one of my favourite poets: 'A friend may well be reckoned to be the masterpiece of Nature.'

'Oh, Alfred,' gasped Clara. 'You certainly know how to make love to a girl. So few males know how to attack the clitoris properly.'

'Oh my, surely not,' said Alfred, who seemed to be winding himself up for a lecture—I was familiar with the symptoms from learning English with dear Doctor White—and he cleared his throat and spake forth. I will repeat his words *verbatim* as far as I can remember as I hope they may be of interest to gallant young chaps not as experienced as us old fogies in *l'art de faire l'amour*.

He began: 'Now every girl possesses one and any girl can show you exactly where it is—and far the best idea is simply to ask advice rather than pore over the pages of an anatomy book for medical students. I would hope that the girl you ask would be impressed that you care and that she would also realise that no part of her body is more sensitive than her little clitty.

'The clitoris is located between the labia near the opening of the vagina. As you begin to rub your hand over her cunny lips after massaging her breasts, you will always find that she will quite jump with pleasure when you touch this tiny nub of erectile tissue.

'To become expert at caressing the clitty requires the same attention and concentration as one would focus on the titties.

'The clitoris is far more elusive and difficult to handle, for probably before you even reach it your girl will be juicing so that everything at the vaginal entrance will be extremely slippery with her lubricants. You may not be able to see what you are doing and will be operating entirely by feel and touch, and strict attention must be paid to the response of the girl.'

'You are so wise, Alfred,' cooed Clara, 'my own clitty is my balancing point. When a man puts his finger on it he puts me into perfect suspension. Time and place simply disappear and I am in an entranced state of ecstasy,' she murmured, putting out her hand to caress my prick, which was now beginning to rise again after all its heroic labours.

'Thank you,' said Alfred, and he continued: 'So by her reaction, one can tell when the clitty has been stimulated, for she will stiffen or moan beneath your touch. When this happens, the best thing to do is to keep your hand exactly where it is and then tentatively move your finger—yes, just a single finger—around the clitoral area. When she reacts again with an expression of pleasure you will know that the slippery target has been found. Extreme gentleness and tender care are now needed. The digital movements should be continued to maximise her pleasure.

'She may have an orgasm beneath your fingertips as she is being caressed. This is nothing to occasion any alarm. If she does achieve a climax, I would suggest immediately suspending any massage of the clitty, for during orgasm and immediately afterwards the stimulation is often not pleasurable just as direct stimulation after ejaculation for a man does very little to please him. It does not matter if the girl reaches a peak, for in my experience girls possess a far greater capability for multiple orgasmic activity than men, so she can reach for the ultimate again during actual intercourse.

'One final point—some girls can become over-excited during clitoral stimulation, or there may be times when she does not require so much massage. The result is that she is put into a frenzy to reach orgasm but cannot except by immediate full intercourse, and that is time to proceed without any further foreplay. It is essential, after all, not to torture a girl by caressing and touching a clitty to a point that no longer provides pleasure.'

All this talking about clitties had fired both Clara and

myself and by the time Alfred had concluded his fascinating little lecture, Clara had grasped my prick and was busy frigging away at my swollen shaft which had now stiffened into full erectness. I reached out for Clara's beautiful breasts which, although not the largest I have ever had the pleasure to fondle, were incredibly firm, each jutting cone capped with a swollen pink aureole the size of a ripe strawberry. We eschewed any preliminaries despite Alfred's wise words and, positioning a pillow under her firm young bum and spreading her legs high and wide, Clara held her cunny lips open whilst I eased the purple dome of my bursting prick into her juicy wet slit. I pressed in and she writhed; I caught her knees in my hands and leaned my full weight into her, ramming the engorged barrel of my cock forward until it was firmly wedged right up to the tight pouch of my balls. Clara spent at once, raking my back with her fingernails whilst I rocked back and forth between her spread white thighs. I then varied my thrusts, pushing into her with short, sharp jerks, savouring the voluptuous sensation of her tight love-tube gripping my bulging prick. I was unable to hold on for very much longer and soon I felt wild sensations darting through me, and with a heartfelt sigh of joy I spurted my load deep inside her.

Clara was truly the most insatiable girl I have ever had the privilege to fuck, for although I was now *hors de combat*, Alfred was ready and willing to take my place. She turned over and lay on her belly, thrusting her firm white bottom cheeks bulging up to our delighted view. Alfred positioned himself behind her, moving his hand up and down his magnificently domed cock.

'I love your arse, Clara,' he breathed. 'It is a woman's arse, not one of those *petite derrières* which are not so good for fucking.'

He pulled her buttocks apart—and lodged that huge dome not up her bum-hole as I thought he was going to do but firmly into her cunt, moving forward, back, then further forward into her voracious crack. He pushed and rammed until the whole of his thick shaft was enclosed in her sheath, then he rested for a few moments, making his prick throb in its tight receptacle until the natural lubricity asserted itself once more and Clara answered with a wanton heave of her bottom to every thrust of her partner. Alfred clasped his arms around the delicious girl, taking one globe of her bosom in each hand, moulding them delightfully with his fingers and tweaking those upright little nipples to perfection. Soon I could see his face contort as the sperm began boiling up inside his thick shaft and he crashed a torrent of love juice inside her as she heaved up her bottom to receive his manly action with the most athletic abandon.

I heard a noise downstairs and whispered to my two friends that Lucy and Doctor White had returned. None of us thought that, however broad-minded they might be, these two would appreciate what we had been up to whilst they had been out. So Clara and Alfred scampered to their rooms whilst I jumped into bed and turned off the light, so that to all intent and purposes I was deep in the arms of Morpheus when Lucy tiptoed into my room. You may recall, dear reader, that she had promised me a good fucking before we left for the Academy dinner but now here was I, fast asleep and seemingly in no mood for night exercises! I opened my eyes narrowly and saw a look of disappointment upon her sweet face and I felt thoroughly ashamed of myself. I almost smiled as I thought of John Gay's lines that we had studied so assiduously at Nottsgrove:

How happy I could be with either
Were t'other dear chamer away!

But truth will out, and I must confess that at the time, as now, I felt that I had acted like a cad and resolved to make things up to Lucy at the very first opportunity. I was now genuinely sleepy, and in fact there was no way by which I could perform again that night after my previous exertions. So Lucy had to retire unsatisfied and I slept, sated of course with the pleasures that Clara had lavished upon me.

CHAPTER NINE

Tirez le rideau, la farce est joueé—Rabelais

I AWOKE at nine o'clock in the morning and after a good hot bath, I dressed myself and went downstairs where Doctor White was already tucking into his breakfast. I helped myself to some coffee, just a couple of eggs and some toast, and joined him. We had some time to kill before we left but Doctor White was busy reading *The Times*, so making my excuses I went back upstairs to see if my sweet Lucy had woken up, for Mr Newman had informed me that she had not yet taken any breakfast.

I was outside her door when I thought I heard a gasp from inside, and the creaking of bedsprings. I frowned—for surely Lucy would not have wanted to fuck Alfred again; and in any case, he was surely as sated as I had felt after the previous night's fun and frolics. I noticed that there was no key in the keyhole and I will admit that I bent down and peered through the orifice. And what a surprise was in store—though goodness knows I surely deserved it, and as many people say, eavesdroppers rarely hear any good of themselves. Perhaps, dear reader, you may guess at what I beheld—on the bed, absolutely naked lay Clara and Lucy, face to face lying almost motionless, their arousal stimulated by the gentle brush of nipples and the mingled warmth of loins not yet joined. Then as Lucy's hands went round her waist, Clara groaned: 'Oh, darling, take me!'

Cupping Clara's lovely buttocks, Lucy pulled her firmly against her own receptive flesh. Their lips met, parted and their heads twisted and turned in a mashing of lips. Clara's hands came up and fastened upon Lucy's soft breasts, squeezing, caressing and tweaking the stiffened nipples between finger and thumb. Clara's face was clenched up as she swung her head from side to side, and low whimpering sounds burst from her as Lucy's attentive lips stole across her cheeks, down the side of her neck, moist on her throat's little cavity before moving to enclose each turgid nipple in turn. Then her attention progressed downwards across her quivering belly until her shoulders were between her raised, spread legs. Lucy nuzzled her full lips around the curly dark bush of Clara's cunt and Clara's own hands clasped Lucy's head pulling it down as she flashed her tongue round the damp bush of pubic hair.

I opened the door quietly so as to better see this exhibition and crept into the room, closing the door very quietly behind me. The girls did not see or hear me and Clara moaned as her pussy seemed to open wide and she lifted her bottom to help Lucy slip her tongue through the pink lips as she licked between the inner grooves of the velvety cunny in long thrusting strokes. Clara's pussy was by now gushing love juice and Lucy slipped first one, then two and three fingers into her crack. Clara began to thrash about the bed in a wild ecstasy until the eruption inside her subsided and Lucy ceased her ministrations for a moment. Clara gasped out: 'Oh, Lucy, heavens, pull my clitty, hard!'

Lucy attacked her clitty, driving her tongue right into the ring of her cunny and then as the little love-bean broke from its pod, she gripped it in her fingers and tugged it quite vigorously. Then she lowered her mouth again and sucked and nibbled at it, her tongue now driving fast round the juicy crack from which dribbled a steady flow of love juice as Clara writhed her hips wildly beneath her.

The girls were so engrossed in their love-making that I was forced to cough to attract their attention. They were somewhat surprised to see me but neither of them betrayed more than a hint of embarrassment at being caught together acting as tribades.

'Goodness me, I never heard you come in, Andrew,' said Lucy, with a hint of a flush on her face.

'I hope you locked the door behind you,' said Clara coolly.

'I most certainly did,' I replied.

Clara smiled and jumped out of bed and went to the sideboard upon which rested a bottle of champagne and some glasses.

'Who will join me?' she asked, popping the cork expertly. We all three drank a toast to each other's health and as you can imagine, I quickly undressed to keep my two girls company in bed. Barely had I finished my glass of Mumm '83 (Alfred kept a fine cellar) when Lucy was on her knees in front of me, forcing apart my legs and saying: 'I don't want you to think that Clara has supplanted you in my affections, my dear. We have enjoyed some fun together but Clara will agree, I am sure, that in the final analysis there is no real substitute for a rock-hard thick cock!'

She swooped her pretty blonde-haired head down and began to slurp greedily at my swelling prick, which throbbed furiously in her sweet mouth. She sucked deeper and deeper, letting it slide thickly against her tongue whilst her lips savoured the juicy lollipop with noisy, uninhibited pleasure. I kissed her head as it bobbed up and down in front of me, but then Clara leaned over and kissed me furiously on the lips, and then taking one of her spanking breasts, pushed it towards me, gently easing the tawny nipple into my mouth. I stroked her thighs and then worked my finger in and out of her juicy cunt whilst at the same time taking my prick out of Lucy's mouth and squeezing it firmly into her wet pussy. I thrust faster and faster, pushing my prick in as hard as I could so that my balls banged against her lovely bottom while my tricky fingers slid in and out of Clara's sopping muff. I grunted with delight as I shot a marvellous load of creamy sperm into Lucy. Our juices mingled happily and our hairy pubes crashed together and rubbed against each other as she milked my cock. But poor Clara was not satisfied with the mere fingering of her quimmy so I heaved myself off Lucy (who quite understood that Clara deserved more) and Clara pulled my head between her legs, licking and sucking the swollen labia. My tongue lashed juicily around her hairy bush and in and out of her slit. My lips nibbled at her clitty and Clara's hips jerked backwards and forwards, gyrating wildly as my tongue tickled round her hole till she could stand it no longer.

'Fuck me,' she screamed. 'Please fuck me, now, quickly.'

Fortunately, my cock was now rampant, aided by some furious sucking by Lucy, and I thrust it deep into her dripping cunny. I pumped my raging tool in and out of the sodden bush but I came very quickly; though it was enough, for we climaxed together as I heaved my glutinous cum through her cunny lips for a full fifteen seconds. I sank back exhausted and try as they may, the girls could not raise Priapus again, so they were forced to play by themselves with a five inch dildo. Lucy ran it up and down the cleavage of Clara's bottom whilst playing with her cunny lips with her hand. Then she switched hands and, frigging Clara's bum, she slipped the dildo between the slightly open lips of the luscious-looking vermilion gap. This seemed to electrify Clara who reached up to fondle Lucy's succulent brown nipples which were as firm as little bullets to the grasp. They ran a delightful course, filled with voluptuous excitement, finishing in a mutual spend but of course, even an expertly handled dildo is not as good as a true cock and I was called again to partake of the feat of love.

Thus we passed a most delicious morning, refreshing ourselves from time to time with champagne and ices, for the worship of Venus and Priapus requires the continual stimulation of the most invigorating viands and liquids.

As the time came for our departure, Lucy and I dressed quickly and went downstairs to say farewell to Alfred Kleiman and to thank him once again for his generous hospitality. He was unable to travel with us back to King's Cross but insisted that we use his carriage as he had only to walk down Regent Street to meet Professor Bagell, his colleague from Vienna, who was in London for a few days to address a learned gathering. Mr Newman, the quiet butler who I suspect may have had an inkling of the high goings-on in the bedrooms, supervised the loading of our baggage and then Lucy, Doctor White and I stepped up into the fine carriage and we were off back to the railway station.

'Did you read that interesting piece in today's newspaper?' said Doctor White to us.

'Oh dear, I am afraid that I have not seen today's *Times*,' said Lucy gravely.

'Neither have I,' I added somewhat guiltily, as our good old head insisted that we took a keen interest in current affairs.

'You really should have read the article,' said Doctor White but luckily he did not sound too angry. 'Every day you are supposed to read the newspaper. However, as we are out of school I suppose you must be excused. Wait a moment, though, you can purchase a copy at the station.'

'Of course we can. That is indeed fortunate,' I said, trying as hard as I could to sound enthusiastic.

'You can read it on the train,' said Lucy with a cheeky grin.

'And when I have finished, I will pass the paper to you,' I retorted, grinning back.

'Yes, that's right, although I cannot understand why you are both smiling,' said Doctor White. 'Nevertheless, I have my copy here and I must say that it is real progress when an article like this appears in our most respected newspaper. It is all about the need for further education for women, Lucy, a subject near and dear to your heart, is it not, my dear? Listen and I will read it to you. It says, "*While we may hope that social opinion may ever continue opposed to the women's movement in its most extravagant forms—those forms which endeavour to set up an unnatural, and therefore an impossible rivalry with men in the struggles of practical life—we may also hope that social opinion will soon become unanimous in its encouragement of the high education of women. Of the distinctively feminine qualities of mind which are admired as such by all, ignorance is certainly not one.*" '

'That is quite encouraging,' I said to Lucy.

'Yes, that is good as far as it goes, but I hope that society will go further than that. We will not be satisfied by having just one or two female doctors or one or two female lawyers or scientists, novelists or teachers. My fear is that we will be outnumbered by the men who are already entrenched in all the powerful positions.'

'This is a danger,' said Doctor White genially. 'But take journalism as an example of a profession that has opened up somewhat to allow women into its ranks. How many women till lately, however talented and well educated they were, ever dreamed of openly writing in reviews and newspapers? You will agree that to do so would probably have been considered a breach of etiquette a few years back, whereas in the army of modern scribblers for the hosts of ever-multiplying popular papers the petticoats are fairly thronging the ranks. And again, when in the history of the past can one recall the spectacle of women standing upon a public platform and addressing a public assembly and haranguing the crowds? But this is happening now, and the women justly claim an equal right to be there. I think that some progress has been made.'

'You see a happy future?' I asked.

'I most certainly hope so. Yet while I do not pretend to be a prophet, it seems to me that looming through the mists of the future, there are some ugly shapes that seem to be frowning upon us.'

'Do you mean the desperate condition of the masses?' I asked.

'Yes, this is a great problem which the building of a park here and there or putting up a People's Palace or two will simply not suffice to cure. I was speaking about this to Alfred last night, and he was shocked when I told him of how many people lived in destitution in our great city. Why, only last night I went on a short tour of London after we had dropped Lucy back in Golden Square. We passed through a low slum just east of Holborn and we were both sickened by the sight of drunken women reeling about with babies in their arms. We saw girls in petticoats and with scarcely any clothing over their breasts sparring about with great hulking boys. What else have they to do and what else can they know? No wonder there are so many illegitimate births and so many unfortunates on our streets. Little tiny children were wandering abroad late at night from public house to public house looking for their parents.'

'What is the answer?' said Lucy.

'Education, my dear. Education and an interest not only in the worst slums, which I agree of course must be pulled down as soon as possible. But in addition there must be a way of helping those thrifty working people who show no apparent evidence of dire want. At present it would appear that worthy working people who by thrift and industry have raised themselves above the brink of pauperism can have no further help to lift the veil of greater want. In addition of course we also have the sad fact that people quickly forget that more than sympathy is needed to relieve those who have been brought to misfortune often by no fault of their own. There are those who in their detestation of roguery, supposed or real, forget that by a wholesale condemnation of charity and so-called demoralisation, they are running the risk of driving the honest to despair and the peaceful to violence. I sometimes wonder whether these fine rich people are in fact secret supporters of the Anarchists, for it is only in such an interest that misery and hunger should increase.'

With this declaration ringing in our ears we approached King's Cross, and with the aid of Graham, the coachman, and two porters we made our way to the train. We had timed our arrival well and in only some seven or eight minutes we were on our way back to Arkley.

We secured an empty first-class compartment (we always travelled first-class, for however egalitarian his sentiments may have been, Doctor White had an abiding fear of catching a disease from persons less fastidious than he over matters of personal cleanliness), and soon he was deeply engrossed in the newspaper.

'Aren't you going to read what is happening in the great wide world?' he asked us.

'I think Andrew and I are both rather tired, Uncle, and we

shall, you recall, have another late night tonight so we shall take this opportunity to rest.'

'Tonight? What is happening tonight? Oh, bless my soul, I had forgotten about Sir Terence Austin. Isn't he dining with us tonight? Lucy, how fortunate you have jogged my memory. Have you met Sir Terence, Andrew? He is chairman of the Old Nottsgrovian Association and is of course the Member of Parliament for West Bucks.'

'No, sir, I have never met him, but I know the name,' I said. 'Isn't he a rather reactionary sort of chap for a graduate of your academy?'

'Yes, he is very much an old-fashioned man. He calls himself a Liberal Unionist but he is far more resistant to change than most of the Tories. I shall take this opportunity of telling him of my opposition to his stand on the Representation of the People bill currently being discussed.'

'He is against widening the franchise?' asked Lucy, with some surprise.

'Of course he is, though strong opposition won't help his cause, for progress cannot be denied. The strong resistance is due to a dread of the people themselves being able to choose their rulers, allied to the mortification of the aristocrats and rich landlords who rightly anticipate their own deposition from power. They are making a bitter fight of it, it is true. They are especially represented in Parliament just now, and of course they have no wish to lose this exceptional position and power. They confidently predict the ruin of all, but it would be far more ruinous to let the people remain so grossly unrepresented as they are, unless you really want to see a revolution in our country, which I for one do not!'

He paused for breath and then mused upon how Sir Terence came to take up such a political stand so opposite from the Nottsgrove philosophy.

'Of course, he only studied with me for three years,' mused Doctor White. 'Before then he was at Eton which explains a lot.'

'I thought Eton was a good school,' I said.

'It's better now than it used to be. In the bad old days it

205

was an anarchic, dreadful place. The routine fostered drunkenness, vile manners and worse food, unnatural sexual acts, bullying and every degrading philosophy of which one can think. Did you know that whilst at Eton Mr Gladstone wrote a subversive ode to Wat Tyler? At Eton in 1809 eight masters served more than five hundred boys, and birchings were the order of the day (you know my views on the vileness of giving and receiving corporal punishment), and indeed there was one headmaster whom I shall not name who presented his first flogging victim with a case of champagne! Goodness me, we will be at Barnet soon—how quickly time flies when one is enjoying a good conversation.'

'Conversation,' echoed Lucy. 'Uncle, you have talked the whole time yourself! Surely that is not conversation.'

'I don't see why not,' replied Doctor White amiably. 'A conversation always needs one person to listen, and I like to do the talking myself. It prevents arguments and keeps me in a good humour!'

We laughed heartily and prepared to disembark. We were met by old Sharp, the head gardener, who drove us back to the dear old school. We discussed the evening ahead and it was truly fortunate that Mrs Hall, the cook, had not forgotten that Sir Terence was dining with us tonight.

'I think that you, Andrew and young Paul Hill-Wallace should join us. You too, my dear Lucy will be there, will you not?' said Doctor White.

'Of course I will,' said Lucy. 'Sir Terence will be bringing his daughter Agatha, Uncle, but Lady Mabel Austin is in France staying with Lord and Lady Clare, so she will not be with us.'

'Oh, yes, I remember. Well, now, I want you looking smart and behave yourselves as I want Sir Terence to make a generous donation to our coffers. I shall suggest a Sir Terence Austin scholarship to him and I want to conclude the matter over the port.'

I went to Paul's study and told him of the arrangements. He was very pleased to be asked, but naturally he was no great lover of Sir Terence.

'He is a pompous old beggar, Andrew. However, for the sake of the old school, I shall be as polite as I know how, for it will all be for the best of causes!' said Paul.

We had no work for the remainder of the day so I was feeling quite refreshed by the time the party gathered in Doctor White's drawing-room that evening. Sir Terence might have been a somewhat ridiculous politician but though I did not agree with his opinions, I did like the man. Since then I have kept in touch and though my contact till his death some ten years ago was limited to the occasional dinner party, I do remember him now as a very likeable chap with a warm personality. He was well built, indeed he seemed to be half as broad as tall, and his distinctive face was set off by a beak of a nose, and in later years a face deeply creased with smile lines. When I knew him better I understood it to be a parchment of experience. He was a fine raconteur though I was always struck by his willingness to let people talk, and by the interest he showed in others.

Agatha, his daughter, was an extremely pretty girl of just seventeen years, lithe and lovely as a fawn, with masses of tawny brown hair and with a fine freedom in her large blue eyes. She was a marvellous amazon and as we were to find out later, possessed a wonderful amount of animal spirits.

Over the meal I recall Sir Terence talking about the agitation for the State to help build dwellings for the homeless poor. 'If the State is to be summoned not only to provide houses for the labouring classes, but also to supply such erections with merely nominal rents, it will while admittedly doing something on behalf of their physical condition, utterly destroy their moral energies. It will, in fact, be a proclamation that without any efforts of their own, certain people, or rather certain sections of the people shall enter into the enjoyment of many good things altogether at the expense of others. The mischief of all this would be very serious, it would assume many menacing forms and be of wide extent.'

'But if private bounty be insufficient,' said Doctor White, 'surely then the State must do the work, for it is necessary to improve the domiciliary conditions of the labouring classes.'

'Perhaps, perhaps, but it is a melancholy system that debases a large mass of people to the condition of a nursery, where the children look to the mother and the father and do nothing for themselves. This will come to pass if those who should know better do not refrain from giving gigantic hints in speeches and pamphlets of the depth and extent of State benevolence.'

I was bored by all this and to my delight I could see that Agatha and Lucy were equally tired of all this political talk. When Doctor White suggested that we show Agatha round the school (for it was a fine June night and dusk was only just falling) while he and Sir Terence talked about school affairs, I was delighted.

We were soon on familiar terms, and Agatha said to me: 'I think my father is mistaken. I believe that Socialism shows the way ahead, for soon the working people will possess the full power of government through elective institutions to embody in law their economic and material desires.'

I hardly listened to what she was saying but taking her hands in mine, I asked her if she would like to see my study. Fortunately, Lucy had wandered off with Paul, so we were on our own. The dear creature agreed and we walked quietly down to my room. I lit the gas lamp and looked at the beautiful young girl who stood just a foot away from me. Before now I might have been shy but *experientia docet* and I turned her face to mine. She closed those liquid blue eyes and started to kiss me, putting her tongue deep into my mouth. I gasped as to my surprise her hand wandered to the front of my trousers and pressed hard against my swelling cock. I pulled her even closer and kissed her again, my hands kneading the full softness of her buttocks and her tongue darted into my mouth, wrapping itself around mine, sucking and licking as we kissed. I unbuttoned the front of her dress and released into view the most exquisite pair of naked young breasts, lusciously rounded, white as alabaster, crowned with superbly fashioned hard little nipples. I gasped with pleasure and the adorable girl whispered: 'Kiss them, Andrew, I love having my breasts kissed!' So I obliged, kissing and gently sucking the hard nipples, biting gently as she sighed, breathless with pleasure. Somehow, we threw off our clothes in an untidy pile and lay naked on my narrow bed. I continued to lick and suck the lovely nipples, running my hands along her thighs. She turned sideways so that I could insert my hand between her legs and gently I pushed a finger inside her dripping slit. She moved across now so that her cunt was almost above my face as she lowered her head to kiss my pulsating prick. Her soft hands caressed my heavy balls as, with infinite slowness, she licked up and around the length of my shaft, taking ages to reach the uncapped crown. I was inwardly screaming for her to engulf the throbbing knob which she suddenly did, jamming down the foreskin, lashing her tongue round the huge pole that thudded away like a steamhammer. My tongue was now pressed against her cunt and I licked at her slit and moved around the outer lips, gently pushing inside the wet crack until the juice ran out into my open mouth.

I decided to change our positions and I managed to roll off the bed, but the delightful girl kept her lips clamped to my cock and she sank to her knees to continue her sucking rhythm.

'Quickly, let me fuck you now before I come in your mouth!' I said, and gently pulled her up so that she stood before me. I turned her round, somewhat to her puzzlement, but she obediently presented her back to me and I squeezed the cheeks of her curvy bum. I told her to stand with her legs wide apart and to bend over the bed. She did as she was bidden and I enjoyed a lovely view of her open bottom and her pouting quim as the lips of her cunny stretched to expose the flushed inner flesh.

I leaned over her, and she gasped as she felt the hot shaft of my prick wedged between her bum cheeks. I did not try to cork her bum-hole but pushed my cock to find the supple, glistening crack of her cunt, thrusting deeply as she whimpered with joy. Fiercely, I pushed forward, burying the shaft to the very hilt so that my hairy balls banged against her arse cheeks. I held her round the waist until the shaft was completely engulfed, and then I shifted my hands to fondle those superb breasts, rubbing the pink little rosebuds till they were as hard as my prick which was nestling in her juicy crack.

I began to thrust backwards and forwards and I felt Agatha explode into a series of little peaks of delight as I continued to fuck her. Her cunt felt incredibly tight and wet, her channel clinging to my prick, almost preventing me from driving in and out.

We were lost in time as I rode against her, filling her pussy with my rock-hard shaft, pulling back for a moment and then surging forward again and again. I could sense Agatha experiencing orgasm after orgasm but I could feel my cock quiver and my own time to come soon followed as I poured spasm after spasm of hot love juice inside her willing cunny. What a blissful fuck this was, and my cock remained hard as I withdrew and Agatha turned round.

'Oh, how marvellous! Do let's continue,' she said, grasping my prick and rubbing it to full length and strength till it rose hard as iron against my belly. We clambered back on the bed and this time Agatha took charge.

'Let me do the work this time, Andrew. Just lie back and let me fuck your darling prick,' she murmured—and who was I to disobey such a sweet command?

She sat astride me and leaned forward, trailing those magnificent breasts up and down my torso so that her nipples flicked against my skin quite exquisitely. She then lifted her hips and crouched over my thick pole, her cunny directly overhead, poised above the uncapped red dome. Then, positioning my knob, she managed to press it directly onto her clitty, and rotating her body, she edged slightly forward, allowing my rigid prick to enter her. Ever so slowly she lifted and lowered her sopping cunny, and each time my prick went higher and deeper inside her until our bodies melted away in sheer delight. Our senses were now at fever pitch as my strokes jerked her body into a further series of peaks of sensual excitement. It was impossible to hold back as she thrust down to meet my jerking upwards to cram every inch of my hardness inside her. My proud prick spurted jets of creamy spunk up her crack as waves of pleasure coursed through my entire body. We had both climbed the summit of love together and we sank back sated on the soft blankets.

The question was now whether I could rise to the occasion for a third time. Agatha lay on her back, her full, rich breasts not flattening as did the breasts of many girls but standing out full and firm, the jutting nipples erect. Her white belly was firm and flat and her mossy mound a tawny, wild temptation.

I stretched myself alongside and then directly onto her naked body, and my cock began to swell as I rubbed it against that tantalising mound. Her young breasts were springy under my chest and I moved my hips, rotating them as I felt her body quiver beneath me. I made my movements stronger, shifting my weight to my elbows and I held those surging breasts in my hands, rubbing the swollen nipples gently with my thumbs as I heard her breath catch, saw her eyes close and her teeth hold her lower lip. I caressed the nipples more firmly and they hardened even further, stood taller and I could feel the throb of her pulse in her breasts beneath the nipples, deep and thundering.

By now my cock had regained all its grand stiffness and the red uncapped knob thrust eagerly into the dripping wet crack as she threw her legs apart and taking hold of my prick, eased the knob slowly into her eager sheath. I retracted momentarily then crashed down on top of the dear girl and she bucked uncontrollably as I pumped hard, her vaginal muscles caressing my cock as we went faster and faster, and she lifted her hips off the bed and met me stroke for stroke. I could hardly hold her for she possessed a wiry strength and speed of movement that not even my own Lucy could rival. I rode her as she bucked and twisted all the time urging me to thrust deeper, deeper, squealing and gasping with the sheer ecstasy of the sensations. And all the while my cock was twitching, burning in her hot, tight yet gloriously juicy cunny but my shaft was tightening with unexploded passion, reaching for the glorious, pouring moment. As the spunk boiled up inside

211

me, I felt her reach for her sobbing, thrashing release and in the midst of it I hurtled jets of creamy love juice flooding into her, and she shuddered with delight as she milked my prick of every last drop of love juice, pumping my white froth into her dark, secret warmth.

We lay there panting with exhaustion until I realised that we had been gone for more than an hour and that we should be missed. 'Don't worry,' smiled Agatha. 'If I know my father, he will still be engrossed in conversation, and from what Lucy told me, I am sure that she will be enjoying all the fun of a good fucking with your friend Paul.'

'I hope that you enjoyed our gay bout,' I said politely.

'I certainly have,' she replied. 'I really enjoyed sinking down on your magnificent cock. My nerves went all a-tingle as my cunny completely enveloped your darling prick. My, how I pulsed all over as you spunked all that glorious froth into me. When I felt that gorgeous cock drenching me with all that lovely cream, oh, just talking about it is almost making me come again!'

But we both knew there was no time except for a quick hug and kiss as we quickly dressed ourselves and went across to Paul's room. We were just yards away when the door opened and out came Lucy and Paul, both breathing heavily.

'Ah, we wondered where you two had got to. We waited and waited but you never showed,' said Lucy, who looked somewhat flushed.

'I suppose you just sat waiting for us. Perhaps you sat down and played bezique?' I said somewhat sarcastically, though it was in the circumstances more than a little unfair to take up such an attitude.

'Er, yes. Well, shall we rejoin Sir Terence and Doctor White?' said Paul hurriedly.

We said no more and walked briskly back. Lucy and I were fortunately some yards ahead of the other couple when Lucy threw open the door of the diningroom. She had not thought it necessary to knock, but certainly the two people in the room would have preferred us to do so. For an amazing scene met our eyes. The table had been cleared, but it was not

empty. For lying across it, stark naked, flat on his back, was
our noted guest Sir Terence Austin. His chest was covered
with matted black hair and his corpulent belly sagged all over
the place without the restriction of his clothes to keep his
body in shape. But his prick stood up smartly enough, a huge
truncheon of a cock as rigid as a flagpole, and who did we see
with her hands rubbing this great shaft to such fine erectness
but young Elaine who had joined Paul and I with Louella and
Lucy for some frolics some days before! She was dressed, or
rather half-dressed in her black and white maid's uniform,
for Sir Terence had undone all her top buttons and her large
breasts had freed themselves of any covering and stood out,
naked and mouth-wateringly ripe for the touch of lips or
fingers.

'Paul, why don't you take Agatha round the cloisters for a
little stroll,' said Lucy wildly, saying the first words that
entered her brain. 'Go on, the night is so pleasant and there is
no-one in here.' I realised that she had no desire to let Agatha
view her own proud Papa *in flagrante delicto* and added my
approval to her suggestion. Paul dithered and I blocked his
entrance to the room and hissed: 'Or take Agatha back to
your room and ask her to suck your prick!'

Nevertheless, his curiosity was aroused and he peeped in,
but seeing what was in view, he hastily withdrew, dragging a
puzzled but agreeable Agatha back to his study.

When they had left, we entered the room and shut the door
firmly behind us.

'Ahem,' said Lucy, clearing her throat. 'Pray do not let us
interrupt your jollities.'

Elaine smiled and said: 'Very well, Miss Lucy. You are
both very welcome to stay and watch me pleasure Sir
Terence's cock.'

She proceeded to rub the great shaft up and down and Sir
Terence, who had said not a word, kept silent, closing his
eyes. It was rather a foolish business, to let himself be put in
this silly situation but as the old saying has it, a standing prick
has no sense. I wondered whether Doctor White had offered
Elaine's ministrations as a reward for the funding of a

scholarship but immediately I mentally rebuked myself, for the dear old headmaster would never stoop so low; and indeed I was quite wrong to let such an accusation even cross my mind but I must record the thought, however base, as a matter of historical accuracy. What had actually occurred, as I later found out, was that a small pupil had complained of feeling unwell, and as was his wont, Doctor White had gone off to visit the little chap in the sanitarium. Meanwhile, Elaine had come into the room to help clear the table and had caught Sir Terence's randy eye, and the baronet had offered her a sovereign to play with his giant pole. Elaine continued her task, pulling her hand up and down the twitching shaft whilst Sir Terence reached out to fondle her naked titties.

'Oh, harder, my love, harder. Put your other hand round my balls and squeeze very gently,' he cried.

She obliged him by rubbing at a faster pace until a sudden spurt of creamy spunk shot out from the tip of his prick, drenching her hands and liberally anointing the tablecloth.

'Never mind,' said Lucy drily. 'Elaine is an expert at stains as you will remember, Andrew.' Surprisingly for a politician, Sir Terence still said nothing, but his prick spoke volumes as it was still stiff as anything as Elaine cradled it in her hands. He stopped fondling her breasts and pulling her down across him, he undid the buttons at the back of her blouse and he slipped it off her completely.

Her skirt and underdrawers soon followed and the big man stretched out the smiling girl flat on the table next to him.

'Heavens, this is more than I bargained for,' she said with a giggle.

'I will give you a bigger present later,' growled Sir Terence, kissing her breasts and belly and then pressing his lips down onto her bushy mound. I saw his tongue licking at her clitty and Elaine pushed her mound against his own beard as he licked away and began to prise open her pussy lips with his fingers, sinking them slowly into her slit which was already dribbling with juice. She reached out and held his head firmly against her cunny with one hand as she squeezed one of her erect little nipples with the other. Then slowly he moved on top of her and she moved excitedly, opening her legs wide and clamping her feet round onto his back as he guided his throbbing prick into her soaking little nook. She took up the rhythm of his thrusts and soon they were rocking together at such a rate that I became concerned that they would fall off the table! I could see Elaine's legs shake and tremble and knew that she was coming. She continued to squirm under the marvellous surging strokes of his cock and they shouted for joy as they climaxed together, with the big man pumping jet after jet of juice into her eager crack, her hands gripping his large bum cheeks, pushing him deeper and deeper inside her.

We had all been so engrossed, both participants and spectators, that none of us had seen or heard Doctor White enter the room. It would be a kindness to draw a veil over what happened, except to say that the good Doctor White was at pains not to embarrass his guest but on the other hand wished to register his disapproval of the events that had taken place. He was not, after all, averse to girls instructing their partners on the finer points of love-making—after all, Lucy had willingly taken my own virginity and Sir Terence's son, the Honourable Nicholas Austin, would similarly be so instructed if Doctor White thought this to be in his interest at the appropriate time. But Sir Terence had abused his hospitality, when all was said and done.

In the end, little was actually said, but Sir Terence knew that he was guilty of behaviour not befitting a gentleman. He made amends by endowing a scholarship for three poor scholars to study at Nottsgrove so out of it all, some real good came about.

EPILOGUE

DEAR READER, I am now somewhat weary and must perforce finish these memoirs at a later date when I shall recall further memories for your kind perusal. But this must now be the finish of this selection from my experiences at my old *alma mater*.

And now, as I close my book, subduing my desire to yet linger, these sweet faces from my past are still with me and above all one face, that of my own dearest Lucy, will never fade from view. If I close my eyes, I can imagine that she is here beside me in all her beauty. Alas, our paths of life were fated not to cross again, for despite my offer of marriage made when I left University and came into a small inheritance from my Uncle Nicholas, we never were to be intimate again.

Lucy left England many years ago and to the best of my knowledge has never returned to our shores. She set off to the New World with a handsome rogue, Lord Arthur D——, to make a new life for themselves in the wilderness of California amongst the ruffians who settled there after the great Gold Rush of '49.

My life has not been unhappy, let me hasten to add, for I enjoyed many years of happy marriage and my travels have taken me all over Europe where, I must confess, I have dallied many times in bedrooms that were not my own.

My final thanks must be to Sir Lionel T—— for his kind hospitality and use of his fine library and of course to you, my dear readers, for allowing me to recall those fine days spent in the lovely county of Hertfordshire all those years ago.

I make no apologies for my work, though I know that certain so-called friends may disapprove of my frank recollections even though they will, *sub rosa*, buy *The Oyster* eagerly to see if I have scandalised any persons they might know. I regret that they will be disappointed for *de mortuis nil nisi bonum* is my motto.

I close then with the wise words of Molière:

Le scandale du monde est ce qui fait l'offense,
Et ce n'est pas pécher que pécher en silence. *

* It is a public scandal that gives offence, and it is no sin to sin in secret.

LETTER FROM MRS HELENE F. TO THE EDITOR

LIKE MANY genteel but poor country girls, I was simply forced into marriage at the tender age of nineteen to a far more mature gentleman who had already celebrated his fortieth birthday when we climbed into bed on our wedding night.

I know that we rural folk are thought of as mere bumpkins by the inhabitants of the great Metropolis, but I can assure you that most girls living outside the sophisticated world of the West End of London are far more knowledgeable about intimate matters than their sisters in the smart salons of Belgravia.

Suffice it to say, however, that thanks to the enormous weapon of the Vicar's sixteen-year-old son and the equally thick pego of Captain Colin S—— of the Worcestershire Light Infantry, I was by no means a stranger to the delights of a good fucking when I married my husband; but alas, try as the poor dear might, he could never satisfy my appetite in the bedroom and I was forced to resort to buying a dildo from one of the surgical appliance shops in Holywell Street.

Last week I took my afternoon constitutional in the park, but my pleasant stroll was rudely interrupted by a sudden heavy shower of rain which completely drenched my clothes before I could find shelter. I walked briskly home immediately and went into my bedroom and took off all my clothes. I must confess that my body has always been a source of pride and I was soon quite naked. After drying myself with a large towel I lay down on the bed examining my figure. I am told that I am not unattractive, possessing light blue eyes that sparkle, a tiny nose but generously wide red lips. I have been told that I am well-proportioned in leg and limb, with large round globes with dark nipples which I tickled, as I lay on my bed, until they became rock hard. My body arched and spasms of pleasure rippled through me as I thought of Captain Colin S—— and his rock-hard organ, and my hands strayed down between my thighs when there was a knock at the door. It was Elspeth, my maid, who had heard me come in and being a good servant, decided to inquire as to whether there was any service she could perform for me.

I called her in, neglecting the fact that I lay absolutely naked on my bed with my legs wide apart and my hands caressing my nice thick bush. Elspeth came in and her eyes lit up when she saw me.

'Ah, madam,' she cried. 'You have been caught in the rain. I have only just come in myself. May I use your towel to dry myself?'

And the cheeky young girl promptly undressed herself and stood in her proud, naked glory in front of me. She was certainly a beauty, only some eighteen years old with dark black hair over a low forehead. Her beautiful snowy bosom was ornamented with pretty little bubbies, well separated, each looking a little away from the other, each perfectly proportioned and both tapering in lovely curves until they came to two rosebud points. Her belly, smooth, broad and dimpled in the centre with a sweet little button, was like a perfect plain of snow which appeared the more dazzling from the thick growth of dark black hair which curled in rich locks in the triangle of her motte.

Elspeth towelled herself vigorously and when she had finished I asked her if she would like to rest a while with me on the bed. Of course this was what the little minx wanted and in a flash she was cuddling up beside me with her hand roving over my legs. I did not push her away and she moved even closer, brushing her face against mine as her other hand slid round my shoulder. Kissing my cheek, she began stroking her fingers higher up my leg. I tried to tell myself that this was mere idle curiosity, for I did not wish to admit that I was actually enjoying the sensation.

But I could not pretend for long, and when her fingers began rubbing the lips of my cunny, I heard myself sighing with pleasure. After a few moments, instead of simply lying there passively I put my arms around her, holding her gorgeous soft body to me as her fingers continued to rub my quim, sending shivers of excitement right through me. Elspeth began to fondle my naked breasts as our mouths crushed together. Her lips felt smooth and warm and I found it impossible to hold back as her wet tongue slipped inside my mouth and stroked against mine. I pressed my hands to her breasts, letting my fingers sink into the firm, yielding flesh.

This was the first experience of its kind I had ever had although being a regular tribade, Elspeth knew exactly what to do and I imitated her actions as she tweaked one of my nipples between her thumb and forefinger. So I let my other hand rest on her tummy as her fingers glided softly over my damp, hairy mound. Then her mouth came away from mine and she started kissing my neck. The feel of her body and the gentle, though stimulating touch of her fingers were amazingly arousing and every stroke she gave my pussy felt more exciting than the last.

She gazed lovingly at my cunny and, pressing her face between my breasts, she eased her hand between my thighs, parting them wide as she sank her finger into my cunt. Her thumb prodded against my clitty and I squirmed with the thrill of it as her mouth closed round my nipple and her finger slid deeper into my slit.

Elspeth enjoyed a most sensitive touch and she somehow made me forget that what we were doing was frowned upon by so-called normal people. I could not forget that she was a girl, of course, but it did not seem to matter to me as I was completely lost in the pleasure she was giving me and the joy of feeling her soft body nestling against me.

So I pressed my hand upon her mound, delving my fingers down between her fleshy thighs. Now it was her turn to moan with delight as I gently stroked her cunny lips and then slid my finger between them. As I sank it slowly inside her, she pushed herself upwards, arching her back, wriggling her body as though signalling to me to penetrate deeper. With her thumb rubbing at my clitty, she began thrusting her own finger in and out of my quim faster and faster. She was thrilling me so much that I found it difficult to concentrate on what I was doing to her. Her finger may not have been anything like the size of even my husband's short prick, but the way she was using it was just superb.

Suddenly, she began moving her body down and my finger slipped out of her crack. She raised one of her legs and locked her thighs around my knee, writhing her wet crotch back and forth as she pressed her face down into my pussy. Her hands gripped my bum cheeks and she squeezed them firmly, as her lips began kissing my quim. My senses reeled and I started moaning and panting as her tongue flicked against my clitty. I clung to the back of her head, pulling her face tightly against my cunt, while her lips slid between the lips of my pussy. I came off straight away, but her warm tongue prodding through my cleft led me to a little series of tingling peaks. My male lovers had done this to me before but none could beat Elspeth at this jolly game. Elspeth was perhaps the best pussy sucker I have ever come across and I lay back, thoroughly enjoying the delicious sensations until finally she raised her pretty head and climbed down to lie beside me. She appeared to be somewhat exhausted herself, but I think she had achieved a climax.

What happened next was like a dream. Soft lips rested gently at first and then with increasing urgency upon my own. I opened my mouth beneath the persuasive pressure and the next thing of which I was conscious was a warm friction that journeyed knowingly from the base of my throat to the valley between my breasts. I moved my head downwards and Elspeth whimpered as my probing fingers played on her body with an increasingly sure touch. Our limbs entwined and plunged into delight that ebbed and flowed, ebbed and flowed . . . I pulled her long white legs apart and nuzzled my full lips around her curly bush. My own hands clamped round her firm bum cheeks as my tongue flashed unerringly around the damp pubic hair and her pussy seemed to open wide as she lifted her bottom to enable me to slip my tongue through the pink lips, licking between the grooves of her clitty in long, thrusting strokes. Her pussy gushed love juice and each time I tongued her, Elspeth's clitty stiffened, even more eager and pulsating, wanting more and more to explode into a marvellous all-embracing climax. I rubbed harder and harder until the little clitty was hard as a prick to my touch and I slid a second then a third finger down inside her juicy cunt, and spread open the lips as she squealed with delight. Her body was jerking up and down which made it all the more exciting as my face rubbed against her curly motte.

'Ohhhhh!' screamed Elspeth, as I worked my tongue until my jaw ached, but soon the lovely girl heaved violently and got off to a tremendous orgasm and she gently pushed my face away. We turned to each other, our arms sliding easily around our perspiring bodies. Our kiss was softly intimate as we pressed together. Lying on top of Elspeth, I crushed her against me, lightly licking her breasts while I pushed my knees between her legs and spread them. I glided my hips over hers and caught hold of her wrists. Her firm breasts stuck proudly upwards when I pinned her arms high above her head. The swollen nipples glistened with my saliva as I sucked hard upon each one, slowly squirming my own drenched mound against hers. She heaved under me and again her eyes closed with knowing expectation. She opened her legs around my thighs and locked her ankles inside my calves. Then she arched her back slightly as my mouth closed over one of her juicy titties. 'Don't you want a man now?' she mumbled. 'Wouldn't you like to be fucked properly with a big, fat prick?'

'No, no, no,' I squealed as she kicked her legs out straight as we jerked in a frenzy against each other, panting and biting and then screaming as our climaxes came together, first streaking through me, then jumping to Elspeth like a flash of electricity.

My appetite was now insatiable and I leaned over to kiss and nuzzle my lips against the large mound of wet curly hair that covered her love mound bulging between her long legs. Elspeth too wished to continue the fray, and in a moment she was on top of me, rubbing my nipples between her fingers and gently her hands eased open my legs to allow full access to my yearning cunny that was already dripping juice even before she began to stroke my clitty until my little button was protruding stiffly. I lifted myself up and buried my face and kissed her deep cleavage, making her titties shake with desire. I then lay back again, massaging her breasts with my hands, stroking her nipples to new peaks of hardness.

Our pussies ground together as she sucked one of my own hard nipples making me jump with pleasure. I rubbed my pussy even harder against hers until we were almost both on the brink of coming again.

Elspeth gasped and lowered her head towards my sopping crack and slipped her tongue through my aching cleft, prodding my clitty, tonguing me to new peaks. Then suddenly she was on top of me again, pressing her lovely naked body hard against me. Our hands were everywhere, grabbing and squeezing and we writhed together as our bodies locked into each other, demanding release. She jerked her own cunny hard up against mine and I gathered the lovely girl into my arms, her breasts rising and falling from the effects of her desire. I pulled her down and it was now the turn of my mouth to bury itself into the yawning pink slit. I slipped my tongue in and out as Elspeth's arm wrapped itself round me and from behind found my own dripping quim with her long tapering fingers, stabbing them in and out with a fierce intensity that caused me to cry out with delight.

I moved my tongue along the grooves of her pussy, sucking her delicious juices, and we continued to play with each other, engaging in all kinds of intimacies for another full hour. Elspeth possessed large cunny lips, which might have led her to seek friendship with other girls, though I assured her that vaginal structural variations are commonplace. She left our service soon after this blissful afternoon and I have never told my dear husband about this incident. I recount it now as he is, alas, three thousand miles away in America, and will not be returning for at least another month. And as he never reads your excellent journal, I feel certain that my secret is safe in your hands. If any lady reading this missive wishes to contact me for a similar adventure such as I have described, perhaps she could contact me through the good offices of Lady C—— who is well-known for her inclinations regarding pretty girls.